Positively Beautiful

Positively Beautiful

WENDY MILLS

BLOOMSBURY
NEW YORK   LONDON   NEW DELHI   SYDNEY

First published in the United States of America in March 2015
by Bloomsbury Children's Books
www.bloomsbury.com

Bloomsbury is a registered trademark of Bloomsbury Publishing Plc

For information about permission to reproduce selections from this book, write to
Permissions, Bloomsbury Children's Books, 1385 Broadway, New York, New York 10018
Bloomsbury books may be purchased for business or promotional use. For information on
bulk purchases please contact Macmillan Corporate and Premium Sales Department at
specialmarkets@macmillan.com

Library of Congress Cataloging-in-Publication Data
Mills, Wendy.
Positively beautiful / by Wendy Mills.
pages   cm
Summary: Sixteen-year-old Erin's life is fairly normal until she learns that
her mother has breast cancer and she, too, may carry a mutated gene,
so amid high school dramas including betrayal by her best friend,
she must consider preemptive surgery to guarantee she will not be stricken.
ISBN 978-1-61963-341-4 (hardcover) • ISBN 978-1-61963-342-1 (e-book)
[1. Breast—Cancer—Fiction. 2. Cancer—Fiction. 3. Mothers and daughters—
Fiction. 4. High schools—Fiction. 5. Schools—Fiction. 6. Best friends—
Fiction. 7. Friendship—Fiction. 8. Dating (Social customs)—Fiction.
9. Single-parent families—Fiction.] I. Title.
PZ7.M639874Pos 2015   [Fic]—dc23   2014009929

Book design by Amanda Bartlett
Typeset by Westchester Book Composition
Printed and bound in the U.S.A. by Thomson-Shore Inc., Dexter, Michigan
2 4 6 8 10 9 7 5 3 1

All papers used by Bloomsbury Publishing, Inc., are natural, recyclable products
made from wood grown in well-managed forests. The manufacturing processes
conform to the environmental regulations of the country of origin.

This one's for you, Mom

Positively
Beautiful

Part One

CHAPTER ONE

Three reasons you don't want a crystal ball:
1. They're a pain to dust.
2. To look into one you really should dress like a medium. Enough said.
3. Sometimes it's better not to know.

Because once you know something, you can never not know it. Your life becomes *before* and *after*. The mountains you thought were important become barely noticeable pebbles, and things you hadn't even known existed become the Himalayas of your soul.

The next time someone tries to read your future in a crystal ball, just say no.

I wish I had.

It is an ordinary Tuesday morning. I was late to school because Trina had trouble with her garter belt (don't ask), Ms. Garrison is hopped up on an energy drink (as usual), and I had so far managed to go the entire day without saying a word in class (par for the course).

"We did well on this paper, but I think we can do better," Ms. Garrison says, leaning her cushy hip against the side of her desk and tapping her foot to the rhythm of her caffeine buzz. "I know we can!"

Ms. Garrison sometimes speaks in the royal "we," as if there are a couple of personalities in her head and she is speaking for all of them. I think it is her way of connecting with us, to let us know she is *one of us*, that *we are all in this together.*

I begin doodling around my notes on Amy Tan, making the *A* in *Amy* a diamond and shading it in. I'm thinking about my physics test tomorrow, wondering if I should study some more tonight or go do a photo shoot with Trina.

"Erin? Erin Bailey?"

I look up. Ms. Garrison is smiling at me. Everyone else is packing up.

"I said, Erin, would you stay after class for a minute?"

"Absolutely," I say, and someone makes kissy-kissy noises. It isn't mean-spirited, just Herbert Wallace trying to be funny, but it still makes me blush.

After everybody clears out, Ms. Garrison comes around to the front of her desk. She looks me in the eye, all serious. She used to be a professor at Columbia or Harvard, but decided to give up the big city so she could come mold young minds in the sticks. She takes her job seriously, and I have to admit she's one of the best teachers I've ever had.

"Your writing is impressive, Erin." She stares at me expectantly like I'm going to clap like a seal or something. I restrain the urge.

"Ah . . . ," I say. "Thank you?" When my sophomore English teacher suggested I take advanced English this year, I was less than thrilled. Especially when I found out it would be heavy on writing. I've always loved words and the way they make sense, and make you feel, make you understand things, but I just never saw myself as the person *writing* those words.

"The whole essay about parents needing to take ginkgo biloba so they can remember what it was like to be a kid . . . It made me laugh. Your paper was hands-down the best in the class."

I tilt my head to the side so my hair sweeps over my flaming cheeks.

"You know I'm the teacher adviser for the school e-zine, correct?" she says. "We think you would make a great addition to our little crew. I wanted to talk to Faith about this before she left— Oh! There she is. Perfect. Faith, can I talk to you a moment?"

I turn and see Faith Hiller, her shiny black hair cut in bangs across her forehead, her eyes a startling blue. She's smart and pretty, president of everything from the debate club to the student council, and editor of the school e-zine. I'm pretty sure she works on world peace in her free time. She is going places and makes sure everybody knows it.

I get the distinct feeling she's maybe been standing outside the door listening.

"You know Erin, right?" Ms. Garrison puts her hand on my back and I wonder if I'm supposed to curtsy.

Faith walks slowly toward us, and I can feel her cool gaze slide over my dark, jumbled curls, my decidedly-not-designer jeans and gray T-shirt, down to my rotten old tennis shoes. I wish I'd worn the new ones, but they hurt my feet. Faith is tiny and perfect in cute red-and-white-checkered capris and a white peasant blouse that sets off her olive skin.

"Erin?" Faith says, and it's a question.

"I sat behind you in history last year," I say quickly, and wish I hadn't. *When all else fails, keep your mouth shut, Rinnie,* my memaw used to say. Good in theory, damn near impossible to implement. At least I didn't say, *And we were in homeroom together our freshman year and you asked to borrow a pen and didn't give it back.* Or, even better, *Remember in the cafeteria last month when you asked your friend if that girl bothered to look in the mirror before she left the house? That girl was me.*

Faith cocks her head at me, her sleek, black hair swinging. "Oh. Sure. Hiii, Erin." She smiles all bright and big, like a shiny white balloon filled with nothing but air. She's saying, *I have absolutely NO idea who you are, nor do I care. We both know that, right? But let's play nice-nice for Ms. Garrison, shall we?*

Ms. Garrison, bless her Ivy League little heart, is completely clueless.

"Good! We were talking about what a marvelous writer Erin is. What do you think about having her join the e-zine?

We need another reporter now that Trina's left us. What do you think, Faith?"

I try to look all *Trina? Trina who?*, hoping they don't realize Trina is my best friend. It's not that Trina doesn't *feel* bad when she abandons clubs, plans, and projects midstream— she's even bailed in the middle of a haircut because I texted her a picture of a killer rainbow—it's just hard to explain to other people.

"Oh . . ." Faith smiles that empty smile again. "Well . . ." She manages to sound charming and embarrassed at the same time. She's neither. She doesn't want me. Now I know she heard what Ms. Garrison said about my paper being the best in the class, better than Faith's. She may not have known who I was before, but she knows now.

"Erin's really a very talented writer . . ." Ms. Garrison is puzzled by Faith's yawning interest in her idea. Yes, Faith is actually yawning, cute and kitteny, showing a lot of teeth.

"Really, it's okay," I say. "I've got a lot going on—" *Lie, lie, lie . . .*

"Please think about it, dear, we'd be thrilled to have you," Ms. Garrison says, shooting Faith a questioning look.

I flee for the door, feeling Faith's gaze like two sharp knives in my back.

∽

I leave Ms. Garrison's room and Trina grabs my arm in the chaos of the hallways between classes.

"What's up, bee-aaatch," she says, falling in step beside me. Today she's got some sort of Pippi Longstocking thing going on, with a short orange dress, striped leggings, and a cape. And, of course, the purple garter belt.

"I honestly don't know," I say. "I feel like I just left the Twilight Zone, where Ms. Garrison thinks I'm some sort of prizewinning journalist and Faith Hiller wants to decapitate me slowly and painfully." I explain what happened.

"Don't let her get to you. Faith thinks she's all that and a bag of chips," Trina says, patting my arm sympathetically. "Her mom is some corporate hotshot, and Faith thinks that makes her *Ms. Thing*. When I was on the e-zine staff, she acted like I was some sort of servant girl who was supposed to kiss her feet. One day, I even dressed like Nelly Dean, the maid from *Wuthering Heights*. She didn't get it—and she's supposed to be *smart*—but at least I got an excuse to wear that cute lace bonnet." People either love Trina or hate her. She doesn't seem to care either way. "*Anywho*, I've got *NEWS*. Chaz, adorable, smart, going-to-be-Mark-Zuckerberg Chaz . . ."

I try not to smile. Chaz the Spaz. That's what we were calling him yesterday.

"He asked me out. Can you believe it?"

"Of course I can believe it," I say loyally, because I catch her thin edge of uncertainty. Boys don't ask Trina out. Boys don't ask her out because she has a bumpy mole on her cheek, crooked teeth, and an impossibly large nose. Once you get to know her, all you notice is *Trina*, her big personality and even bigger heart. I've known her since I was six, so I don't even notice how she looks anymore, but other people do. I know they do, because we both hear what they say.

"He says he's got some cool place he wants to show me

Saturday night. I told him you and I were doing a movie night—"

"Oh, Trina, we can do that some other—"

"No. It's all good. So he says, 'Why don't you bring her?' The more the merrier, right? He's going to bring somebody too."

"I don't think—"

Trying to get a word in is like holding back waves with a knife. Trina just washes right over you.

"Seriously. You *have* to come. I'm nervous enough as it is. If you come, I won't feel so weird. You'll have a blast, I promise."

"Uh-huh." Like the time she thought I would have a blast when she tried to talk me into bungee jumping. Or the time she thought it would be a blast to go toilet paper evil Mr. James's house. I've seen Chaz the Spaz's friends. I'm not at the pinnacle of high school hierarchy, far from it, but those geeky guys make me look like Queen Victoria. It won't be a blast. I'm certain of it.

"Please? Pretty, pretty please?" She stops in the middle of the hall and throws herself down on her knees in front of me, confusing a herd of freshman who go all wide-eyed and nervous. I shrug at them as Trina looks up at me with her trademark this-is-me-beseeching-you look.

"Look, she's proposing," someone snickers.

"Okay, okay! Get up. *Please.*"

She jumps to her feet like nothing's happened.

"You're going to have a *blast*," she says.

I smile and keep my mouth shut.

CHAPTER TWO

Trina's newest interest, her fashion blog, requires a lot of work. By me. I'm used to Trina's overwhelming short-lived passions, and I know she'll soon move on to something else. As long as it's not skydiving again.

"Okay, how does that look?" Trina poses in the orange dress, cape, and garter belt in front of her old green tank of a Saab (code-named "Retro"). She's got one hand on the hood, and she's staring down at the ground, all pensive. I frame her in my camera and snap a couple of shots, the green-fuzzed March trees in the background.

"Are you going to tell me, or do I have to wait to read it on the blog?" I ask, as she hops up on the hood and does a pinup girl pose. "I got Pippi Longstocking and what? Victoria's Secret model? Wonder Woman?"

Trina's outfits often have a theme. Valentine's Day last year she was Juliet complete with a bloody dagger sticking out of her chest, and another day she was Violet Baudelaire from *Lemony Snicket's A Series of Unfortunate Events*.

"What? A girl can't wear a garter belt and a cape if she feels like it?"

Okay, and sometimes she has no theme whatsoever, just a random assortment of clothing.

Trina is super-skinny, though she eats like a horse. It's because she's always in motion, like a hummingbird that can't stop buzzing around or it will fall out of the sky. Her best feature is her buttery-fine hair the color of daffodils, but as often as not, she dyes it magenta or violet or neon blue. Today it's blond, but she has it clipped with clothespins into two short little pigtails at the base of her neck.

Her phone buzzes and she whips it out. Usually she's adamant we turn off our phones while we're "working," so I'm surprised.

"Chaz is just so *cute*," she says. "He texted, 'I'm thinking about you while I cut the grass.' Isn't that adorable?"

Really? I smile though, because it's nice to see Trina happy like this. I've been asked to a couple of dances—I never went—just guys I knew who didn't have a date either. I've even had a boyfriend, pudgy, sweet Ted Hanson, when I was in ninth grade. After two months, he said he needed his freedom and I was heartbroken for about two seconds, and that was that. Trina, on the other hand, has had no dates, no dances. Zilch.

"So are you going to do the e-zine thing?" she asks after texting Chaz back something (equally adorable I have no doubt) and slipping her phone in her pocket.

"No . . ."

"Why not? It sounds right up your alley. But I know what you're going to say. No. *No, Trina, I don't want to do Reading Olympics even though I read for like hours every night. No, Trina, I don't think we should try out for football.* No, no, no. One of these days you're going to have to say yes to *something.*"

"I know, I'm *so* unreasonable. I'm sure we would have made great quarterbacks."

"It was the *principle.* Anyway, don't get me off on a tangent. You. Writing. You're always writing in your journal, so you must like it. What if you're really good at journalism? You like taking pictures. You like writing. It's a no-brainer. Wouldn't it be fun to try it out and see?"

I wince. "Trina, I know you're on a mission to try everything until you find your true passion, but I'm not. I have to be sure."

"Oh pooh. There's so much out there to *do*, why limit yourself? Though I'm pretty sure I've found my thing. I'm going to be a fashion reporter for *Vogue* or *Cosmopolitan.* Won't that be killer?"

I say nothing as Trina starts doing jumping jacks and gestures at me to take pictures. No point in telling Trina I doubt this fashion blog will last more than a month. She is always so *happy* when she first starts a project, why pop her bubble? I wish I could find something like that, something I was so excited about I wanted to do it every minute of the day. Even if it was only for a week, or a month.

"You can't go to some hoity-toity fashion school, though," I say. "We're talking Emory, or GSU, right?"

"I would never leave my bestie behind," she says, throwing

her arms around me. "We promised we'd go to the same college no matter what, right? Oh, oh! I have an idea! We'll go to the same school as Chaz. Yes!" She pumps her small fist.

I hug her back. "Crazy girl. So tell me about Chaz, already."

She hops onto the hood of the car and sits with her elbow resting on her knee. "Ooh, Erin, he is so cute, don't you think? We've been talking in Visual Arts, but, you know, just kinda 'Hi' and, 'Nice painting of that flower vase.' And then yesterday, out of the blue, he said he had a place he thought I'd like to see. Wait a minute!" She jumps off the car and grabs my arm. "It's a date, right? Maybe he meant as friends? Oh, I'm such an *idiot*. Of course he meant as *friends*." She starts pulling at her hair and I put my hand out to stop her.

"Trina. Either way, he asked you out, right? See where it goes."

"Well, as long as you go, it'll be okay," she says. "Dorkster Twins activate, right?" We bump fists and pack up.

She's bummed though, and we don't say much else.

∽∾

It's almost six o'clock and Mom's still not home. Laptop and books are spread across my desk as I try to work on physics. It's not my favorite subject. Actually, if Newton were still alive, and I ever met him, my hope would be that it would be on a dark road, with me in a speeding car. *How's that for testing speed and velocity, Mr. Newton?*

After a while, I even turn off Netflix so I can concentrate, but I find myself staring at the picture of my dad on the wall above my desk. He's standing beside the red plane, the one I remember from when I was a kid. The wind must have been blowing pretty hard, because the dark, curly scraps of his hair are standing on end. How long before he died was that picture taken? I have no idea. Mom and I rarely talk about Dad. The only clear memories I have of him are the times he took me up in his plane, which I adored. I was fearless at six.

I hear the front door open and abandon physics to go meet Mom.

She's forgotten to take off her lab coat at work again, and there is a big green patch of spilled who-knows-what down her left boob. She's a marine biologist, and is currently working on algae that eat waste, i.e., poop.

"Hey, Rinnie," she says tiredly. "Sorry I'm late. How was school?"

"Unreal."

She takes off her glasses and puts them absentmindedly on the foyer table. "I'm going to change. I was thinking Dino's tonight? I don't feel like cooking."

This isn't unusual, but something's off.

"What's wrong?" I look at her more closely. "Are you tired again?"

She hesitates, then looks away. "No, everything's fine. Let's go grab a pizza and you can tell me all about your day. Maybe later we can watch *The Princess Bride*? I'm in the mood for a good movie." She picks up her briefcase and heads for the kitchen. I am still standing in the middle of the foyer.

"What is it?" I do not even recognize my own voice. It sounds hollow and crystal, like something fragile that might break.

She turns to look at me. I read the lines and furrows on her face as easily as words on a page. I know her that well, and I know this is bad, whatever it is.

"What is it?" I whisper.

"Let's go get some pizza, and we can talk about it." She brushes a strand of hair out of my face.

I begin to shake my head back and forth. "Tell me, just tell me, please?"

She sighs and looks over my shoulder for a moment. Then she looks back at me.

"I have cancer," she says simply.

And my life cracks into *before* and *after* just like that.

CHAPTER THREE

Mom insists we go get pizza after dropping her bombshell. Like I have any desire to eat pizza after she tells me *she has cancer*. But I can tell Mom doesn't want to cook, that she wants to be *doing* something, *anything*, so I agree.

In the car, I babble questions.

"How'd you get it? No wait, that's stupid. I mean, what kind do you have? How'd you find out? Have they told you, you know, like, if you're going to—" I can't go on. I can't say *if you're going to die?* But that's the question, isn't it? And I don't want to know. I really, really don't want to know.

"I have breast cancer." Mom's hands are gripping the steering wheel like it is the last absolute thing on this planet. "I found a lump, and I went in, and they did a biopsy and some tests and . . ." She pauses, and swallows hard. "It's cancer. I wanted to tell you sooner, but . . ." She shakes her head. "Anyway. I have surgery next week, a . . . a mastectomy."

"Wait a minute. Wait. A mastectomy? You mean, they're going to cut off your . . . breast?"

She nods. "Yes. It needs to be removed. Right now, that's all I know."

I can tell it isn't though. Not when her hands are tight on the steering wheel, her knuckles white, Memaw's sapphire ring she always wears looking like it's about to bite through her skin.

"What aren't you telling me?" I whisper. "Don't you know how much worse it is for me to think you're hiding something from me? I'm almost seventeen years old, I can take it. I need to know. I need to know *everything.*"

Mom uses one hand to give me a calm-down pat.

"I had breast cancer about eight years ago. I had a lumpectomy, and radiation, and they got it all. I didn't tell you because you were only nine at the time, and you were already going through such a hard time with your dad's death, and with school and all, so I didn't want to pile anything else on you. Later . . . I didn't want to think about it."

"Is that . . . is that why Memaw came and stayed with us for a little while? I remember that."

I remember sweet-potato pies, big, soft hugs, and no-nonsense words when I started on my I-don't-wanna-go-to-school-today whine.

Mom's throat is working, like she is trying not to cry. A hot prickle of tears stings my eyes. Mom always gets emotional about my memaw, who died of ovarian cancer when I was twelve. Mom still hasn't gotten over it. The funny thing is, they never seemed to get along all that great when Memaw was alive. They were so different, Memaw with her big country accent and flowery housedresses and high school education, and then there was Mom with her doctorate and nice house and manicured hands. It was like Mom set out to be as different from her mother as possible, but in the end, when Memaw was dying, Mom realized how much she loved her. I miss Memaw— *a lot*—and I know Mom does too.

Is that the way it's going to be for me? If Mom dies, will I ever be able to think about her without wanting to cry? I'll be crying for the rest of my life.

I hiccup a sob and Mom reaches over and grabs my hand. "It's going to be okay," she whispers.

But it isn't. It is never going to be okay. Never, ever again.

"Okay, what, it's back?" I ask when I can talk around the baseball in my throat.

"The lump is in the other breast. So, no, this is a new cancer."

The word sounds awful. I can't comprehend it. It's like she's speaking another language.

Mom squeezes my hand so tight Memaw's ring cuts into my palm, but I don't care. The pain feels good. The pain feels real, and nothing else does.

"I'm sorry, *sorry*," Mom says. "I never meant to do this to you." Like she did it on purpose, but I can tell she's thinking about Memaw dying on *her*.

Losing Memaw was awful. Dad, too, though I only remember the pain in a fuzzy, six-year-old way.

Losing Mom . . . that's unthinkable. She's all I have left.

Dino's is our favorite pizza joint, but we try to save it for special occasions, because otherwise we would eat there every night. Now I wish we hadn't come. Now I will forever think about this place as where *Mom told me the news.*

There is a line, like always, and I get stuck in the doorway, awkwardly holding the door open with my foot while people come out and we inch forward. Signs cover the door, and because I am a compulsive reader, I stand and read them while my mom continues to die in front of me.

Dino's, a Great Place to Have a Party! Pictures of happy, clueless Little Leaguers chowing down on pizza and wings.

Lost Cat. Black and White, Answers to Sherlock. I stare at the picture of the fat, long-haired cat, trying to figure out why someone would name him Sherlock. Is he good at finding things? Like his owner would lose a shoe, and presto, Sherlock would show up with the shoe in his mouth and sit there looking all *aw shucks, it's nothing*? Would he know just by looking at me that my heart is breaking?

The line inches forward some more, and I study an orange flier with a picture of a man and an airplane. Planes always remind me of my dad, and my heart twists a little.

The flier says: *Learn to Fly! Lessons for people from 16 to 100.*

Funny. The old fart standing unsmiling in front of his plane doesn't *look* suicidal. I probably don't look like I just heard the worst news of my life, either. I wonder how many people are walking around with a big bruise where their heart is and no one even notices. It feels bizarre. It feels like the whole world should be talking quietly. I want to go over and smack the kids at the birthday party. *Don't you know my mom has cancer? Be quiet! Look sad, for God's sake.*

Then we are inside, and making our way to a table.

"What do you want?" Mom asks brightly, like Dino's is going to make it all better, like pizza will *save the day.*

"I don't care." I'm angry, for some reason, but I don't know why. My head is buzzing. Everything seems so unreal I want to stab myself with a fork to see if I can still feel anything.

"Erin," Mom says after the waitress leaves carting our menus and our order.

I look at her.

"It's okay to *feel* things. It's okay to be sad, to be angry, to want to kick something. I want you to know you can always come to me with any questions you have. And . . ." She looks away, sees someone she knows, and flashes a quick, meaningless smile. Then she's back to me. "I made you an appointment to meet with the school counselor. You'll be meeting with him every week for a while, so you have an outlet for your feelings."

"Are you kidding me?" I say it too loud, and the emo girl sitting behind my mother turns and gives me a dirty look. I glare at her, and she shrugs, like, *What you going to do, huh?*

"I think it's important that you have someone to talk to, someone other than me. I mean, I want you to talk to me too, but you need someone else you can say anything to. Someone safe."

"I can talk to Trina." *Trina.* She's going to be devastated. Trina and her mom don't get along, so Trina has sort of adopted Mom as her own.

"I want you to go to counseling. Will you do it for me, Erin?" Mom asks quietly.

Already, she is playing the cancer card.

"Okay." I look down at the table and Mom sighs.

We eat some pizza and Mom tells me more about what is going to happen. Surgery definitely, chemotherapy, maybe radiation. "We'll know more about the treatment after the surgery," she says, picking at her pizza.

"Will your hair fall out?" I ask.

"I don't know."

That scares me. If she doesn't know what to expect, how can I?

I don't notice the popular kids until I'm walking out. Faith is there, darkly effervescent, holding court among the best and prettiest of our school.

Faith looks up and right through me.

I follow after my mother, feeling as if suddenly I can't walk right. I bend my neck so my hair hides my face. My legs feel robotic and my arms don't seem to know how to swing like they should.

When I get to the door, I hesitate, and then rip off one of the little tabs attached to the *Learn to Fly!* sign. I don't let Mom see, because *I* don't even know why I'm doing it.

But somehow, flying away suddenly seems very appealing.

CHAPTER FOUR

Mom's surgery isn't until Monday, and she seems intent on getting back to *life as it was before.* Life isn't like it was before, but with Mom doing a pretty good imitation of an ostrich (Do they really stick their heads in the sand? *Why?*), I can't really say anything.

On Saturday, I start obsessing about my breasts. More specifically, that there is a lump in the right one. Not that they are so big that a lump wouldn't stand out like a bunion on your big toe, but still. Still. Something is there. I am sure of it.

"I think I have a lump," I announce when Trina answers her phone.

"You do not," she says.

"Seriously. I can feel it. Round and hard like a pebble."

"I'll be right there."

She comes over, and feels my breast.

"No lump."

"Are you sure?"

"No lump and you are *seriously* going insane."

"Like you wouldn't if your mom had cancer."

Her eyes well up. When I first told her the news, she rushed right over and hugged my mom and sobbed. Mom loves Trina, but I could tell all that emotion made her uncomfortable. But she was real nice about it, holding Trina and patting her back until she stopped crying.

"Her surgery's Monday, right? I can't believe they're going to cut off her breast."

"Evidently they wanted to cut off *both* breasts, but she said no. I heard her talking to Aunt Jill and she said she can't see cutting off a healthy breast just to be safe." ("What, I'm supposed to cut off my head if I get a headache?") "Jill's coming tomorrow, and I'm trying to talk Mom into letting me skip school Monday, but she's really not embracing the idea." Like I could go to school and concentrate while Mom is getting her boob hacked off.

"I'll ask my mom if I can come too," Trina says, but we both know she's already missed too much school this year. She always seems to find something more important to do than go to school. "Uh . . . so do you still want to come with me and Chaz tonight? Honestly, I get it if you don't. It'll be okay." She sits crisscross-applesauce behind me and uses her fingers to dig into my shoulders. I roll my neck and she massages the tense muscles.

But I can tell she wants me to go really bad. She can't shake the feeling that this isn't actually a date, and now she's worried if she shows up without me it'll make her look stupid. And desperate.

"Of course I do," I say, though all I want to do is curl up in a ball and howl.

"Do you want to talk about what to wear?" She's hesitant, and I feel bad, like she has to tiptoe through a verbal minefield to talk to me.

"Sure." I try to sound enthusiastic.

"Good!" She jumps up and bounces to my closet. "I don't know who he's bringing, but you need to wear something awesomely sexy so Mystery Guy says, 'Wow, I want to hit *that*.' " She deepens her voice and tries to sound masculine, but it comes out echoey and creepy.

"If he talked to me like that I think I'd get up and run," I say. "That sounds like someone wanting to show me his puppy inside a white-paneled van."

"Seriously, though. Clothes?"

"I thought maybe jeans and a T-shirt," I say, knowing it won't be good enough for Trina. I have no desire to dress to be noticed, while Trina seems to think her clothes will distract attention from her face.

"How 'bout this?" She holds up a white lace dress with a heart on it. She found it for me at a thrift store, but I've never worn it. "It'll show your cleavage."

I push my boobs together, and we both look at the disappointing result in the V of my shirt. I think of my mother. She's *losing* a breast, and I'm worried about what mine look like in a stupid dress?

"Jeans'll be fine," I say. "I might even wear my new tennis shoes."

"Jeans . . . ," she says. "Oh, Erin."

"Look, what's wrong with jeans? Jeans say, 'I don't care what you think of me, but have you noticed my butt?'"

"Dorkster Twins activate," she says resignedly, and we touch our knuckles together.

Trina isn't going to change, and neither am I.

After Trina leaves to get dressed (she's keeping her outfit tonight a secret—I'm a little scared), I go downstairs. Mom is sitting at the kitchen table with a glass of orange juice and a science journal. Spaghetti sauce is bubbling on the stove, and I turn it down. Mom burns more meals than not.

"Are you wearing makeup?" she asks.

"Can you tell? How's the zit?" I started with some concealer, and before I knew it, I was up to lip gloss and eyeliner. Trina will be ecstatic.

I try to see if the zit is visible in the reflection of the stainless steel refrigerator. And there it is. Wonderful. I step back and look at myself in the distorted reflection: a girl, me, on the shortish side, a little pudgy around the middle, round face, chunky glasses, and medium-length curly black hair.

"What zit?" Mom says. "Push your hair back. Stop hiding your beautiful face. Are you and Trina doing something? Invite her back over, if you want, and we can eat spaghetti and watch *Sixteen Candles*." Mom is a complete eighties-movie buff, and Trina and I get a kick out of making fun of the big hair and shoulder pads.

"Remember, I'm supposed to go with Trina and meet some

people? But I don't have to. Really. It's no big deal. I'll call her and tell her I'm staying here."

"No, no! That sounds like a lot more fun. Where are you going?"

"I have *no* idea. Evidently it's a surprise."

Mom frowns. She doesn't like surprises.

Me either.

I wonder then whether she needs me here so she won't think about her surgery on Monday. My chest starts feeling funny, like maybe I'm not getting enough oxygen.

Mom reads me instantly. "Erin, it's going to be okay. *I'm* going to be okay."

"But you don't know that!" I cry. "You say that, but *you don't know!*"

"You're right, I don't." She takes me in her arms and rocks me back and forth like she did when I was a little kid and I'd wake up screaming from the nameless, ferocious nightmares.

This time, though, the nightmare has a name.

Cancer.

"What do we do now?" I whisper.

"We go on. We live our lives. There's nothing else to do," she says, and I start crying again.

CHAPTER FIVE

Chaz pulls up in my driveway a little after six. He's driving an old Mustang, all decked out.

"Nice car," Mom says, peering out the window.

I give her a quick hug and say, "See you later, alligator."

"After a while, crocodile," she answers. She started this when I was little and petrified to go to school because I was afraid she was going to up and die while I was learning addition, like my dad did. "We don't say good-bye because we know we're going to see each other again soon, right, Rinnie? Go to school, and when you get done, I'll be waiting for you."

For some stupid reason it stuck. We still don't say good-bye.

Trina gives me an oh-my-God face when she gets out to let me in the back. She's relatively sedate tonight, in white bloomers that come to her knees, a green spidery-thin shirt she's belted with a piece of rope, and her hair in a bun. She's wearing the big green glasses she always wears when she's feeling shy.

"Hi, Chaz, nice car," I say as I climb into the empty back-seat.

"You like it?" Chazs peers over his shoulder at me with his gray, caught-in-the-headlights eyes.

"Well, sure, it's a 1966 Mustang Pony Coupe. What's not to like?"

"Erin's got a thing for old cars," Trina says as Chaz pulls out of my driveway.

Not really, but it's easier than explaining the truth. My dad's 1965 Mustang convertible is parked in our garage. It doesn't run, and lately Mom has been talking about selling it to free up the garage for her potting table. Every time she says anything about it though, I change the subject. Last year, as I neared my sixteenth birthday, I started researching old Mustangs to see how expensive it would be to fix. My birthday came, I got a Corolla, and somehow I stopped thinking about fixing it. But I can't see selling it. When I was little I used to take off the cover and sit inside and pretend my dad was still alive. I would close my eyes and say, *Yes, Daddy, ice cream sounds really nice. Maybe then we can go to the airport and watch the planes fly? Please? Oh, silly Daddy, of course I love you too.*

"My dad left me a '65 Mustang," I say, and leave out the rest.

"I'd like to see it sometime." Chaz swings a long arm over the back of the seat to look at me and socks Trina in the face. "Oh, I'm sorry! Are you okay?"

"Drive, Chaz, drive!" she says, rearranging her glasses, which have been knocked askew.

That's why he's Chaz the Spaz. It's like he's got a motor inside him that's herky-jerky. It goes really fast sometimes, spinning his tall, lanky frame into a frenzy, and then it stutters, leaving his long arms and legs flailing helplessly. He's really not bad looking, though. He's got tight golden curls cut close to his scalp, and nice cheekbones (except for the bloom of acne), and wears I'm-a-nerd-and-proud-of-it glasses. He snaps constantly to some unrhythmic song in his head, which makes you want to break his fingers. Trina, of course, thinks this is cute.

"Seriously, though, I'd love to see it." *Snap, snap*, even as he drives through the tree-lined streets. We live inside the "Perimeter," meaning inside Interstate 285, which encircles metro Atlanta, but our city has a small-town feel, with a little bit of history thrown in. There are a few buildings that hark back to the Civil War, at least the ones that survived Sherman. Of course, a lot of people in Atlanta feel like the Civil War was maybe ten, fifteen years ago, rather than a hundred and fifty.

"I bet Michael would too," Chaz continues after a moment. "He's the car man, really. He restored this baby." He pats the dashboard affectionately. "I did the research and dug out the specs and all, but he's the hands-on guy."

"Michael . . . ?" I say.

"Michael Lundstrom. You know him, right?" he says all casual, but Trina shoots me a triumphant glance. She knows I've had a secret crush on Michael Lundstrom since he was my lab partner last year.

"I know who he is," I say, making a face back at Trina, who looks like she is about to do an emergency eject out of her seat. *Chaz and Michael Lundstrom are friends.* Who would have thought?

"There he is. We'll ask him," Chaz continues as he pulls into the driveway of a picture-perfect restored Victorian and Michael comes loping down the walk.

Trina pumps her fist and mouths "Score!" at me. Now I get all the funny, oh-so-meaningful looks. Chaz must have told her who was coming with us tonight.

My heart starts doing the funky chicken in my chest. Michael is hands-down my desert-island boy. He could catch fish and make fires and we would have deep, dreamy conversations. Not that I've ever had any sort of conversation with him—other than "Hand me that test tube" and "Wow, that polymer putty sure is sticky"—but I am confident our conversations would be deep. And dreamy.

Michael used to be one of the most popular guys in school, soccer cocaptain, smart, and cute. He and Faith Hiller were our class's golden couple, and there was never any doubt that the two of them would go off to some great college and reign there as king and queen. But something changed. Last year, he quit the soccer team and he and Faith broke up. Now he sits by himself at lunch and walks the halls alone.

That hasn't changed what he looks like—*hot*—and if anything, his aloneness only makes him more attractive to me. I get walking the halls alone.

"Hey, Michael," Chaz says, "this is Trina."

He sounds little-boy proud, showing off his shiny new toy to a friend.

"Hi, Michael, like the T-shirt," Trina says. "Morbid much?"

That's Trina for you.

Michael settles back into his seat and I can *smell* him, all musk and patchouli. He sweeps his hair out of his eyes and stares at Trina for a moment. He's got a little dimple in the cleft of his chin. Perfect. I mean, just *perfect*.

He looks down at his shirt, and I follow his gaze. It's a black T-shirt with a crumbled building outlined in silver with a grim reaper dancing on top. Below it says, GAME OVER. There is nothing else on the shirt to indicate what it means.

"I drew it," he says, following the edge of the building with his long, tanned finger.

"Michael is going to be an architect," Chaz says. "I mean, he wants to be an architect more than I want to be a video-game designer." His tone holds a note of awe. Michael's level of dedication to architecture must be extreme.

"Wow," I say, my sole contribution to the conversation so far.

Michael turns to look at me, his gaze smoky charcoal. He's all straight dark hair and eyes you could just drown in. It doesn't hurt that he's muscular in all the right places and walks like some sort of panther, *pacing* down the hallway like he owns it. I've seen people literally get out of his way, but he doesn't seem to notice.

"Hi, Michael." I hold out my hand. "Remember me? I'm Erin."

My hand hangs there like I'm waiting for him to kiss it, and his brow furrows.

"Got it," he says, taking my hand and giving it a little shake. "Chemistry last year. You're pretty smart."

I duck my head, feeling the blood burning in my cheeks.

"She *is* smart," Trina gushes. "If only all of us could make straight As." She sighs dramatically, giving me a you-can-thank-me-later look, and then asks brightly, "How do you and Chaz know each other?"

"We met a couple summers ago. Michael was . . . hanging out," Chaz says, glancing into the rearview mirror at Michael and then back to the road as we pass the entry arch for Agnes Scott College.

I see Trina narrow her eyes at him, but she doesn't say anything. For now. Leave Trina alone for five minutes with a wall and she'll know its life story. It won't take her long to worm the details out of Chaz.

"Me and Erin have been friends since we were six," she says. "Best friends forever, right?" She looks back over her shoulder and grins at me.

∽

Six years old . . . me crying on the playground because my dad was dead. I didn't really understand death yet, just that he wasn't going to come to see me anymore. He was gone. It was different from the Mommy-and-Daddy-can't-live-together-anymore gone that happened when I was four, though I wasn't sure why he couldn't visit me from heaven. Was heaven farther than Druid Hills, where he moved after the divorce? Anyway, I was pretty sure it was all my fault, this going-away-forever thing. In my six-year-old world, you did things right, and life was good. You did something wrong, and you got punished. I figured I must have done something really bad for my daddy to be taken away. I decided I would be *really, really* good from then on. Maybe then they wouldn't take away Mommy too.

There I was crying on the swing, and Trina came up to me.

"Why're you crying?"

"I'm not crying."

"Yes you are."

"Are not!"

I keep crying and she sits beside me, knee to knee.

"My daddy died," I say.

She's quiet for a while. Then, "Your daddy can play with my turtle Buddy up in heaven, okay? And you can come play with me."

And I did. And we've been friends ever since.

"All right!" Trina says, never quiet for more than five seconds. "Can you tell us where we're going yet?"

"Uh . . . no. Don't you like surprises?" Chaz says, looking over his shoulder at me and Michael, narrowly missing a car full of bless-your-heart grandmas turning into the Edgewood Retail District.

I get an amused vibe from Michael, though his expression is still dark. Come to think of it, I'm not sure I've ever seen him smile. He's dark and broody, like a Heathcliff/Rochester character.

"I *love* surprises," Trina says. "One time I even hid cookies from myself so it would be a surprise when I found them."

Chaz laughs, a delighted burble. Oh wow, he's a goner. Good for Trina.

Chaz and Trina chat as if Michael and I aren't even there. Michael is staring out the window, and I do the same on my side. He never said much to me as my lab partner either.

I wonder what Mom is doing, and then I try not to think about my mother because all it does is make me want to cry. It's too late, though, because now I've got a picture in my head of her in a coffin, looking pale and peaceful, and I can't get rid of it.

"What?" Michael says.

I realize I'm shaking my head back and forth, trying to jar loose the image.

"Ah . . . nothing. I'm thinking about—" My mind is not working. I don't want to tell him about my mom. I don't want anybody to know about my mom. It's just too private, too personal to share.

His eyes are a really dark brown, almost black, like velvet night as he looks at me. I think he can tell my brain-wheels are spinning like crazy but nothing's coming out. He says, "I was thinking about this thing I heard, about a kid who went crazy and killed a bunch of people? They called him the Question Mark Kid, 'cause he would put down a question mark instead of his name."

"Seriously, you got any other sunny thoughts for the day? For kicks let's talk about killing puppies," I say without thinking.

He doesn't exactly smile, but his lips quirk a little. "No, I guess I just like the idea of not being anybody but a question mark. You get to define who you are, nobody else does."

"Of course, if being a question mark means you want to kill a bunch of innocent people, then you have to wonder whether it's such a good thing. Can I just tell you this conversation got a little creepy?" I ask. "Should I be thinking about contacting the authorities?"

His lips quirk again and we fall silent. But it's more comfortable this time, strangely enough.

∾

We go over I-20 and we're near EAV, East Atlanta Village. Mom and I used to go to the farmers' market on Thursdays, but it's been a while since we've gone.

Chaz pulls into a parking lot beside a church. This isn't what I was expecting. EAV is known for its funky bars, and I *was* wondering if Chaz knew a way to sneak us in. Of course, Chaz doesn't seem like the barhopping, fake-ID kind of guy, but you never know.

Church, though?

The sun is setting, shadows thickening the air, and the parking lot is empty. Across the street is an abandoned old school, brick and square. Someone has spray-painted a very lifelike grim reaper beside the front steps.

It takes me a minute, then I get it.

"Your shirt," I say to Michael. "That's the building on your shirt!"

CHAPTER SIX

"I started this group," Chaz says, after Trina glances at Michael's shirt and makes the connection to the decrepit building across the street. "We call ourselves, uh, the Excaps, Explorers of Creepy-Ass Places. We're urban explorers, and there's a bunch of people doing this all over the country. So, the Excaps, we basically explore abandoned landmarks around Atlanta and take pictures. Extreme pictures. Ones that most people would never see if we didn't do it. It's exciting. Sometimes we even have to run from the police." He's all proud. Big, bad Chaz, the rebel. "I thought you'd like to see one of our favorite buildings."

I look over at Michael, but he doesn't seem like he's paying any attention.

Chaz sees me, though. "Michael isn't really part of Excaps, he just likes . . ." He trails off.

Michael looks around, an amused tilt to his mouth. "Michael likes creepy-ass places," he says.

Chaz looks at Trina, and you can tell it's important she understand. She does, of course. It's right up her alley.

"Awesome," she breathes. "How cool is that? Are we going in?"

"I thought we would. Do you want to? Really?"

"Yes!"

I knew she would say that. And, oh no, what do I do? I don't want to go inside the building. It's boarded up, it looks dark and dangerous, and it's *got* to be illegal. It's not my thing, *at all.* But they are getting out, and how big a dweeb will I look like if I say I want to stay in the car?

So I get out and hug my elbows in the brisk breeze, wishing I'd thought to bring a jacket. I trail behind as they wait for a couple of cars to pass, and then cross the road to the sidewalk in front of the school. It looks old, a sturdy brick building sheltered by trees, with a few rickety steps leading up to the front doors. There are a ton of boarded-up windows, tall and narrow, and white skinny letters spell out OHN B. GORDON SCHOOL above the small triangular overhang.

Dusk throws thick, charcoal shadows into the secret places of the building. I shiver. I don't like this.

Chaz, however, is like a kid in a candy store. "Come around here, that's where we get in."

He leads us around the building to a door and pushes it open with a slam of his palm. Even though I can still hear cars passing out front, somehow the air feels quiet here, muffled. There's a feeling of stagnant time, a bubble of the past here in the present.

I hate horror movies. They always end badly. You're always

yelling at the screen, *No, don't go in there!* Did no one else hear the little voices screaming, *No, you idiot, don't go inside!*

Apparently not. One by one, they slip through the door, right past the NO TRESPASSING sign, as if it's written in Sanskrit. I stare at it and Michael looks back at me.

"If you don't look at it," he says, "it's not really there."

"What, is it like one of those tree-falls-in-the-forest kind of things?" But I squeeze through after them anyway.

Inside, we're in a hallway, tall and narrow with crumbled plaster and trash littered across the floor. At some point, kids were running down this hall to make the bell. Now it looks like a bomb went off. Above us, ceiling tiles hang precariously from thin strands of metal. Rectangles of dim light spill through the doorless openings onto the floor, a parade of sunshine boxes marching down the hallway.

"This is the John B. Gordon School," Chaz says. "It was built in 1909, and they used it all the way up until the nineties. Then they closed the doors."

"It looks like they up and walked away," I say. "Why did they leave all this stuff?" Schoolbooks lie on the floor, and a bulletin board on the wall advertises a Christmas program dated 1995.

"Seems strange, huh?" Chaz busts out three flashlights from his backpack and hands them to us. He pulls a strap over his head that holds a light like a big Cyclops eye in the middle of his forehead. I stifle the urge to giggle, because he looks real serious about the whole thing.

"Just in case," Chaz says, and I don't feel like giggling anymore. I clutch my flashlight so hard my fingers hurt.

He pulls out a camera. I wish I'd brought mine. I always feel safer with a camera between me and everything else. I dig out my phone; though the camera on it pretty much blows, at least it's something.

"All we take away is pictures," Chaz says solemnly. "No souvenirs. Don't change anything. The point is to leave this place exactly the same for the next people to find."

As graffiti covers the walls (are those *gang signs*? Really?), and the place frankly looks like a demolition crew already went through it once, it seems a little pointless, but Trina and I nod. Michael looks bored.

Chaz grabs Trina's hand, and they disappear into one of the open doorways. Michael looks at me and shrugs. He starts off down the hall and I follow.

It's hard to see anything to like about this place. It's decrepit and abandoned, full of dust and broken pipes and rusted fluorescent lights drooping toward the floor. The paint is flaking off the walls, and the floor is littered with pieces of ceiling tiles and garbage. A doll rests facedown on the bottom step of the stairs leading to the second floor. What little girl left that and never came back? Ivy drapes over the urinals in the boys' bathroom, and I shudder because somehow the green vines seem greedy and grasping.

Michael and I are quiet as we move through the echoing hallways. In one classroom, a neat row of small coat hooks line the wall, and a name tag next to one reads DERRICK. It seems strange to think that twenty years ago a kid named Derrick hung his coat in this room. In one room the chalkboard is a pristine green, as if just waiting for a teacher to pick up a piece of chalk and start writing equations. Colorful squares and triangles line the walls of the stairwells, and a collage of animal pictures hangs beside a tree growing in the middle of a classroom.

Weeds rustle in the auditorium and glass crackles under our feet. One end of the big room is open to the sky, and heavy lights dangle from wires, looking like some sort of bizarre wind chimes swaying in the breeze.

"You don't take pictures?" I ask Michael after a while. "I thought that was the whole point of this."

"Not for me," he says and starts walking again without saying *what* the point is for him.

We end up in a room with a few rusted desks and a humongous teddy bear in the corner, covered with plaster dust and slowly moldering. Fading light the color of dried blood pours thickly through a window with no glass, and the wind whistles and moans through the cracks of the building. It's getting darker and I flick the flashlight on and off again. Just to make sure it works.

Michael sits with his back against a wall and studies the bear. I stand awkwardly. No way am I sitting on the floor.

Michael hasn't spoken much and basically, I suck at talking to guys. I don't have a lot of experience and it always shows.

I cough a little dust out of my throat. "Uh . . . what's with the teddy bear?"

Michael shrugs. "No clue. It's been here ever since we started coming."

"Oh."

Think, Erin, think! "So, you want to be an architect, huh?"

He doesn't say anything for a minute. Then, "Yeah. My dad was an architect."

I, of all people, should have realized what that meant. Instead, I go, "What does he do now?"

"He's dead," he says flatly.

"Oh." I back up until I hit one of the little rusted desks. I lean against it, a balancing act between my butt and the desk to keep us both from crashing to the floor. "Mine too."

He looks at me, the first time I think he really has the whole night. It's like I was some sort of paper doll to him before and now all of a sudden I became a real person.

"When did he die?" he asks after a moment.

"When I was six. I don't remember him much. He flew fighter jets, and then was some sort of National Aerobatic Champion. He liked country-western music and sappy poetry, and he died in a motorcycle accident." It was a quick sum-up of a man's whole life. I didn't know much more, not really, just vague, warm memories. What if one day I had to sum up Mom's life?

She was a good mom and she liked helping the world in her lab. The thing she loved best was to sit at home with me and watch corny movies. She died of breast cancer.

I take off my glasses, fighting back the tears.

"Hey," he says from across the room, "you should do that more often."

"What?" I turn to look at him.

"Take off your glasses. You have nice eyes. I noticed them . . . before. Blue, but they kind of have a purple tint to them, like grapes."

"My eyes look like grapes?" But what I was thinking was, *You noticed me before? When?*

He gets up and comes toward me, but I'll never know what he was going to do or say because we hear Chaz's voice and running footsteps in the hall.

"Guys," Chaz says. "There's someone else here. Probably bums. I think we should go."

Michael looks around. "I'll go check it out."

We wait five minutes and then Michael is back, moving quicker. "They're here for the night. We need to go. One of them is talking to his hand."

We leave quickly, back the way we came into the chilly night air. I notice that Michael isn't wearing his jacket anymore, and I wonder about that.

Voices, the smell of smoke, and crazy laughter follow us out.

CHAPTER SEVEN

Mom looks up from *Sixteen Candles* as Trina and I come in.

"How was it, girls?"

"Chaz brought *Michael Lundstrom*, Ms. B. Hottest guy in school? And I think he likes Erin! At least he talked to her more than he talked to anybody this year." Trina flops down at my mom's feet. I sit on the couch beside her and Mom pats my knee.

"Why wouldn't he like Erin?" Mom's sweet but she's delusional.

"Chaz definitely likes Trina," I say. "They were holding hands."

Trina blushes, which is rare. She jumps to her feet. "I am *hungry*. Feed me, Erin, or lose me forever!" She drags me to my feet and into the kitchen.

"Wait a minute, didn't they take you to dinner while you were out?" Mom calls after us, but we let the door swing shut behind us like we didn't hear her.

"I got the scoop," Trina whispers as I pull out the leftover spaghetti and pop it into the microwave.

"What?"

Trina sits cross-legged on a kitchen chair. "Michael. Didn't you wonder about his story?"

I shrug. I figured he had a story, just like the rest of us.

"His dad *killed* himself, the summer before our sophomore year. That's why he changed so much. Chaz met him on an urban explorer website, and when they met up at one of their abandoned buildings, Chaz said he almost fell out when he saw it was Michael. But Michael was cool, didn't make a big deal about being popular, not that he is anymore. Chaz said when they met, Michael talked about death a lot. I guess he's better now but he's still all . . . *melancholy*."

"That's terrible," I say. "I guess some people's stories are sadder than others."

"But they all end the same, right?" Trina jumps up to get the spaghetti out of the microwave, then turns back to look at me, her face stricken. "Aw, man, Erin, I'm sorry. I didn't mean . . ." She trails off while I keep my face blank.

Yes, the stories all end the same way. Every one of them, but some sooner than others, like a good book where someone has torn out the last pages.

∽৶

Monday morning, Dr. Chu is drawing with a felt-tip marker on my mom's breast.

"Erin, you're welcome to go on out to the waiting room if

you want." Mom looks scared, but like she is trying real hard to *keep it together for the kid.*

I smile, and try to look like it is the most natural thing in the world for my mom to be sitting on the edge of the bed with her hospital gown around her waist and a nurse and doctor practically drawing smiley faces on her boob.

"Wouldn't want to take the wrong one off," the nurse quips and I debate smacking her.

"We wouldn't want that," I say. "Maybe you should write 'excess baggage' across the one you're taking off."

Dr. Chu ignores me, but the nurse looks over and smiles real tight, like, *We both know you're being a smart-ass but I'm going to give you leeway because your mom's sitting right here with marker all over the boob she's about to lose. See this understanding smile? This is me giving you leeway, butt-munch.*

"Done," Dr. Chu announces and hands the pen back to the nurse. "I will see you soon." She pats my mom's shoulder and strides out, looking determined and competent in her child-size white coat.

"All right, what's next?" my mom asks the nurse, all fake cheery. "Are we ready to get this party started?"

"Someone will be along shortly and take you to surgery," the nurse says.

"When you say 'shortly,' can we safely assume that's the same 'shortly' you used when my mom asked you for some ice chips and it took, like, two hours?" I ask.

"Erin," my mom says tiredly and I shut up.

The nurse gives me an evil look behind my mom's back and flounces out.

"I'm sorry," I say immediately.

"I know," my mom says. "I know this is hard on you. I wish you had gone to school today. There's nothing much you can do here."

"I don't want you to be alone." For the first time, though, I see my mother might rather I not be here.

"I wish Aunt Jill could have been here," I say.

"Me too," my mom says. "But Malcolm is very sick, and I understand."

Jill (not my real aunt but she's been my mom's best friend since before I was born) moved to Seattle five years ago to start her own lab. She ended up marrying, and now has a bouncing three-year-old, who, because of Jill's sincere belief that immunizations are the bane of the civilized world, has come down with measles. So, no Jill.

Like me, Mom has acquaintances, but she puts all of her efforts into one best friend. She and Jill met in grad school, and I know Jill hates not being here. But since she can't, and Memaw is dead, that leaves me sitting here beside Mom holding her hand. Blue fire flashes on my finger and I look down at Memaw's sapphire ring. They made Mom take it off when we got here, and she wanted me to wear it. I didn't want to. It makes me feel weird, the logic being: Mom got the ring because her mother died, ergo it is bad mojo for me to be wearing it right before Mom goes into surgery.

Mom glances nervously at the door as someone goes by. "I'll probably be out of it later," she says. "Don't wait around if you're ready to go on over to Trina's for the night."

"I'd rather stay here."

"I know." Mom squeezes my hand. I feel her shiver and I pull the blanket up from the foot of the bed and she drapes it over her shoulders like a shawl.

"Momma, you need your lucky socks." I rummage in her bag until I find the fluffy pair embroidered with reindeer I gave her for Christmas when I was five or six. Dad helped me pick them out for her. Was it his last Christmas? It scares me that I don't remember.

I put them on her and we wait in silence. My chest is starting to get tight and my heart is pounding and I wonder if it's possible to have a heart attack when you're only sixteen. I'm holding on to Mom's hand and all of a sudden I'm not sure I'll be able to let go when they come to take her. What if this is the last time I see her? What if something goes terribly wrong in there and she doesn't come out?

"You know I love you, right?" Mom's voice shakes a little so I know she's thinking the same thing.

"Me too," I say.

With a clatter, an orderly comes in with a rolling bed and helps Mom onto it. I grab her hand again while he tucks the blanket around her. Her face is pale and frightened but she tries to smile for me.

"See you later, alligator," she says softly.

"After a while, crocodile." Tears are slipping down my face because I can't make them stop.

"This train is a-leaving," the orderly says. "Woo-wooo." He makes like he's pulling a train whistle and pushes Mom out the door. I hold her hand until our arms are stretched tight, and then I have to let go.

I cruise the Internet, and wait and wait and wait. They call it a waiting room for a reason.

Trina texts: u ok?

Me: I want this to be a dream, a nightmare I can wake up from

Trina: Hang in there. Luv u

They said it would be at least two hours. It's been five minutes.

I sigh and pick up *Jane Eyre* and try to get into it. It's one of my favorites, which is why I brought it.

A doctor comes in, and I tense, but he goes over to talk to a woman on the other side of the room, and the woman is all smiles, and the doctor tries not to look like he has a God complex, but he totally does.

I try to concentrate on Jane's story. Knowing it turns out okay is the only way I get through it.

Dr. Chu rushes in three hours, six minutes, and twenty-eight seconds after I entered the waiting room.

"She is doing fine. Recovering now, but fine." Dr. Chu is not one to waste time or words. "You can see her when she gets back to her room. We will let you know. Fine? Fine. Good."

She turns and leaves and I try not to cry.

But I do anyway.

CHAPTER EIGHT

"What's up, girl?" Trina asks as she slides into the seat across from me, putting her Hello Kitty lunch bag on the table. Today she's wearing a plaid shirt over a red taffeta dress with "laugh" written in black eyeliner under one eye and "cry" under the other.

"Nothing." I stare down at my soy burger. Splashed with ketchup to make it edible, it looks like some sort of organ, maybe a heart, bleeding across my tray. I pick at the fried okra, which I usually love, but today, nothing tastes right.

It's been four days since Mom's surgery. We have to wait until her follow-up appointment, which is still a week away, to find out what happens next. When Dr. Chu came in after Mom's surgery, she rattled off a bunch of words like "ancillary lymph dissection," "frozen sections," and "metastasis," and Mom's face got still and quiet, but whenever I asked her questions she said, *We need to wait and see what the lab work shows.*

"How you holding up?" Trina reaches over and touches my hand. I'm still wearing Memaw's ring and I stare at it. Evidently the story behind the ring is that Memaw always wanted a sapphire ring, but Granddad was too cheap to buy one. After he died, she used his insurance money to buy the biggest and brightest sapphire she could find. Memaw used to say, *I hate lemonade, so when life hands me lemons I throw 'em away and buy some apples instead.*

"I can't stand this waiting," I say. "It's *killing* me. I just want to know. But then I'm afraid it's going to be bad news, and I'm going to wish I *didn't* know. It's a no-win."

I look up and catch Michael's eye by accident. He's sitting by himself at the back of the cafeteria with his chair leaned back against the wall. He gives me a smoky stare and nods.

I nod back, and then duck my head to hide my face. We've not spoken again since the night of the creepy-ass school expedition. I don't know what I was expecting, but he's as remote to me as ever.

"Before Chaz gets here," Trina says in a low voice, "I wanted to tell you something."

Trina and Chaz have become an instant couple. She's thrown herself into him with the same passion she pursues anything new. I'm happy for her, I really am, but I wish it hadn't happened right now. Right now sucks and I need my best friend.

"Faith found out you and Michael were together the other night. She thinks it was like a date or something. She got all jealous, from what Chaz says. She told Michael she didn't know what he was doing, playing around with a nothing like you."

Trina looks mad, which is always a funny expression on her small, determined face. "Have I told you lately how much I dislike that chick?"

"What? Are you kidding me? It *was* nothing." I look over at the popular kids' table where Faith is laughing and waving her hands around. She looks gorgeous, even as she chows down on her burger. I'm pretty sure she looks adorable as she sits on the pot.

"You don't want to get on her bad side, girl, that's all I'm saying. Remember what happened to Julie Harris last year."

Last year, head cheerleader Julie Harris decided to run against Faith for student council, looking to fluff up her college application. Someone started a rumor just before the election that Julie's dad was a cross-dresser with a fetish for small dogs. The fact that Julie's family owned several small dogs only added plausibility to the story. No one could prove Faith started the rumor, but Julie lost the election and transferred to another school her junior year.

Faith hasn't said another word to me since Ms. Garrison's disastrous invitation to join the e-zine. I told Ms. Garrison I couldn't do it, but I've seen Faith watching me. Now, my heart sinks as I realize she has *another* reason not to like me.

"If she's so into Michael, why did they break up?" I see Chaz making his way over to us, a gaggle of computer geeks trailing behind him like ducks. He flicks a salute at Michael, and Michael nods back. I would never have even noticed the small exchange if I wasn't looking for it.

"I'm not sure what happened. Chaz won't tell me." She looks peeved. Chaz is pretty much ready to dive in front of a bus for her at this point, so either Chaz doesn't know or Michael told him to keep his lips zipped. "But he *did* say Michael was kinda broken up about it. I think Faith is all, *I don't want him, but you can't have him,* you know?"

I can't imagine anyone *not* wanting Michael. But then, Faith being Faith, she probably dropped Michael like a ton of bricks when he stopped being shiny and glossy like her.

"Well, Faith's got nothing to worry about. He hasn't said a word to me all week. I mean, what's she worried about? Look at her. Look at me. There's no comparison. He would be stupid not to date her."

Trina elbows me. "Jeez, chick, stop drinking the pity-me Kool-Aid. You're smart, you're pretty, it's *definitely* possible he could like you. Just watch Faith. She's ice-cold. Chaz says Faith is just like her mom, and neither one of them likes to lose. At anything."

"Oh lovely," I say. "Just what I needed to hear."

Trina flicks my ear. "Stop it. You'll be fine. Did I tell you? Chaz is planning another Excap excursion this Saturday night. Just us, like last week. Somewhere different. Michael says he'll come."

Another creepy-ass building? No, thank you. But I can't help it, my gaze is drawn to Michael, who is buying a Gatorade from the guy selling drinks to raise money for the JROTC.

"I don't like leaving Mom at home by herself at night," I say. "I mean, she's making me go to school, but I don't want to leave her at night."

"I understand. If you decide to go, let me know."

I notice Trina's not quite as anxious for me to go this time, now that she knows Chaz is into her.

But I don't want to go anyway, right?

∽⌒

When I get home, I grab a banana and climb the stairs to my mom's room. The phone rings and I speed up. Maybe it's the doctor, maybe they got the lab work back early and she's calling to tell Mom everything is A-OK. Maybe it was even a false alarm.

I hear her say, "Oh, Jill, my God, it's terrible," and I stop just outside of her bedroom. It's bad, then. Suddenly, I don't want to go into the room. I slide down the wall and sit with my arms around my knees.

"Cancer and this worry on top of *that* . . . I guess it just didn't seem real before. I didn't want to think about it. But now . . . What do I tell Erin? She's going to need to know at some point. She's only sixteen, though. Okay, almost seventeen. But when should I tell her? The counselor said she couldn't even get tested until she's eighteen, and really, it's better to wait until she's twenty-five."

Tested?

There's a pause as she listens, then: "I know there's time, it's just . . . I feel so bad. It'll be awful if I gave her this. She only *got* her breasts a few years ago. How do I tell her this?" Her voice shakes a little.

WTF? My face is hot. Why are they talking about *my* breasts?

Mom says good-bye and hangs up.

I look down at my banana. It's completely squished in my hand.

I get to my feet and push open the door. She's still holding the phone, and she looks up, startled.

"Erin!"

"What's going on? What were you talking to Aunt Jill about? Why should I get tested? For what?"

"It's nothing, Erin. Don't worry about it." She looks sick and guilty.

I stand in the middle of the room. Only one other time in my life have I *known* Mom was lying to me. It was when Memaw was dying and I went to visit her in the hospital. Mom swore up and down Memaw would be okay. But I knew Mom was lying. Mom doesn't fib about the little things.

But she will lie about the big ones if she thinks she's protecting me.

"What do I need to know about? What do I need to get tested for?" I can't seem to stop squeezing the banana and it begins to leak pulpy mess onto my palm.

"Erin . . ."

She has to tell me. She *has* to.

"Mom, whatever it is, you've got to tell me, or I'm going to imagine the worst."

She sighs. "I wasn't going to tell you. Not yet. I haven't wanted to think about it, and I thought we had plenty of time. I don't know how . . . to tell you this."

"Just say it."

She closes her eyes and leans back on the pillow.

"You asked me how I got cancer, and that was actually a very good question. After Memaw died, my doctor decided to test me for something called a BRCA gene mutation." She pronounces it *brackah.* "The BRCA gene is responsible for suppressing tumors in breast tissue, and when it doesn't work right, when it's mutated . . . well, it makes a person prone to breast cancer. Me having cancer so young, and then Memaw dying of ovarian cancer . . . it just made sense for me to get tested. I did and I was positive for the BRCA gene mutation. My body doesn't know how to fight off cancer in my breasts. That's why I got cancer at such a young age the first time, and why it's back in the other breast now. We think Memaw probably had it too."

She looks at me like I'm supposed to get something.

I don't.

"Memaw had it? But she had ovarian cancer. I don't get it."

"If you have a mutation in the BRCA gene, you are also prone to ovarian cancer. While Memaw never got tested for the gene mutation, it's pretty likely she had it and passed it down to me. We'll never know for sure, though." She pauses, studying my face, then she sighs and continues. "There are many mutations of the BRCA gene, but I have one that is usually seen in people of Ashkenazi Jewish ancestry, which is unusual because we're not Jewish. I know that my grandfather, your great-grandfather, came from Poland during World War II, so maybe that's where it came from and he passed it down to Memaw. I don't know. We'll probably never know. All we know is that I inherited a gene mutation that makes it more likely that I'll get cancer."

It's not like I'm stupid. All this talk of ancestors passing down faulty genes finally sinks in. "Wait a minute, wait a minute . . ." My voice is shaky and my chest feels like it is pumped up full and tight with hot air. "You and Memaw . . . Does that mean I have it too?"

Mom pats the bed beside her and I sit, because I can't stand anymore.

I get it now. I get why she didn't want to tell me.

Mom talks some more about the gene thing, telling me there is a good chance I don't have it, and anyway I don't need to worry about it, because it isn't something I need to think about until I am older, she hated keeping secrets from me, she hopes I'm not mad at her, it's hard being a mom and making the right decisions, and she loves me so *very very much.*

We're both crying by the end. I hug her knees because she is still in too much pain to hug her the normal way and she strokes my hair and says, "It's going to be all right, *I promise it's going to be all right.*"

CHAPTER NINE

Friday afternoon, I go to a bookstore. Usually I go with Trina, but she's off with Chaz. I haven't told her yet about the gene. It's stupid, but for some reason I was waiting for her to ask what was wrong today at school. Like she's supposed to be psychic and know. But we're the Dorkster Twins, so yes, I guess I do expect her to know when something's wrong with me.

I grab a caramel macchiato and think about a muffin, and then decide on the muffin, despite the little fat ring I have rolling over the top of my jeans. I wander the aisles, finding the Health section, and flip though the books on breast cancer. Some of them look heavy and serious, some not, like *Breast Cancer for Dummies* and *Totally Pink Mad Libs*. I guess some people find breast cancer absolutely hilarious. Or maybe they just need a good laugh.

Feeling dissatisfied, I find a comfy chair and pull out my

laptop. I search "BRCA gene" and come up with a ton of websites. I start reading, and before long I want to throw up.

Mom says people with this mutated gene are "prone to breast cancer." She didn't tell me people who are positive for the BRCA gene can have up to an 80 percent chance of getting breast cancer. How could she have left that out? She didn't tell me a lot of women who test positive decide to lop off their breasts, and take out their ovaries for good measure, even *before* they get cancer.

I feel like I've been kicked in the stomach. I sit, just breathing for a few minutes. A clerk comes by and I must have looked pretty terrible, because she goes, "Honey, are you okay?"

Just read my fortune cookie, I almost say, *and it's a real bummer.*

"I'm fine," I say instead, and she nods and moves off.

Maybe I don't have the gene. There's a 50 percent chance I *don't*, after all. But I keep thinking about little tumors gleefully growing RIGHT NOW while my stupid mutated BRCA genes run around in circles wringing their hands going *I dunno, what do we do?*

I look back at the computer. I'm on a BRCA website, and I notice they have a forum for young "previvors," which is apparently what they call people with the gene before they have cancer.

I click on it, and most of the posts are from women in their twenties and thirties. They're talking about getting their breasts taken off, perfectly healthy breasts, because they don't want to worry about cancer. Some of them are talking about when to have their ovaries taken out because they also have up to 45 percent chance of getting ovarian cancer. *Do I have time to have children? Will I go into menopause?*

I want to throw up again.

I scroll through the messages back a couple of months, but nobody's my age. Surely, there's got to be someone like me out there who is worried about having the gene?

I sign up using "Thissucks" as my user name. The cursor blinks over the comment section, and then I start typing:

> Life sucks, and then you die.
> Words of a wise Greek philosopher or a 1980s thrash metal band? You decide. That's how I'm feeling right now. I found out my mom has breast cancer, and now that I may have this stupid BRCA gene that means *I* might get breast cancer. I don't know what to think. I don't know what to do. I'm sixteen and thinking about whether I'm going to have to cut off my breasts. Should I get tested? My mom says no, not right now, I need to wait. But I can't stand *not knowing*. How do you live with that? How do you live your life knowing that you might have an 80 percent chance of getting cancer?

I hesitate, then stab Send.

∞

I'm still shaking when I get home. Tiny trembles, aftershocks, that keep quivering along my skin in waves.

I check on my mom, but she's sleeping. The pain medication makes her tired.

Settling down on the couch, I pull up my e-mail and am surprised to see several messages in response to my post on the BRCA website. I'm already starting to feel stupid for posting anything.

I read through them, most of them from adults giving me encouragement but telling me I can't get tested until I'm at least eighteen, and really I should wait until I'm twenty-one or even twenty-five, and to put it out of my mind until I'm older. I scroll through these impatiently. Really? I'm just supposed to NOT think about this until I'm at *least* eighteen? They don't understand. They're all ancient. They don't know what it feels like to be sixteen and find out you might have to cut off your boobs.

The last is from someone with the screen name "Ashley!!!"

When I turned eighteen a couple of months ago, my mom told me I could have the BRCA mutation. My mom had breast cancer but is in remission. Her twin sister, my aunt, just died of it. My grandmother died of breast cancer five years ago. I have a little sister who's going to be finding out in a year she could have this gene mutation.

I got tested a week after my mom told me. I thought there was no way I could have it. I thought I was invincible. I'm the strong one, I'm the one who takes care of everybody else. I thought it would make my mom feel better to know that I didn't have it.

I'm positive. I have the mutation.

Here's the thing. I saw a dolphin jump the other day, flying through the air like she thought she could keep on going and fly to the moon. She crashed down in a big splash of water and then she did it again. You could tell she was having a blast. I started thinking: does she think about death? Do animals feel joy because they don't think about death or because they live with it every day?

I'm learning how to live with this. It's not easy, but hey, nothing is.

CHAPTER TEN

Mom is sleeping when Chaz and Trina pick me up Saturday night. I wasn't going to go, I really didn't *want* to go, but when Trina called to say Michael had asked whether I was going . . . I decided to go. Mom spends most of her time sleeping, all doped up with pain medicine, so she won't even miss me. I want to see Michael again but . . . couldn't we just go to the movies or something?

Trina gives me a Dorkster Twin fist bump as I crawl into the backseat, and Chaz grins at me. He's dressed all in black, like some sort of ninja warrior. I can tell he really gets off on this exploring stuff. Even Trina has gotten into the spirit of the thing; she's wearing a camouflage tank top with tight black pants and a wide black belt.

"Hey," is all Michael says as he slides into the backseat beside me a few minutes later.

"Where we going this time?" Trina asks, bouncing up and

down in her seat like a little jack-in-the-box. She's holding Chaz's hand and he looks proud as a peacock with new tail feathers, as Memaw used to say.

"It's an old prison farm in southeast Atlanta," Chaz says, turning onto Candler Street.

"You know, I grew up here, and it's always like, *really?* when people visit and want to see Peachtree Street and CNN and the Underground and all that. I mean, who cares? This stuff is all so much more *real*," Trina says.

"I didn't know death and decay was your thing," I say sourly, and then wish I hadn't. Trina throws me a hurt look and everyone is quiet for a while.

I can't help it. I'm not getting it. And it's later this time, so it's going to get dark while we're there. Trina even packed a picnic basket, and Michael is carrying a cooler. The plan is to hang out at some dark, dank building long past sunset. F-U-N.

I pat my bag where I've stashed my flashlight. I put new batteries in it, and I've only checked it, oh, about twenty times. It should work. I've also got my camera. I *am* looking forward to taking some pictures, if nothing else.

Well, maybe there is something else I'm looking forward to. I glance at Michael out of the corner of my eye. He's in jeans and a black T-shirt, with a dark blue bandanna over his hair. A tiny skull on a black cord hangs around his neck. The broody thing really works for him.

He must have sensed me looking at him, because he turns with a stare as dark as coal. "Chaz says your dad left you a '65 Mustang. You don't drive it?"

I like the way he doesn't do small talk. He says what he wants to say. "It's not running. It's pretty cruddy and Mom wants to sell it since it's taking up space in the garage."

"Maybe I can help you with it. I like working on cars," he says.

"Sure. I mean, yes. Anytime." I'm flustered and he can tell. His lip does that upward quirk, and he turns to look out the window. I nurse the small glow inside me.

"Michael is a *genius* at cars. Michael is a genius at everything, the jerk," Chaz says. "He'll be designing award-winning skyscrapers when he's twenty-five, watch."

Michael shrugs.

I see Chaz's eyes in the rearview mirror and I can tell he's about to say something else, but decides not to.

Trina chatters away as the roads become increasingly desolate and the trees crowd close. Shadows flicker over the car, and I close my eyes, trying to tell myself, *This is going to be all right.* Just then, Chaz pulls off the side of the deserted road and jumps out of the car like the Energizer Bunny. Trina gives me a one-armed hug as I slowly get out.

"You going to be okay?" she whispers. Her breath smells like peppermint and I can tell she's just chewed a mint. *Someone is expecting a kiss.* I think about asking her for a mint, then decide not to.

I nod. No, I'm not sure I'm going to be fine, but once again, I'm here. I can't just sit in the car. Please, someone, next time, tell me to stay at home.

We walk down an overgrown road through the trees, and the squat prison buildings come into view. They're covered with graffiti and kudzu, and surrounded by a parking lot that is almost completely overrun with grass and bushes.

"A giraffe and an elephant named Maude are buried here somewhere," Chaz says, gesturing vaguely toward the rolling land around the crumbling remains of buildings. "This used to be the burying ground for circus animals that were too big to cremate."

It's a warmer-than-normal evening, and the cicadas hum as the sun droops in the sky, the shine of its bloom dull and crimson. The faint roll of thunder in the distance vibrates gently in my chest and birds chirp merrily, at odds with the sincere need I feel to whisper.

Leaves crunch under my feet as I follow the others toward a long white building with barred windows and no roof on the second floor.

"Some bums caught it on fire a while back." Chaz shakes his head, like anybody actually *cares* that half the decrepit old building burned down.

We enter the building through the front entrance, covered by a cheery portico that not only protects the front door but an abandoned old boat as well.

Nobody mentions the boat, so I don't either.

Inside are large open rooms, framed by banks of windows covered only with bars. Rusted pipes droop from the ceiling, and floor tiles slip and slide under our feet. A few small metal bunk beds lie on their sides and bloated water-stained paperbacks lie open as if waiting for someone to come back and finish reading them. The prison laundry is full of rusty washers and dryers, massive enough for me to crawl inside. A pile of what must have been fifty seat cushions molders in a corner, and thousands of sheets of paper litter the floor.

I pick one up and read that Thomas West, born November 8, 1956, was admitted into the prison in 1987, in possession of "a wallet and one honest face."

I let the paper flutter back to the floor.

"Check out the art," Michael says, the first thing he's said since we entered the building.

It's hard to miss the street art. Colorful spray-can paintings cover every available wall, full of big bubble letters and vibrant blues, green, reds, and oranges. Faces peer at us from walls, and strange vivid paintings sprawl the length of entire rooms.

We stop at the entrance of a long narrow hallway, dark and dripping in the fading light. Someone has painted a man— boy?—dressed all in gray, crouching on the ground clutching his head in his hands. Above his head, it reads "I'm so ronery."

"Ronery?" Trina says. "What's that mean?"

Chaz laughs, a sputtering hiccuping sound. "It's from *Team America: World Police*? He's trying to say 'lonely.' *I'm so lonely.*"

Trina slips her hand in Chaz's, and he pulls her close. I busy myself with my camera. By the time I've snapped several shots, Trina and Chaz have moved off.

Michael is still near me, by a wall. I walk over to him and see the paint is peeling off the wall, erasing the painted squiggles on top and revealing an empty canvas underneath.

Without speaking, Michael heads down the dark narrow hallway and I follow. At one point, he stops and offers me his hand over a large puddle. The feel of his warm hand sends tingles through me from head to feet.

We pass cell after cell, tiny rooms only big enough for one person. Each cell has a metal shelf attached to the wall for a bed and a rusty metal table, and some still have toilets.

Michael heads up a flight of steps, and I hesitate. It's getting darker, and the stairs look dicey. I debate turning on my flashlight, but instead hurry up after Michael, who is looking at a painting of a puffer fish in the stairwell.

Upstairs, we go down another hall and Michael stops in front of a cell door.

"This is my favorite," he says.

I step inside the tiny cell. There's no door, but still it feels creepy. What grabs my attention right away is the picture someone has painted on the wall. It's a bearded man in an orange prison suit, and the artist has painted him sitting on the metal bunk with his elbows on his knees. Above him are several lines, crosshatched, as if he's been marking the days he's been imprisoned. A dialogue bubble reads "Mama Tried."

"I know that one," I say. "My dad and I used to listen to old country-western music all the time. That's from a Merle Haggard song. It's about a kid whose mom tried her best, but he still ended up in prison when he was twenty-one."

Michael nods, looking faintly impressed. "I had to look it up. But yeah, that's what it's from."

I pull out my camera, but the cell is so narrow I have to back up close to Michael to get the shot. He could have moved, but he doesn't, and I can feel the heat of him. I try to concentrate on the picture, but I'm distracted by his warm breath on the back of my neck. I wish I got a mint from Trina. My skin buzzes from the closeness.

After taking several shots, I have no more excuse to stand so close to him so I walk over to the back of the cell and examine the green flaky paint that looks like some sort of surrealistic painting, all swirly and textured.

"My mom never tried one goddamn day in her life," Michael says suddenly.

I turn to look at him, surprised by the bitterness in his voice.

"My mom never wanted me, I don't think. I mean, it was cool when I was a kid—I was like an accessory—but once I got older, all she cares about is shopping and drinking wine with her friends. I don't think she even cared that much when my dad died, 'cause she got to spend more time doing what *she* wanted."

Michael looks away. I wonder what it would be like to have your dad commit suicide. I still feel guilty about my dad dying, and I know it wasn't my fault. *Logically*, I know that, but it still feels like maybe I did something wrong. But Michael's dad killed himself. How hard would that be to take?

"I'm going to get into a school as far away from here as possible, and after I graduate, I'm gone. I feel like that guy." Michael points at the picture of the inmate. "I'm counting my time, waiting to get out of prison."

I don't know what to say. I hate it when I can't think of anything to say. He's opening up to me and I got *nothing*.

He looks at me, and I can almost feel the touch of his eyes, like the tip of a dark feather drifting over me.

"I think it's cool you want to be an architect," I say; "I'm sure you'll get into an awesome school." God, "cool" and "awesome" in the same sentence. He must think I'm an idiot.

"What's your deal?" he asks. "What do you do?"

For a horrible moment, my mind is blank. What *do* I do? What could I possibly have to say that would interest him? My life is so boring, it's surprising it doesn't put *me* to sleep. "I write!" I blurt out. "I like to write."

He nods slowly and then says, "Anyway, there's more to see. And I want a beer." He leaves abruptly, and I scramble to keep up.

It's dark. Too dark. My breath is coming in quick pants as I follow after the shadow that used to be Michael. I can't even tell for sure if it's him or not anymore. My feet catch on planks of wood and metal bars, and an odd mewling sound comes from inside me. I stop and rummage in my bag for my flashlight. Once I flick it on I feel a whole lot better. Michael is at the top of the stairs by the puffer fish, waiting for me.

I go toward him and he disappears down the dark stairway. By the time I get to the top, he's gone. How did he get down so fast?

The walls are crawling with mold and seem way too narrow. The stairs look unsafe. Did I really think it was a good idea to climb them? *Really?*

Taking a deep breath, I start down. I hear a crack underneath my foot and throw myself sideways against the wall for support.

The flashlight falls from my fingers and goes out when it hits the ground.

It's dark. Pitch-dark.

I try not to scream.

Then I do.

Even with my eyes squeezed shut, I can sense the flashlight beam sweep over me, then I hear footsteps.

I stop screaming, but only because I've stuffed my fist in my mouth.

"Hey," Michael says. "Hey, what's up? Are you okay?"

He crouches down near me, but not touching. I open my eyes, and I'm looking at an ant making its laborious way across a stretch of wall that must seem like a thousand miles to it. I stare at it, willing myself to calm down.

"Breathe," he says. "In and out."

I concentrate on breathing, in and out, and my heart begins to slow.

Michael sits down on the step below me, stretching his legs out in front of him. He studies me in the gloom.

"It's the dark?"

I nod, just barely.

He touches my hand lightly, a quick stroke of his fingers on my palm, and I somehow sense he gets it, what the dark feels like to me.

"What's going on?" Chaz and Trina appear at the bottom of the stairs.

"I thought she was right behind me, so I went on. I think she dropped the flashlight," Michael says.

"Oh *no*." Trina comes thundering up the stairs and kneels beside me, throwing her arms around me. "It's okay, honey, it's okay."

I feel better, and stupid. I feel like a little kid, scared of the dark, but I've been like this since I was six. I sleep with the lights on, and even then it's hard, because I know the darkness is pressing hungrily against the windows. I do a lot of reading at night. It gets me through.

But this has never happened to me in front of other people, and my whole body is hot with embarrassment. I force myself to my feet, feeling Trina's arm around me like a protective cloak.

"I'm okay." I try to laugh. Hollow and fake. "Sorry about that. I'm okay."

But I'm not. And I haven't been for a long time.

CHAPTER ELEVEN

"This must really suck for you," Mr. Jarad says.

"Uh . . . okay?" I say.

"Wow. Hey, are you into baseball at all?"

I stare at him. My first session with the school counselor is not going at *all* the way I thought it would. I was expecting a woman in a sensible pantsuit and glasses taking lots of cryptic notes as she said profound things like, *And how did that make you feel?* Mr. Jarad, however, looks like he just came in from coaching football or baseball or something else sporty, and would rather have me do jumping jacks than talk.

He reaches over, grabs a baseball, and swings his legs up onto the coffee table between us. He throws the ball up and down. I watch, fascinated.

"No? Not into baseball? Okay, this kid, fresh from the minors, comes up to the big leagues. And to teach him a lesson, the pitcher throws one at him. Hits him square in the arm. So the kid, he takes his walk to first, and then makes it all the way around to score one for the team. Then he passes out, because the ball shattered his elbow."

Mr. Jarad stares at me expectantly. "Uh . . . bummer?" *What a waste of freaking time* is what I'm thinking but I try to look interested. This is getting me out of trig and I promised Mom.

"What I'm thinking is you might be feeling a little like that kid." He tosses the baseball up and down, concentrating on it, not me. "Not a lot of time under your belt, and here comes this pitch out of nowhere that knocks you into next Wednesday. But you don't have much choice, do you? You have to keep on going, even though you're hurting bad inside."

He stops.

I am quiet for a minute, and then the words spill out, like verbal vomit.

"Tomorrow is Mom's appointment to find out how bad the cancer is. Mom won't let me go with her to the appointment, and I don't understand why not. She's in a lot of pain, and you can tell she's just waiting to find out what happens next, that she can't think about anything else until she knows. It's been ten days, and all we've been doing is *waiting.* And she wants me to go to school and act like everything is A-OK."

He's looking at me now but the ball is still going up and down with a soft *thwack, thwack, thwack.* I stare at it for a minute and keep talking, barely aware of what I'm saying.

"She doesn't want me to help her, you know, to the

bathroom, or change her tube thingy that's draining all this yellow gunk from her chest. Then she starts crying, she's in so much pain. I can tell she wants to be strong for me, but she hurts so bad she can't help herself. Maybe she doesn't want me home during the day. Maybe it's so hard to be strong for me that I'm making it harder for her. Or maybe she *needs* me there so she can be strong. I don't know. Either way I know I have to be strong for her but I'm not sure how long I can be and I can't stand this *waiting*."

I'm breathing hard and I can feel him looking at me.

"And I know I shouldn't be thinking about this right now, but I can't get it out of my head that I might have this gene mutation like she's got and soon it'll be my turn to be going through all this. I think of the *waiting* I'll have to do until I finally get cancer and I'm not sure I can take it. I don't even know if I have the mutation or not, but all this not-knowing is about to drive me insane. I want to scream and scream and scream."

"Why don't you?" Mr. Jarad says. "Go somewhere where no one can hear you and scream to your heart's content."

"What is this, primal therapy? I can't go somewhere and scream. People would think I'm crazy. *I* would think I'm crazy."

He shrugs. *Thwack, thwack, thwack.*

"I found a website where I can do a BRCA test online and no one would know about it. You're *supposed* to go talk to a genetic counselor and Mom said I could go if I want to, but I know they'll just tell me not to think about it and wait until

I'm older. That's what everybody has been saying. Do they really think I can *not* think about it? Really? Maybe some people can, but not me. It's *all* I can think about. And, really, I'm still not sure whether I even *want* to know, and it feels stupid and selfish for me to be thinking about all this when my mom can barely pee by herself and she needs me so much. I'm just so afraid . . ."

Mr. Jarad looks at me. "What are you afraid of?"

"Huh?" I glare at him, but he's not being sarcastic. "What do you think? I'm afraid my mom is going to die." My breath hitches just saying it. "Okay, I'm not always the best daughter, I forget to pick up my stuff and sometimes I'm bitchy to her, but . . . I can't lose her. I can't lose her too."

He's quiet while I concentrate on *not* crying. And then I do, and he hands me a tissue.

"Erin, when you're feeling like this," he says, "you need to be careful with yourself. Teens in your position have a tendency to engage in risk-taking behavior, like drinking and driving, and drugs. Here's my tip for the day: go somewhere and scream instead."

∽

I ditch school after my session with Mr. Jarad. I don't really mean to. I tell Ms. Brown, the front office secretary, I forgot my trig homework in my car and she looks at me all pity-eyed.

"Oh dear," she says, her words fluttery. Ms. Brown is not that old, but everything about her shakes and quivers, from her flyaway hair to her trembling hands and voice. "I'm *so* sorry about your mother. We've let your teachers know, and please feel free to come talk to Mr. Jarad whenever you need to."

One of Faith's friends, a blond clone in super-skinny jeans, has come into the office, and she leans on the counter, unabashedly listening.

"I can't imagine how you must feel," Ms. Brown goes on, her voice sounding as if it is being fed through a high-powered fan. "If it were my mother—"

"Thank you, Ms. Brown!" I say loudly, interrupting her. "I'm just going to go get my trig homework, okay?" *Shut-upshutupshutup.*

"Of course, dear," she says and turns to the clone, who is eyeing me thoughtfully.

I go out to the parking lot and sit in my car for a while.

Then I drive away.

I don't know where I'm going. I just drive. I end up at Stone Mountain Lake at this cool spot Mom used to take me and Trina when we were kids, right by a decrepit old rope swing. I stare at the lake, glimmering blue like the sapphire ring I'm still wearing. After a while I get on the swing and go back and forth, back and forth. I kind of want to jump in the water but I have all my clothes on. I swing higher and higher thinking I might fall in by accident, but I never do.

I stay at the lake for a while. I try to scream a little bit but it comes out a weird squawk, like a duck fart, so I close my mouth and just scream in my head some more.

I have to go back to school to get my books, and it's strange walking the halls without the yelling, jostling mass of people. There's still a few kids hanging out, waiting for various after-school clubs to start, and I nod at a couple people I know as I hurry to my locker. As I grab my books, I see Michael coming down the hall out of the corner of my eye. Without thinking, I slam the locker shut and rush the other way. It's been four days since I broke down at the abandoned prison, and I've been avoiding Michael. I feel bad I ruined everybody's night when they had to take me home early.

I can hear his steps behind me, but he doesn't call out. It will be hard to avoid him in the parking lot, and I'm starting to feel shaky and weepy. I don't want him to see me like this.

I see the double doors to the auditorium and I slip through them, wincing as they clang shut behind me. The auditorium is dark except for a few dim lights spotlighting chairs and tables on the stage. I hurry toward them, my heart pounding.

Just as I reach the stage, I hear the door open behind me and I turn to see Michael standing in the doorway. He's in the shadows, but I know it's him as he walks slowly toward me down the long aisle. I stand beside the stage, holding my elbows, feeling stupid and young.

"What's up?" he says as he nears me. "I got the feeling you were running away from me."

"What? No, no, no," I say, trying for, *Are you kidding, me run from you?*

"Look," he says, "about the other night. There's nothing to be ashamed of. Plenty of people don't like the dark."

"Not everybody's such a freak about it though," I say.

He shrugs. "Then they have other things to be a freak about."

I look at him, because his tone is peculiar. "What are you a freak about?"

He comes up beside me and leans against the stage. I turn, and I'm too close to him, but I don't want to back up. I'm practically standing between his legs, but he doesn't seem to notice.

"I stay up all night drawing plans and then building them as models," he says. "That's my dirty little secret. I'm so tired by the time I get to school, I can barely stay awake, but I can't seem to stop. It's all I want to do."

He grabs my hand and pulls me closer so now I'm not *practically* standing between his legs, I *am* standing between his legs. I feel like I can't breathe. His eyes are dark and shadowed in the dim light.

"See," he says, "everybody's got their thing . . ." He almost whispers it though, because he's pulling me even closer as he says it and I know, I *know* we're going to kiss and my head is going crazy with *ohmygodohmygodohmygod.*

The door bangs open and a group of chattering people enter the auditorium. They go silent when they see us, and I jump away from Michael, feeling my cheeks flare.

Faith stands there with the rest of the debate club, and her face is pale white.

"What's he doing with *her*?" someone says, not trying to be quiet.

"Wow, Faith, who knew your replacement would be a *dork*,"

someone else says, and it's hard to miss the glee. These friends of Faith don't mind seeing her brought down a peg.

Before anybody else can say anything, I flee down a side aisle and escape out the back door into the parking lot.

This is bad, very bad.

CHAPTER TWELVE

Mom is awake, doing arm exercises, wincing as she does them. If she doesn't do the exercises, her arm will swell up like a balloon, but you can tell it's excruciating.

"How are you doing, Rinnie?"

"All good," I lie.

The phone rings and we both jump, and then break out in half-hysterical laughter.

It's the school. I can tell right off because Mom goes from a hiccuping "H-h-h-ello?" to "Yes?" in a stronger voice and she's eyeing me. I squirm. I really didn't think through this whole ditching-school thing.

Mom hangs up and looks at me. She doesn't say anything.

"Okay," I say. "Yes, I ditched school. I went to see the school counselor, I want you to know. I did *that*. And then I was sort of . . . upset, I guess. So I left."

Her face crumples a little, and I wish I told her there was this movie I just *had* to see. Then she wouldn't think it was her fault I am becoming a juvenile delinquent.

"I should put you on restriction or something, shouldn't I?" She starts doing the arm exercises again, her face sweaty with the pain.

"Probably."

She sighs. "Look, this is hard on both of us. Promise you won't do it again and we'll leave it at that. Okay?"

"Okay," I say.

She looks away. "I know this is hard for you . . . especially after what happened with your dad. You seem so lost to me sometimes."

"I'm right here," I say. "Didn't need bread crumbs or anything to find my way back."

"No . . ." She shakes her head and concentrates on her arm exercises for a minute. Up, over her head, down by her side. "Are you sure you don't want to join the school e-zine? I think it's very exciting that they asked you. And it would be a good way for you to engage."

"Engage in what?"

"In the *world*, Erin," she says because she knows I know what she's talking about. It's not the first time we've been on this conversational merry-go-round. Usually it's because I read so much. The e-zine thing is just a new twist.

"I think I'll go engage in a graham cracker," I say. "Do you want one?"

School the next day is a nightmare. First of all, Mom's appointment is today, and as much as I begged, she wouldn't let me go with her.

Second, I find out in third period when someone says, "Hey it's Va-jay-jay Girl!" that everybody thinks I got caught in the girls' locker room looking at my own vagina in the mirror.

It is just bizarre enough to be believable.

People believe.

Unfortunately, I know exactly where the rumor came from. Yesterday, during gym, I started my period. I stood on the bench in the locker room so I could look at the back of my pants in the mirror to make sure I hadn't bled through. Missy Keller came in about that time and saw me. Later, I saw her whispering to Faith, looking at me, and laughing.

It's all Faith needed.

I can feel the eyes on me as I pass and hear the whispers that follow in my wake. I'm sweating as I make it through the salad-bar line and look around for Trina. She is sitting with Chaz and a crowd of his geek friends, and she waves me over. I can hear the snickers as I walk across the cafeteria and I hear someone say, "There goes Va-jay-jay Girl!"

Chaz's table gets quiet as I approach. Trina is too busy trying to move people over so there's room for me to notice the eye rolling and smirks going around.

"Scoot," Trina says to Chaz. "Make room for Erin."

"Hey, no, don't move," I say. "I was just coming over to say hi." Which I totally wasn't. "It's such a pretty day I thought I'd eat outside."

"Are you sure?" Trina asks. "You want me to come? I'll come. Hold on." She grabs her tray.

"No, no, I'll be fine. Need to get some sun, right?"

As I walk away, I hear someone from the redneck table say, "She's trying to get sun where the sun don't shine," and everybody laughs. I pass Molly Jenkins and her crew, kids I used to hang out with in elementary school, and she gives me a sympathetic shrug. Everyone's heard. *Everyone.*

I'm hoping Trina will come sit with me, but she doesn't. Only seniors are allowed to sit outside, but there are too many kids for the monitors to know who is in what grade, so as long as you don't look like a giggly, clueless freshman, you're okay.

I wonder if Trina has heard the rumor and my new nickname. I still haven't told her about the BRCA gene. I feel mean and small, treasuring my secret and my resentment. *If she loved me she would know something's wrong.*

I sit at a picnic table by myself. I'm not hungry but I don't want to sit there and look pitiful. I try calling Mom, but she must be sleeping, because she doesn't pick up. Her appointment isn't for another two hours. I reread the e-mail from Ashley!!!, the chick from the BRCA forum. I haven't e-mailed her back. I wasn't sure what to say.

Now I type.

My mom didn't plan on telling me about the gene until I was older. In some ways I wish she had kept it a secret, but then I feel angry at her for even THINKING of keeping something like that from me. But now I don't know what to do. She says she doesn't want me to think

about it. I don't think I can stand it. The waiting. I could
get tested for the gene by that online place and Mom
wouldn't even know.

Are you glad you got tested? Or do you wish you
didn't know you are positive? I'm Pandora right now,
wondering whether or not to open the box.

Ashley!!! e-mails back almost immediately:

I wish I had an answer for you. I don't.

Easiest would be not to ever know about the gene at
all. That's the kid in me, I guess. Once I knew, there was
no going back to oblivious. I got tested because I wanted
to know one way or another. Now that I know, I try to live
my life like it's a nonissue. When it's time, I'll do the
surveillance.

Honestly? I don't think about death. I think about living.

Me:

I keep thinking of getting cancer like my mom. It's so
hard watching her go through this. We're still waiting to
see how bad the cancer is and it's so HARD to sit around
and wait. I want to be doing something, anything.

Ashley!!!:

So . . . I went kite surfing yesterday. You stand on a board
about the size of a surfboard and you hold on to a sail

and you go zipping across the water like you're not even connected to it. And sometimes you're not, sometimes you hit a wave and you go flying through the air and it's just like you're flying. You don't *think* when you're out there, you just feel.

But here's the thing. Yesterday was windy, I mean, REAL windy. It has to be windy to go kite surfing anyway, but it was seriously blowing. It was scary, and I'm standing on the shore trying to decide whether or not I wanted to do it. I hate to admit it, but I stood there a long time, trying to decide. And then I went ahead and did it, and it was scary, yeah, but not nearly as bad as I thought it was going to be. Really? The worrying was worse than the actual thing.

"You saving the whole table?" Michael straddles the bench so he's facing me.

"Watch out, you sat on my imaginary friend." I look up and give him a little smile.

Michael pushes his dark hair out of his eyes. His lip twitches but he doesn't smile.

"One day I'll make you laugh," I say. "Evidently I'm good at it. Evidently I make a *lot* of people laugh."

"People are stupid. You can't worry about them."

"Oh yes I can."

He shrugs. "No one believes it, anyway."

"Oh yes they do."

He looks at me steadily. "Anyway, I just wanted to come say hi. So. Hi."

"Hi," I say. It's moral support and I'll take it.

He leaves and Faith comes out of the cafeteria in time to see me staring at his butt as he walks away.

If looks could kill, I'd be a bag of bones smoking on the ground.

∽

I'm walking out to my car with Chaz and Trina after school, hurrying because I want to get home to Mom and hear what the doctor said, when Faith comes toward us.

"Chaz!" she calls.

"Uh-oh," I say, "Dorkster Twins activate."

I wait for the fist bump, but Trina is staring at Faith. "I like her outfit," she says, almost to herself. Trina has been dressing more . . . normal lately. I hadn't really thought about it, but the red pantsuit she is wearing is pretty tame, even with her hair up in a high, bright blue ponytail.

She avoids my look of amazement.

"Heeeyy, Chaz." Faith tucks her dark, shiny hair behind a delicate little ear. "Just wanted to tell you I'm throwing a little party at that school—what's it called? The one you and Michael took me to by EAV?"

"Uh . . . the John B. Gordon School?" Chaz is confused.

"That's it. I figured you could be there to show us how to get in, okay?"

Chaz frowns. "At the school? A party? Why?" *Snap, snap* go his fingers.

"I thought it was pretty cool. How fun and goth would it be all lit up with candles? Something different. My friends have no imagination when it comes to parties. I wish I thought of it over Halloween."

"You can't mess it up," Chaz says, still perturbed. "You have to pick up all the trash."

Faith smiles, her white, white smile. "Of course. I know how strongly you feel about leaving nothing but our footprints. I hear that all the time in my Sierra Club meetings. I get it. After you get us inside, why don't you hang out? And, you can bring your friend if you want." She smiles all crocodile at Trina, who looks faintly stunned.

"Hey thanks, Faith, sure," Chaz says. "Sounds like fun and yeah, we'll be there." He's flustered enough to make it clear he's not used to this sort of attention from Faith. I wonder how she treated him when she was dating Michael.

"Thanks, Faith, that sounds like *loads* of fun," Trina gushes. Someone has taken over her body.

Faith smiles queenly and lets her glance fall on me before turning away. No, I am not invited.

"Who gives a crap about your stupid party?" I say without thinking.

Chaz steps back from me like I might be contagious.

Faith turns around slowly. She says nothing for a moment while she looks me up and down.

"Who are you again?" she says. "The party is just for my friends. I'm sorry but I'd rather not have any losers there. You understand, right?"

This is said in such a sweet voice it takes a moment for the words to sink in. She's gone before I think of anything to say. Naturally.

"Oh no, Erin, why'd you do that?" Trina asks. "I told you you needed to watch her. God, I should have said something. I should have stuck up for you. What is wrong with me?" She grabs her ponytail and yanks on it, hard.

"Stop it," I say tiredly. "It's okay." I can't blame her because I didn't say anything either. But I do blame her, just a little.

"I won't go to her party," Trina promises. "I don't even *want* to go." But her tone is unconvincing.

"No," I say, shaking my head. "It's no big deal. You guys go. It sounds like fun."

"Are you sure?" Trina studies my face.

I shrug and try to smile. "I've got to go. I'll talk to you later."

"I wish you hadn't said that to her, Erin," Chaz says as I walk away. "*Epic* fail."

But I can't worry about it right then, because I'm too focused on getting home to Mom.

I should have worried, though. I should have realized Faith wasn't done with me.

CHAPTER THIRTEEN

"What did they say?" I blurt as I burst through the kitchen door.

But I can see it's bad. I stop, and it's like I'm waiting to get hit, my stomach muscles all tight and my breath coming in short punches.

"It's . . . a little worse than they thought. More extensive, more aggressive, more . . . everything." Mom looks up at me, her face taut and pale.

"All right. What next?" I try for all upbeat, like *no big deal*.

"Chemo," she says. "Then radiation. We'll beat it, it's just going to be a little bit harder."

She's crying, and I'm crying, and I hug her, but it's hard because of the bandages and the tube and so we sort of rock back and forth as best we can.

The next morning before school I order a genetic test. The website says it will take a couple of days for the kit to arrive. Then I have to spit into a tube and send it back to them and it'll take two to four weeks to find out if I have the mutation.

I'm not sure I'm going to do it. I don't know if I want to do it.

But if I have the test, at least I *can* do it. I can't take the limbo anymore. I don't want to be standing on the edge of the water wondering how bad it's going to be. Sink or swim, I want to *do* something.

As I go to get up from my desk, a piece of paper flutters to the ground. It's the number for the flying school I got at Dino's, the day my mom told me she had cancer. I still don't even know why I got it.

I look up at the picture of Dad standing by his red plane with his dark, curly hair just like mine and the big smile on his face. That's what I remember about Dad. He was always smiling, always laughing. And yet he did dangerous things, like flying fighter jet missions over Iraq. After he got out of the military, he took up aerobatic flying as a hobby, which meant flips and rolls and stalls and all sorts of crazy stuff. He teased death every day, and one day death got tired of playing.

Do animals feel joy because they don't think about death or because they live with it every day?

I wish I could ask Dad. I think he'd know.

I remember how it felt when I was up in the plane. I loved looking down at the world from up in the air. It all made sense up there, somehow, even when we were flying upside down and doing loop-de-loops and my parents told me *they loved me, they did, but Mommy and Daddy needed to live apart.*

Flying with my dad was the best time of my life. How sad is that? The best time of my life happened when I was six years old.

I want to feel like that again.

Without letting myself think too much about it, I pick up the phone and dial the number.

"What the hell?" is the gruff answer.

"I, uh, want to sign up for flying lessons," I say, confused. "Do I . . . have the right number?"

"At six thirty in the morning? Are you kidding me?"

"Oh I'm sorry, I didn't realize . . ." I feel stupid, my cheeks glowing hotly. "I'll call back later."

I won't though. I already know that. And it is kind of a relief. I tried, at least.

"Wait a minute, wait a minute," the man grumbles right as I go to hang up. "How about Saturday, a week from tomorrow. What's your name? Speak up!"

"Erin," I manage.

"Erin. E-r-i-n. Ten o'clock. Sharp. And if you're under eighteen, you need to have your parents sign a consent form so they won't sue my ass off if you die. Got it? Good."

He hangs up on me.

I stare at the phone.

What have I done?

That afternoon I call Aunt Jill on my way home from school.

"Hey, Rinnie," she says, her voice loud and cheerful as usual. Immediately I conjure her round, smiling face framed by long, dark hair streaked with gray. Jill always smells faintly of sweat, because she uses a crystal instead of deodorant, and washes her hands so much you start wondering what kind of creepy-crawly stuff she's working on in her lab. She comes across as kooky sometimes, but she's a supersmart microbiologist who started her own successful research company.

"How're you holding up?"

"Uh . . . fine, I guess. Listen. I need some advice."

"Shoot. Wait. Malcolm? Mommy needs some mommy time right now. Remember, we talked about this? Just because Mommy is on the phone doesn't mean you have to talk on the phone too."

I hear some incoherent little-kid mumbling, and then Jill says, "Okay. What's up? I have about five minutes until he figures out how to pick the lock."

"I want to fly!" I say. "I don't know why, but I've been thinking about it a lot, and I even registered for lessons, but I need Mom to sign some sort of parental consent form. And you know what *she's* going to say."

"Wowie. I wondered if your dad was ever going to make an appearance in you. You know why your mom's going to say no, right?"

"Because it's dangerous." It makes me almost sick—with dread, excitement?—just thinking about it.

Jill makes a buzzing raspberry sound. "Wrong answer. Try again."

I frown. "Because my dad flew? I remember them fighting about it a lot before they got a divorce. After, too, when he took me up."

"You're getting closer. Your mom . . . I knew her before she met your dad. She was on a mission to get away from that crappy little town where she grew up. She wanted a career—a good one, mind you, so she'd never have to worry about being poor again."

"Mom was poor?" I frown. I guess I knew Memaw and Granddad didn't have a whole lot of money, but Mom never said anything about being *poor*, as in I'm-hungry-and-I-have-no-shoes poor.

"Yes, she was poor." Jill's voice is firm. "She got her degree and her good job, and then she started looking around for a nice, stable husband because she wanted to have a family. She met your dad, and at first he seemed like the answer to her prayers. He was calm and steady, he had a good business, flying private charters. He seemed secure, and that's what she wanted. I've never seen two people so in love. And for a while it worked, but ultimately . . . your dad had something in him that needed to go fast. In the air, in his life, everything. He needed that element of danger to make him feel alive. And your mom . . . your mom has to feel safe. It's what makes her tick. And once your dad started taking you up in the plane . . . it was too much for her."

I never thought about it, but she's right. Mom is happiest when she's in her comfort zone, which seems to include mainly watching movies at home with me and going to work. We never went anywhere on vacation, though we would do fun stuff around Atlanta like go to the zoo, or the aquarium, or the botanical gardens. Has Mom even been out of the state of Georgia? How could she have fallen in love with someone like my dad?

"She even asked him to stop flying," Jill continues, "and he did for a while, but he was so unhappy . . . I think she always felt guilty she asked him to stop. And mad he couldn't, not really.

"So, here's the thing. You could have chosen about anything else, oh, say, recreational knife juggling, and she'd take it better than the flying. That's why she's going to resist. Because she still feels like flying is what took him away from her."

"I never knew . . ."

"Yeah, well, I think it's time you *did* know. Malcolm, sweetie, the door is locked for a reason." I hear an outraged howl.

"Can I ask you something, Rinnie?" Jill says over the stuck-pig screeching.

"What?"

"Why did you sign up for flying lessons? I'm proud of you, honey, I am, but I'm just wondering why you're doing it."

I am quiet for a minute. In the background, Malcolm's rage has turned into pitiful sobbing. "Up there, it was just me and Dad and all that sky. It was like we could do anything, go anywhere. I liked that feeling."

"*Okay*, Malcolm—gotta go, Rinnie. Good luck, girl, and I'll talk to you real soon— *Here* I am, don't *cry*, baby, I'm right here . . ."

The phone goes dead.

CHAPTER FOURTEEN

The day before Mom starts her first round of chemotherapy I decide to talk to her about the flying lessons. If I don't do it now, I'll have to cancel the lesson on Saturday.

The last week has not been good. On the plus side, Mom is feeling better. It's been several weeks since her mastectomy, and she can't wear a prosthetic breast yet, so she's been wearing bulky sweatshirts to try to hide her uneven cleavage. She had to go earlier this week for a procedure to put a port in her chest. It's a small disc under the skin above her breast that allows the doctor to inject the chemo without running an IV every time. She said it was no big deal, but if that's not a big deal, how bad will the rest of it be?

On the minus side, school hasn't gotten any better. People aren't actively laughing as I walk by anymore, but I know the nickname Va-jay-jay Girl has stuck. Trina was horrified when she finally heard about it, but there was nothing she could do.

And it's not like I saw a whole lot of Trina this week anyway. She's trying to be fair, trying to still spend time with me, but I can see she wants to be with Chaz. It hurts. I've been avoiding her so she doesn't have to choose.

Michael hasn't been at school most of the week, and when he does show up he looks tired and drawn. I wonder if he's working on his models. He's nodded at me a couple of times, but we haven't talked. Who wants to talk to Va-jay-jay Girl?

I close my physics book. Mom is stirring beef Stroganoff, my favorite, on the stove and checking her e-mail. She's been working at home for the past few weeks, but plans to go back to work as much as she can through the chemo. If she's lucky, the chemo won't be bad—it affects people differently so you never can tell.

"I miss Jill," Mom says suddenly. "I wish she hadn't moved so far away."

I know she is wishing Jill could be here tomorrow.

"We could have moved to Seattle," I say. "When she started her new company. She wanted you to come." Lately, I'd be just as happy if we lived on the other side of the country.

Mom frowns. "It's such a long way."

"But you would have been with Jill."

Mom says nothing. She's never even gone to Seattle to visit Jill.

"I want to learn how to fly," I blurt out.

She stares at me in astonishment. "You want to do what?"

"I've signed up for flying lessons. I'm supposed to start Saturday. I need you to sign this parent consent form. I'm using the money I saved from working at the yogurt shop, so you don't have to pay for it or anything, but I . . . want to do this."

She closes her eyes and presses two fingers to her temple.

"I don't think it's a good idea, Rinnie. Not right now. We can talk about it later, after all this is over." She gestures vaguely at her chest.

"No! Don't you understand? I *need* to do it now. I need . . . something else right now."

"Rinnie . . . I understand, I do. But can't you do something else to keep your mind off all of this? Something less dangerous?"

"It's not that dangerous. I won't be doing crazy aerobatic stuff like Dad did, I just want to learn how to fly. I remember when Dad took me up when I was a kid. And he brought me home that time and you were so mad at him. It was the best day of my life, but then you two wouldn't stop arguing after that so I knew it was my fault. My fault you got a divorce." My voice hiccups.

"Oh no, Rinnie, it wasn't your fault! I was worried about your safety. It was bad enough when he flew, but to take you . . . You don't know what it's like to be a mother. I wanted to protect you, to make sure you were secure and happy. I wanted you to always feel safe because I didn't when I was a little girl."

"I'm not a little girl anymore," I say in a low voice. "Mom, this is something I really want to do."

She's quiet for a long time, staring at me, but she's not really looking at me, she's seeing something else.

"I'll sign," she says, and her voice is real quiet. "I'll sign it, but you've got to understand. I can't watch you fly. I couldn't watch your dad fly at the end, and I *won't* be able to watch you."

～♆〜

The next morning, I go with my mom to her first chemo appointment. She didn't want me to go, but I could tell she didn't want to go by herself either, so she lets me.

"Oh good, you brought a chemo buddy," says Sherry, the nurse.

Mom is poked and prodded and given last-minute instructions, all of which she has already heard. *Take your temperature often, your immune system will be compromised. Flush twice for a couple of days, the chemo drugs are toxic. Replace shower curtains, use gloves to wash dishes, change your toothbrush often, and slather on hand sanitizer—you must avoid germs. Drink water! Exercise!*

We are led to the large chemotherapy room, which is filled with reclining chairs like in a dentist's office, with curtains you can draw closed if you want, though most of the curtains are open. There are figurines of angels everywhere, crowding the windowsills. A basket on a table is full of colorful yarn hats, and a sign invites patients to take one, courtesy of the Ladies Lunch Bunch.

"As you know, you'll have six rounds of chemo, three weeks apart," Sherry says, snapping on her gloves. "You'll have at least a few days after each round where you *will not* feel good. Keep in mind that oftentimes chemo gets worse with succeeding sessions. I want to be upfront with you so you know what you're facing." She turns back to hooking a bag on the metal stand beside my mom's chair.

It's quiet, people softly talking or lying with their eyes closed listening with earbuds in. Everyone has water bottles, and a few patients are sipping a shake or nibbling dry toast. One woman has a strange cap on, and as I watch, a younger woman opens a cooler and exchanges the cap for one from inside the cooler.

"It's called a cold cap. It's to help keep her hair from falling out," Sherry says.

Mom's doctor has told her the type of chemo she will be taking could cause her hair to fall out. She had it cut short last week, and we've looked at wigs but she's waiting to see if she'll need one.

Mom sucks on a lemon drop as Sherry threads a catheter into the port in Mom's chest and sets up a bag. Sherry stays for a while and chats, but she's holding a medication box and she is studying Mom closely as she talks. The doctor mentioned that some people have bad allergic reactions during their first chemo treatment. After a while, Sherry seems to decide Mom is going to be fine and moves off. I'm left holding Mom's hand while the IV *drips . . . drips . . . drips . . .* Mom downloaded *Dirty Dancing* to watch on her tablet, but the medicine they gave her to help with the side effects of the chemo seems to have made her drowsy and she lies with her eyes closed.

At one point a bell rings and I turn to see a pale, puffy-faced woman with a scarf tied over her head pulling a rope attached to a bell mounted to the wall.

People clap, and then cheer, and Mom and I look at each other in bemusement.

"You get to ring the bell when you're done with your

chemo," Sherry says as she drops a goody bag on the table beside Mom.

Inside is some hand sanitizer and more lemon drops, as well as a book called *Not Now, I'm Having a No Hair Day*, and Mom and I giggle over the cartoons until she dozes off.

When we are done, Sherry helps my mom up. "Remember, we have pretty good drugs to control the side effects of chemo. Not like the bad old days. Some people are able to go back to work the next day. But others feel it more. You need to take it easy until we see how you're going to react," she says.

As I drive us carefully home, Mom gets ashen and clammy and finally asks me to pull over. She throws up and after a while we drive on.

Then she has to stop to throw up again.

And I see chemo isn't going to be easy for my mother.

Not one little bit.

CHAPTER FIFTEEN

The day after my mom gets her first chemotherapy treatment, I go for my first flying lesson.

"Let's go." My instructor, Stewart Call-Me-Stew, points at a small tin can with wings. It reminds me of a VW Beetle, some-how, round and yellow and like maybe it was built right there in the seventies. It's a four-seater, but it's hard to believe that four normal-size people could fit into it.

"Go?" I ask.

"Flying. You thought we were maybe going on a picnic today?" Stew is bitter wrapped up in a soft taco of sarcasm. In his fifties—sixties?—he's got short gray hair and sunglasses, and he's dressed like he's expecting someone to give him points on anal-compulsiveness, all ironed and buttoned tight over his substantial stomach.

"I figured we would be . . . in a classroom today?" I say. "I didn't think . . ." Seriously, I didn't think we would actually be going up in the AIR already. My stomach starts doing somersaults.

Stew is driving me in front of him, clapping his hands, like he's Lassie and I'm the dumb sheep. My phone dings and I check to see if it's from Trina. She knows I'm flying today, but we haven't talked since she called yesterday to ask how my mom's chemotherapy had gone and to ask if I was *sure* I didn't mind if she went to Faith's party tonight.

"Are you kidding me? What's with you kids? Can't you go for more than two minutes without looking at your phone?"

"Uh . . . sorry?"

I slip the phone back in my pocket, but not before I see the message is from Ashley, who I've been e-mailing a lot this past week.

flying high?

The words make me smile. At least someone is excited about my learning to fly. My mother doesn't even want to hear about it, and Trina said I was "plane insane." Ha, ha, ha.

Ashley thinks it's the coolest thing since sliced bread. Somehow I'm not surprised. It sounds like something she'd like.

"What do you think, you just jump in like it's a car?" Stew barks at me. He's chewing gum like he's starving, all smacking and gnashing of teeth.

"I don't . . . no?"

"Even before you get in a car, you're supposed to kick a tire or two, maybe check the oil every once in a while. With a plane, it's even more important. Up there, were you expecting to pull into the nearest service station if something goes wrong?"

I am rapidly seeing the futility of answering any of Call-Me-Stew's questions. They are meant solely to amuse him. He's already told me he doesn't like kids, never has, never will, we're all ungrateful brats, thank you very much.

I follow him around as he checks out the plane. He stabs a stubby finger at various mysterious things as he rapid-fires info in my direction, as well as the smell of stale beer. I stuff my hands into my pockets to hide their shaking.

So why haven't I already said *sayonara*? Why can't I just make like a tree and leave? Here's the thing: I *want* to fly that plane, more than just about anything. I *like* the canary yellow plane, it looks sassy and punk, like Tweety Bird. It makes me smile. I haven't had a lot of giggles lately, what with Mom puking up her guts and whispering when she doesn't think I can hear, "I think it would be easier to just *die*."

"Let's do this," Stew says, with an expression on his worn, lined face like this is about as fun as a pop quiz.

"Now I can get in?" I ask.

"Yes, get in."

"You sure? We don't need to check the windshield wipers or something?"

"Get *in*. Smart-ass," he says, looking perturbed.

I grin at him sweetly, which throws him off, and climb into the plane.

"You got your parents stashed somewhere? Your age, they're usually following their little chicks around with a camera." He heaves his jiggling belly into the seat beside me.

"Nope."

Mom, the last I saw her, was leaning over the toilet, heaving, heaving, heaving. And when I tried to put a wet washcloth on her forehead after she brought up a bare spittle of bile, she screamed hoarsely, "Just go, go, Erin, *I can't have you here right now.*" So no, Call-Me-Stew, my mom is too sick right now to be able to care what the heck I do.

He shrugs and starts rattling off another long list of information I sincerely hope isn't vital, as I'm so nervous I'm only catching about half of it. Then he starts spitting nonsensical words into the radio like "November Six One Seven Niner Romeo" and I hear someone through my headphones answer back, "Cleared for takeoff."

And then we're moving. Stew stops at the end of a runway, craning his neck around to look out all the windows. He revs the engine so hard it rattles everything in the plane. I notice my window is being held shut with a twist of clothes hanger, and a piece of tinfoil covers some gadget on the dash. Not all warm-and-fuzzy-making, but on the other hand, it makes me like Tweety Bird the Plane even more.

I'm not entirely sure if the whole-body shaking is from the engine or coming from inside me. I debate asking Stew to take me back to the hangar.

But it's too late.

We're rolling, and the little plane is racing down the runway, and with a sudden dip in my stomach—*Oh no, am I going to throw up?*—we've left the earth. We're in the air. We're touching the sky.

It is freaking awesome.

I clutch the door handle as the ground falls away and the buildings get smaller and smaller, just like I remembered. The engine roars and we bump over pockets of turbulence as we make our ascent and it's amazing how quickly everything below us begins to blur together. I think about all those people living life in their own little squares, and not understanding that all the squares are connected, going on and on as far as the eye can see.

I remember a poem my dad liked.

Oh, I have slipped the surly bonds of earth,
And danced the skies on laughter-silvered wings;
Sunward I've climbed, and joined the tumbling mirth
Of sun-split clouds,—and done a hundred things
You have not dreamed of . . .

I used to beg Dad to read the poem to me at bedtime and he would tousle my hair and say, *Rinnie, don't worry, you'll do a hundred things I've never even dreamed of. Go to sleep now, and think about dancing in the sky . . .*

Stew steers us into a steep turn and I hold my breath because it seems like we're going to drop sideways straight into the ground. I have this irrational fear Stew is going to fall on me because it seems like he's hanging above me. I'm pressed against the door, hoping desperately it won't spring open and dump me into all that air down there. I see Stone Mountain in the distance, but I can't make out the humongous carvings of the Confederate war heroes. Then we swing around into another sharp turn and all I can see out my side window is endless sky and I claw for the handle to keep from tumbling into Stew's lap, even though rationally I know my seatbelt is holding me in place.

We straighten out and bounce over air bumps like a stone skipping across the surface of the water. Stew shoots me a sideways glance and I see that he's smirking just a little. I wonder how many students he scares off this way, because I definitely get the feeling he's trying to.

"Well?" he says through the headphones.

"Cool," I say. "Very, very cool." I try to look all nonchalant, like this isn't the best thing I can remember doing in . . . well, ever.

He nods and his expression changes, becomes less smug and more thoughtful. Maybe he was expecting me to throw up. I'm still holding the paper barf bag he shoved at me when I got in the plane. Maybe he is expecting me to be terrified. I've been terrified for weeks. This fear seems *clean*, somehow. Pure. Not putrid and creeping.

"Your turn." He lifts his hands off the yoke on his side.

"Say what?" I stare at him in horror. My hands clamp over the yoke in front of me and somehow I push it forward. The nose dives, and my stomach comes to rest somewhere in the vicinity of my throat.

"Oh man!" I snatch my hands away from the yoke. We are totally going down.

"Pull back." Stew grins at me. He's enjoying this, the sick sadistic bastard.

Since he seems content to watch us dive into the ground

without lifting a finger to stop us, I grab at the yoke and pull it back.

Too much. Too fast.

My stomach careens as the plane yanks up toward the sun.

"You planning on making it into orbit?" Stew says, fishing in his shirt pocket for another stick of gum. He seems completely unconcerned that a loud alarm has starting blaring. "We're getting ready to stall."

"Oh my God!" I yell, and push down again.

Now we're diving toward the earth faster and faster, and I start wondering if this is the end.

"Slow and easy," Stew says, popping the gum into his mouth.

I pull back slightly and the plane starts leveling out. I pull back some more but somehow I've twisted the yoke and we're flying tilted to the right.

Stew shows me a gauge on the dash that shows how far off center we are, and I turn the yoke back to the left a little. I experiment, back and forth, fascinated by how responsive the plane is to my touch. *I'm* controlling it, *I'm* in charge as we careen through the sky at over a hundred miles per hour. I manage to get us level and turn a big, delighted grin toward Stew.

"Now you're flying straight," Stew says, chomping on his gum in satisfaction.

CHAPTER SIXTEEN

When I get home, Mom is sitting at the table with a glass of water in front of her. Her face is white and her hand shakes as she takes a determined drink, but she is dressed and her hair is damp. Shower. Good.

"How was the flying lesson?" she asks tightly.

"Out of this world," I say. "Stew says I'm a natural. Okay, he didn't say that, he asked if I'd flown a plane before, and when I said no, he acted like he didn't believe me, but still. I think I did good."

She smiles, but it looks more like a grimace. She doesn't like this. I know it, and I feel bad. How can I explain that flying makes me feel brave, when nothing else does?

"I want you to know I appreciate all your help," she says. "I know this is . . . hard. I love you, Rinnie, you know that, right?"

My throat is closing up and I nod. She holds out an arm,

and I go to her. We hug clumsily, me standing, her sitting. It almost feels safe again, like it used to, but she is shaking and smells funny.

Upstairs I put on some music and write in my journal. I've always enjoyed writing, but until Ms. Garrison's class, I didn't think I was any *good* at it.

The little test tube I got in the mail from the gene-testing place is sitting beside my computer. All I have to do is spit in it and mail it back. I play with the cool, smooth tube, rolling it between my fingers. I take the top off it and put it up to my mouth.

I put it back. Not yet. Not yet.

I check and I have a text from Ashley. We exchanged phone numbers last week, so we could text. So far, we haven't talked on the phone. I've thought about calling her a couple of times, but it feels awkward, so I don't.

Ashley's fishing with her dad, and I text her back that I just finished flying and it was *beautiful.*

Nothing from Trina. I know she must be thinking about what to wear to Faith's party at the abandoned school. Trina said I should come, that the school wasn't Faith's, she couldn't kick me out, but, *really?*

Michael might be there.

I fall asleep with my phone clutched in my hand. When I wake up, my mom is vomiting again. I put my pillow over my head, but I can still hear her. It goes on and on, and after a while I get up to go check on her.

The door is locked. A first. I stand outside and listen to her try to bring up a lung.

I knock tentatively. "Mom? You okay?"

Like she's going to call back, *Just fine, honey! No worries. My new recreational activity is seeing whether I can bring up the lining of my stomach. You should try it!*

She doesn't answer. I jiggle the handle. "Mom?"

"Erin, I need to be alone for a little bit," she says, and groans softly.

I stand outside the door for a while longer listening to her retch.

"I'm going out, okay?" I call. "I'll be back later."

She heaves, and I imagine her hanging her head over the toilet, maybe laying her face on the cold rim.

"Okay . . . that's fine." No *Where are you going? When do you expect to be back?*

I go to my room and look in my closet. The white lacy dress, the one with the heart on it and the Cyndi Lauper–retro feel, is unlike anything in my wardrobe. I throw it on and go.

∞

It should take twenty minutes to get to the John B. Gordon School. It takes me thirty because I get lost, but I finally find Metropolitan Avenue and the church across the street from the school. A bunch of cars huddle together in the church parking lot, and I can smell smoke, though the school looks dark and deserted.

I pick my way around to the door, clutching my flashlight. I want to sneak in and find Trina or Michael without anyone else noticing me. No need to make a big entrance.

"Look, it's Va-jay-jay Girl!" someone shouts as I come into the big auditorium. The end open to the sky is eerily lit with candles.

Right off I see I'm overdressed. I'm wearing too many clothes, anyway. These girls are sleek and tanned in tiny mini-skirts and halter tops that bare their stomachs and backs even though it's not that warm. I want to turn around and leave, but it's too late.

I smile, like it's the funniest thing in the world to be known as Vagina Girl, and walk into the crowd. After a minute, they seem to forget about me, as football captain Sean Mitchell shows up by the fire barrel with a beer bong. I pretend to be super-interested as a girl gets down on her knees and puts the long tube in her mouth while Sean stands over her pouring beer into the funnel.

Classy.

I see Trina with her back to me. She looks almost . . . normal. Her dress is blue and tight and shimmery, with a long fringe swinging around her knees. A flapper. That's what she was going for. I could totally see Daisy Buchanan wearing it. Trina doesn't quite look like the other girls (since when did she *want* to?), but at least she's in the ballpark. I look like Dorothy in Oz next to her and I wish I could clickety-click my ratty sneakers and *be home* but it's too late.

"Errriiinnn." Trina's mom believes in serving wine to kids at dinner to stave off incipient alcoholism (*and how's that working out for you, huh, Ms. Howard?*) so I've seen Trina buzzed after a glass of wine, but she is officially *trashed* tonight.

"She's got balls, I'll give her that," Chaz murmurs as I approach, snapping his fingers in agitation.

"Errrin," Trina says again and gets weepy. She throws her arms around me and we both stumble and almost fall. "I'm so sorry about your mom. I think about her *all* the time, and you too. I know we haven't been hanging out a lot lately, but I want you to know I really miss you."

"Me too." I gently push her away. She's swaying like the ground is rocking beneath her.

"How's she DOING?" she says in a drunk's idea of a whisper, which is more like a breathy shout.

"Let's not talk about it now, okay?" I say. "I really don't want to talk about it."

She nods owlishly. "I understand. You don't want anyone to know. My lips are *sealed.*" She zips up her mouth and throws away the key. "Faith really did an amazing job, didn't she?" She pats the red-velvet throw that has transformed a camp chair into steampunk and cool.

"I'm surprised she's not worried about getting busted. That'll throw a wrench in her Stanford dream, wouldn't it?"

"Chaz says she does crazy stuff all the time, like she's daring something bad to happen, but it never does," Trina says, and her tone is actually admiring.

"Good for her," I say, and don't mean it. Cool, beautiful, and fearless too? I want to smack Faith. Trina too, really. What in the heck is wrong with her? When did she become Faith's biggest fan?

"You want a beer? Michael brought a ton," Trina asks.

I hesitate, then nod. "Why not?"

Two beers later I'm feeling warm and buzzed. Chaz and Trina have gone to collect beer cans people keep throwing on the ground but I have a feeling they might be looking for a dark corner somewhere to continue their make-out session. Their groping had gotten semipornographic. I am happy for Trina. Happyhappy*happy*.

I talk a little bit with Carrie Smith, who's one of those popular girls who are truly nice, but she moves off after a while and I find a seat on a bench near the fire barrel, close to some people so it doesn't look like I'm by myself.

"Hey." Michael sits down next to me. I scooch over and he scooches right along with me. He's drunk, but he's wearing it better than Trina.

"Didn't expect to see you here," he says, and I'm very aware of his thigh touching mine.

"Me either." And because I'm feeling loose and clever, I say, "But I am!"

His leg feels warm and solid next to mine. Behind me I hear Faith saying, "Seriously? What is *she* doing here?"

"Michael said she's cool," someone says. "Chill out."

I feel Faith's gaze on the back of my head as I sit with Michael. "Chaz is really freaking out about people leaving trash everywhere," he says.

"I know," I say. "He's really big on the '*Don't leave anything but footprints*' thing."

"It's all going to fall down anyway; I don't see how it matters. But, hey, if it matters to him, I guess it matters."

I giggle, and immediately regret it. "I've been wondering . . . why do you like these old buildings? I just don't get it."

He's quiet. Then, "I guess because I'm interested in designing buildings, I want to see how they die."

"I—"

"Hey, Michael," Faith says, coming up behind us. "Can I talk to you a minute?" Michael looks at me, but gets up. Faith puts her hand on Michael's arm and draws him toward a group of her friends.

Michael doesn't even look back at me. But Faith does.

And I shiver.

∞

I get another beer out of the cooler and watch Michael lean against the wall unsmiling as Faith leans close to him. Her expression is serious, his is unreadable. The beer is kicking in and someone even asks me if I want to do a beer bong.

For some reason I do.

Evidently, I am pretty good at it, because I remember doing the third one with a bunch of people standing around chanting, "Go, Va-jay-jay Girl, go!"

Afterward, I pick my way down a dark hallway, clutching my flashlight. Everything is fuzzy and tilted. I want to find Trina, I *need* to find Trina.

Light spills from a doorway, and I head there. It's a bathroom, and someone has put the big teddy bear on one of the toilets. The bear looks forlorn and awkward, its black eyes staring at the floor.

"Erin!" Chaz says, playing his flashlight over the bear. "Why? Why would they do this?" He looks ready to cry.

"It's okay, we'll just put him back where he was." My words feel swirly and distant.

"But it's not the same, don't you see? He's been in that classroom for, like, *years*. You can put him back, but it won't be the same."

I'm feeling dizzy. I go closer to the teddy bear and trip and Chaz puts out his arms.

"Whoa, watch it," he says. He's holding me up, and I look up at him, and his face is so kind, and no one loves me, and everything is bad, and I reach up and bring his face down to mine with two hands and kiss him.

He stiffens, but he doesn't pull away. I throw my arms around his neck and kiss him harder, pressing myself against him.

A light flashes and I turn, my eyes startled with splashed light. Chaz says, "Oh crap," under his breath and shines the flashlight on Faith, who is standing at the door, grinning broadly.

She holds her phone, and while Chaz and I gape at her, she snaps another picture.

"What a cute couple you make!" she says, and disappears before we can say anything.

"Erin . . . ," Chaz says, and his voice is full of accusation.

"Oh God." I feel like I need to throw up. "*Trina* . . ."

Just then we hear running feet and shouts of "Cops! Come on, get out of here, it's the police!"

CHAPTER SEVENTEEN

I wake up feeling like crap. I'm in my own bed, but I don't know how I got there. I don't remember coming home. Did I *drive*?

I stumble to the bathroom and look at myself in the mirror. I'm still wearing the same dress from last night, but orange vomit stains dribble down the front of it. My hair is bird's-nest tangled and my eyes look hollow and dead. I pull off the dress and throw it on the floor. After a moment, I pick it up and throw it in the trash.

I don't remember *anything*. Then I do, a little. Flashes. Doing a beer bong. Talking to . . . oh no, no, *kissing* Chaz. What did I do?

I start crying, big heaving sobs, because now it's all coming back to me and I'm such a loser. *LoserloserloserLOSER.*

Once the police showed up, we scattered for our cars like fleeing cockroaches. Chaz took me home, because I was too messed up to drive. He barely said a word the whole ride home. Trina, all unknowing what a terrible friend I am, chattered on about the excitement. She seemed bubbly, happy. What kind of person am I?

Chaz had to pull over so I could throw up on the side of the road. Then at home, stumbling in, trying to be quiet. Mom was retching and she didn't hear me, and we were puking in chorus. Like mother, like daughter. Like mother, like daughter, in everything.

I want to curl up and die.

I lie back down on my bed and go to sleep instead.

I sleep most of the way through Sunday. Sunday night I call Lynn Mitchell, a friend from the yogurt shop I've known since elementary school, and ask her to give me a ride to my car. She's happy to do it and grills me the entire way about the party, envious that I was there and she wasn't.

If you only knew.

Monday morning, I don't want to go to school. I haven't heard from Trina, so I don't know if Faith did anything with the picture. Has Chaz told her I kissed him? I don't know if *I'm* going to tell her. I know I should, but it's so much easier not to.

I don't want to go to school. I really, really don't want to go to school.

I check on Mom, and she's sleeping. That's what she's been doing most of the time, anyway. That and throwing up. I fill up her glass of water and leave some cantaloupe beside her bed. That's all she seems able to keep down. She looks so white and still that I panic and lean down close to her mouth so I can feel the faint brush of her breath on my cheek. She's alive. I kiss her cheek and go downstairs and call the school to tell them I will be absent today. Because they think I'm my mom, they say that's A-OK.

I leave through the garage, running my fingers over my dad's Mustang as I pass. I sit in my car for a few minutes, and then I just drive. I don't know where I'm going. That seems to be the story of my life lately.

Ashley: u ok?

She texted a couple of times yesterday but I didn't answer. I didn't want to talk to anybody. A couple weeks ago, I tried to find her on Facebook, but she doesn't have a page. We've been e-mailing a lot about the BRCA gene, but not about our private lives. I know she lives in Florida, on the coast, because she's always talking about the water and fishing. For all I know she could be like Faith. Or maybe she is as much of a dorkster as I am. No, not that either. She's something else completely, I think, but I don't know what.

Without thinking too much about it, I pull into a grocery store parking lot. I open an e-mail and pour it all out to her. The party. Beer bong. Kissing best friend's boyfriend. Michael. Mom throwing up. That I am alone.

I hit Send and turn up the music, watching people come in and out of the store. They are busy, harried, and none of them notice me. They push carts, fuss at children, juggle bags, and not a single one knows I'm alive.

Fifteen minutes later, I get an e-mail from Ashley:

I've got this place, a place I go to when things get too insane. I went there a lot when my mom was doing chemo. It's an island, *my* island, though I'm guessing the state would disagree. The water smells of mud and green and things living and dead, and the air is happy-bright, the way it gets when it touches the sea. When I'm there, it's not so much that I forget all the bad stuff, it's more like I remember all the good stuff. I wish you could see it. Not everybody feels the magic, but I think you would.

You need to find your good place. In your head, or an actual place. It's there.

You just have to find it.

I sit and think about that. *Can we go to the airport and see the planes fly, Daddy?*

So I go to the airport and sit in the parking lot and watch the planes take off and fly. It's Monday morning, and because it's a small airport, there aren't a whole lot of planes. Still, it makes me happy to watch.

After a while, someone taps on my window and I look up, startled, to see Stew standing impatiently beside my car.

I roll down the window.

"Did we have a lesson today?" He smoothes his shirt over his big belly and taps his foot like I'm keeping him from something.

"Uh . . . no," I say. "I just came to watch the planes. I used to . . . I used to watch with my dad."

He doesn't say anything for a moment, absentmindedly

patting his pocket where he finds a pack of gum. "Your dad didn't want to come out and see you fly the other day?"

"He's dead," I say. "He was a pilot too, but he died."

He rocks back and forth on his heels as he looks at me, chewing his gum in fast, rapid chomps. Then he says, "You gonna sit out here all morning or you going to make yourself useful and help me wash my planes?"

I get out and help him wash the planes. We don't say much, and after Stew covers some ports on the planes with tape, he disappears into his office long enough for me to think he might have taken a nap, but I don't mind. Splashing the planes with water from the hose and then scrubbing them down is mindless work. Perfect. The bottoms of the planes are covered with grease and it takes all my concentration to scrub it off. Stew comes out to tell me to not clean the windows in circles but up and down to prevent glare and then he disappears again.

Once I finish washing them, Stew walks out of his office and tosses me a can of wax.

I start all over again with the wax. Stew sits in a rolling office chair and starts telling me about the planes. *This is a Cessna 172, the most popular plane in the world; over there's a Cessna 152, which we call the Land-o-Matic, it's so easy to land; that's a Piper Tomahawk, the Air Force guys love that one 'cause it's got big-airplane-style handling . . .* He rolls from plane to plane as he talks and at first I wish he would be quiet, as I am in a no-thought zone, but after a while I start listening. It's interesting; I bet my dad knew all this stuff.

"You want to learn to fly, you're going to need a get a

medical and a student pilot certification before you solo, and you need to study for the written test." He goes into his office and brings out a pile of books so high it's hard to see his face over the stack. He dumps them on the workbench beside me. "You can do a ground school course, online if you want, or I can work with you on these."

I look at the stack of books. Seriously?

He picks up the can of wax and goes to work, occasionally pointing out parts of the plane: *The ailerons turn you, the flaps slow you, the stabilizers balance you . . .*

When we are done, Stew thanks me gruffly.

"No problem," I say. "If you need help again, let me know."

He nods and picks up a wrench and I head for the parking lot.

"Hey!"

I turn around.

"You're Justin Bailey's daughter, right?" he says, standing by a plane, looking at me with his hand shading his eyes.

I turn around and stare at him in disbelief. "How did you . . . ?"

"Last name Bailey. Dead pilot dad. Thought so," he says and turns away without another word.

CHAPTER EIGHTEEN

Three weeks later, Faith still hasn't posted the picture. I know, somehow I know, that she's holding on to it as ammunition. It feels like blackmail. *Stay away from him, and we'll forget the whole you-kissing-your-best-friend's-boyfriend thing, okay?*

I need to tell Trina, I know it, but somehow I can't.

The doorbell rings and I hear Trina downstairs, loud and in a hurry, as always. She's talking to Mom and Jill and I want to hide under the covers and pretend to be asleep.

Jill is here because Mom starts her second round of chemo tomorrow.

Five more rounds to go.

Five. More. To. Go.

I'm happy Jill is here this time. I dread how sick Mom will get, how terrible she will feel, and that there is nothing I can do about it.

Trina comes up the stairs and I tense, preparing myself.

We haven't talked a whole lot since the night I kissed Chaz. I'm not sure she's noticed, not really, because I've been trying to act normal (*Busy, busy, busy,* my tone says whenever we meet in the hall. *I love you, I do, but I've got so much to do! Right now! See you later!*), and she's been so wrapped up in Chaz. She's invited me out with them a couple of times, but I've said no. I don't want to face Chaz.

I've spent the last three weeks taking flying lessons with Stew every chance I get and helping him out around the hangar when I'm not flying. It's been the only time I've been able to breathe without feeling as if someone's sitting on my chest.

Trina comes in, and her face is serious. My heart sinks. Did Chaz tell her?

"Hi, bee-aaatch," she says, but it's solemn.

"Hey," I say. "What's up?"

Because I have to know now, if she knows. I can't stand it.

She looks confused. She didn't used to need a reason to come visit.

"I thought . . . we haven't been hanging out as much lately. I wanted to see how you were doing. You know, with your mom and all."

She doesn't know. Somehow I'm not relieved.

"She's got another chemo session tomorrow, but Jill's going with her this time," I say. "And Jill is going to stay for the next couple of days, when it's bad. I'm really glad about that."

She nods, fiddling with her phone, sneaking a quick glance at the screen. Evidently there's not a text from Chaz, but give him five minutes and he'll think of something. They text constantly. "Good." She wanders around my room, and I hold my breath as she picks up the glass tube on my desk, but she puts it back down without saying anything. I feel guilt about so much, about what happened with Chaz, about not telling her about the BRCA gene mutation . . .

"Want to do something tomorrow night? It's your big one-seven, we gotta celebrate."

"I guess," I say.

She looks at me for a long moment. "Are you okay? I mean . . . really? Things don't seem right between us anymore. I know I've been spending a lot of time with Chaz, but . . ."

Now *she's* feeling guilty and it's all my fault.

"I found out I might have this gene mutation," I say, because if not that, I'll have to tell her about kissing Chaz.

She listens as I tell her the entire story.

"That's *terrible*," she says, throwing her arm around my neck and hugging me hard. "And some people cut off their *breasts*? *Before* they get cancer? Seriously, I can't imagine." She steps back and clutches her boobs in both hands. "Have you told Michael?"

"I haven't talked to Michael since the party three weeks ago." And the fact that she doesn't know this shows how far apart we've grown.

I don't know whether Michael's avoiding me, or if that's just the way he is. He nods at me in the hall, but that's about it. Or maybe he knows what Faith is capable of, and he's staying away from me for a reason. To protect me. I don't know.

And what would he think about you if you had no breasts? The thought comes unbidden. If I get tested and I am positive, chopping off my breasts is the only way to really make sure I don't end up going through what my mom is going through.

How cute do you think he would find you if you had no breasts?

I shudder and Trina sees me. She climbs on the bed behind me and rubs my shoulders and then puts her arms around me. "It's going to be okay. I know it's terrible, but it's going to be okay."

But she doesn't know that. No one does.

∽⌒

Trina stays for a while, and it's almost like it used to be. She talks happily about Chaz and some Internet game he designed, and they're playing it, and Chaz is a king and Trina's a warrior princess and they're on a mission to save the world. She stays for birthday cake—Mom made me one tonight because she's afraid she won't feel like it tomorrow—and we talk about going thrifting, and we almost do, but Chaz calls, and he wants to go to a movie. Trina asks if I mind and I say, "Of course I don't care. You go on." Then she wants me to go, like I'm going to go sit and watch them grope each other, so I say no.

After she leaves, I e-mail Ashley.

I told my best friend about the BRCA gene mutation and she was real sweet about it, I mean she really *cared*, but it didn't help. I thought it would. For some reason I thought when I told her that it would make it less bad, that she would tell me it's not as bad as I think it is. But she was horrified, too, so now I know it's not just me.

I can't decide whether I want to get tested or not. I have the test kit, and I haven't told my mom, because she somehow thinks I've forgotten about it all. I don't want to worry her.

I just don't know. I'm not sure I can stand this waiting anymore. Waiting until I'm twenty-one, even eighteen, is just too freaking long.

I go downstairs and Jill and my mom are weeping together on the couch, all curled up under one blanket. They've demolished the rest of my birthday cake; all that's left is just crumbs on the coffee table.

"What are you *doing*?" They are watching *Beaches*, an old movie about two lifelong friends who find out one of them is sick. And then she dies. *And then she freaking dies.* "Seriously? Why are you guys watching this?"

"Come sit down," Jill says, scooting over so I can sit beside them. "We were all keyed up about tomorrow, so we decided it would be better just to cry."

My mom nods, tears streaming down her face.

So I sit with them while Mom strokes my hair and the woman dies, and it's so horrible I start crying too.

We're all crying, and laughing at ourselves, and for some reason it makes it better.

CHAPTER NINETEEN

The next day it's my seventeenth birthday, and I fail a physics test. I never fail tests. Never.

I can't say anything to Mom, because she had chemotherapy today and feels like crap. Jill is on the phone when I come in, twirling her long gray-streaked hair around one finger. She waves distractedly, before continuing. "She's got a slight fever, should we be worried?"

I sit beside Mom and hold her hand. She is sitting up, and clutching her chest: heartburn. At least she isn't vomiting yet. The doctors promised they would adjust her medicine to reduce the nausea, and so far, so good.

"Hey, birthday girl," she says, and then Jill comes in with a glass of water and some hand sanitizer. They forget about me, and finally I leave.

I go downstairs to the garage, singing, "Happy birthday to

me," and pull the cover off Dad's Mustang. I've been doing this a lot lately, sitting in the car. It scares me how little I remember about my dad. If something happens to Mom, will I forget her too?

I sit for a while, my mind a blank, silvery nothingness, and then my e-mail dings and I see it's from Ashley.

"However mean your life is, meet it and live it; do not shun it and call it hard names." I have this as my screen saver where I can see it every day. Thoreau was no dummy.

I can't tell you whether or not you should get tested now. Nobody can, even though the experts will tell you to wait, wait, wait. I'm glad my little sister doesn't know. I'm glad I didn't know until I was eighteen. But seriously? We're all going to die someday, right? I mean, I could walk in front of a bus tomorrow, and so could you. None of us knows how much longer we have.

So, what would I tell you if you were my little sister? Live for today. That's how I get through.

Someone knocks on the side door to the garage and I look up. It's Michael and I jump as if I've been Tased. I get out of the car, doing a rapid inventory of my appearance—curly hair standing on end, no makeup, hopefully no visible zits—and open the door.

"What are you doing here?" I say stupidly.

He looks over my shoulder at the Mustang. "I came to see that." He walks in and stands and looks at the car for a minute. Then he walks around it, running his fingers over the rust spots, peering inside at the torn and faded upholstery. He pops the hood and looks at the engine. He pokes and prods for a while, then shakes his head and slams the hood shut. "It's trash. Might as well sell it for parts."

It's what Mom has been saying for the past couple of years but I don't want to hear it. "I don't really want to do that. It was my dad's. He was going to fix it up."

Michael leans against the hood of the car and looks at me, his long fingers smudged with grease, his eyes serious. "You can't hang on to memories," he says. "When they're gone, they're gone."

"That's why you're determined to be an architect?" I say without thinking. "To forget your dad?"

He doesn't say anything and I'm afraid I've gone too far.

Then, "My mom harped on my dad all the time. He didn't make enough money. He didn't dress well enough. She didn't like his friends. Sometimes I get why he took a header off that building."

We're quiet then. Really, what can you say to that? For some reason I think about Trina, and me kissing Chaz. Does Michael know? I don't want him to know. What would he think about me then?

His phone rings and he pulls it out and glances at the screen. He sort of grimaces, and then says, "Hold on," as he turns away and answers it. "Yeah?" He listens for a minute. "I'm at . . . a friend's house right now so I don't think that'll work." He listens some more and kind of glances at me. "Yeah, okay, that's where I am." He sighs. "I guess. Fifteen minutes."

He slips the phone back in his pocket without saying goodbye. "Faith's mom is onto her about her grades and Faith's having a heart attack because she doesn't think she's going to get into Stanford. Always drama."

My heart is breaking for poor little Faith. Instead I say, "It's nice that you guys can still be friends after you broke up. Her mom doesn't sound too great, though."

"Yeah . . . her mom's a real piece of work. Always pushing Faith to get ahead, to be better than everyone else. I guess she and I have crappy moms in common. I better go."

But he doesn't leave, he just stands there. After a moment, he walks toward me and stands real close to me. My head is doing the *ohmygod* thing again and then he leans forward and brushes his lips against mine. It's quick and light, but my lips feel as if they are on fire as he heads for the door.

He stops with his hand on the doorknob. "Faith knows I was here," he says, and it's a warning, plain as day. "We all got this app so everybody knew where everybody else was. I forgot about it, or I would have turned it off." He hesitates and then opens the door.

"See you around."

He's gone, and I feel like I've been punched.

Faith has her ammunition, and now she has her reason.
I need to talk to Trina.

∞

But when I go inside, my mom has a 104 temperature and Jill
and I have to take her to the emergency room. Two hours
later, Faith publishes the picture of me and Chaz kissing on
the e-zine, titling it, "Aren't they cute?"

CHAPTER TWENTY

Mom spends the weekend in the hospital as the doctors work at getting her infection under control. She is very dehydrated, and they pour gallons of liquids into her through an IV.

I stay at the hospital with her and Jill. I don't know what I would do if Jill wasn't here. She's the one who talks to the doctors, she's the one who talks to the nurses about getting Mom more pain medicine, she's the one who helps Mom to the bathroom and sits with her in there. Mom wants us to go home at night, but both Jill and I refuse. We take turns sleeping in her room on the uncomfortable chair that pulls out into an unconvincing bed. It's still better than the waiting room, where the chairs are all hard vinyl cushions and wood.

I find myself almost calling Trina a dozen times to tell her where I am, but then I remember. I know she's seen the picture of me and Chaz kissing because there's a gazillion messages from her. I don't listen to any of them. I can't. I turn off my phone so I don't have to hear the beeps as each message comes in.

⁓

Sunday afternoon, Mom is well enough to go home. Trina must have been cruising my house, because she shows up an hour later.

"How could you?" she says as she comes into my room.

Trina has been crying. I feel like crying too.

"Oh, Trina, I'm so sorry . . ."

"I should have known! I should have known he wasn't interested in me. It was you the whole time, right? He was interested in you, and he used me to get to you. How could I be so stupid? Of course he doesn't like me. Why would I think he would?" She is whirling around the room like a broken-winged bird, pulling at her hair.

"No, Trina, no." I try to stop her from yanking her hair out. "It's not like that. It was my fault. Have you talked to Chaz? It was *my* fault, not his. I kissed him. He was never interested in me, and he hasn't said two words to me since it happened."

"*You* kissed *him*? *Why?* You know how much I like him. You know how hard it's been for me to find someone. How could you do this? We both know you're prettier than me; did you have to prove it? *Why would you do this?*"

"I don't know," I say miserably. "It was the night of the party at the school. Michael was talking to Faith and somehow . . . My mom was so sick, and everybody was calling me Va-jay-jay Girl, and you and Chaz were so happy . . . I guess I wanted somebody to like me the way Chaz liked you. *I don't know!* I was drunk, and it didn't even make any sense then. Do you think it makes sense to me now? I was stupid. So, so stupid, and I wanted to tell you, but it seemed better not to, because you were so happy."

"The two of you kept this secret from me for *three whole weeks*? My best friend and my boyfriend? I can't believe this. I can't believe *you*, Erin. Who are you? How could you do this? I know you've been jealous because I've been spending so much time with Chaz . . . Is that why you did it? Were you trying to break us up? So that you would have me all to yourself again?" She stops and stares at me intently. I don't like the expression on her face. It's anger, but there's . . . what, pity, as well?

"No! What kind of person do you think I am? I would never try to break the two of you up. I'm happy for you, I really am." I sit back on the edge of the bed, clutching the bedspread in both fists. "Trina, please, I know it was wrong, I know I was terrible, but . . . please. You're my best friend. I don't want to lose you."

"You weren't thinking about me," she says. "What kind of friend is that? You were only thinking of yourself."

"No, no, no," I say, shaking my head.

But I feel a prickle of doubt. Could she be right? Was I so scared of losing Trina I was willing to break them up? Was I that terrible of a person?

I put my head into my hands. I'm crying in earnest now, and so is Trina.

"I'm so sorry." I whisper.

"I am too," she says and walks out.

Outside in the hall, I hear Jill ask Trina if she's okay, but I don't hear what she says.

A knock sounds on my door and Jill comes in, carrying bottles of liquid Benadryl and Maalox that Mom is using to help with her mouth sores. Jill puts them down on my desk and sits beside me on the bed. I'm trying to stop crying and she doesn't say anything, just pats my leg.

"I kissed Trina's boyfriend." My voice hiccups. "And now she hates me."

Jill puts her arm around my shoulder and pulls me close. "Wowie. Okay, calm down. Do you know how many stupid things I've done in my life? I can't even count them all. We all make mistakes. It's part of growing up. Heck, it's part of living. Because you're not truly living if you don't make mistakes now and again. Trina will get over it. I promise. You are too good of friends for this not to blow over."

But I'm not so sure.

~~

Mom starts crying, the aching in her bones is so bad, and Jill goes back to her best friend. I sit and think about what Trina said. Who am I?

I'm rolling the spit tube in my fingers.

Who am I?

This I know: I like the color purple. I'm afraid of the dark. I like to read, and lately I think I might like to write. My mom has breast cancer and may or may not die. I might have the gene and may or may not die because of it.

Very few positives in my life—very few things I know for *sure.*

There is one thing I can know for sure. There is one thing I can nail down in my life one way or another.

I pop the lid off and spit in the tube.

CHAPTER TWENTY-ONE

"What do you think you're doing?" Stew barks at me.

I jump, and Tweety Bird jumps with me as my hands jerk back. "Uh . . . flying?" I answer through the headset, bringing the plane back level.

"Is that what you call it? You're two degrees off course, I'm getting airsick with all the overcorrecting you're doing, and hey, look, there's a cloud ahead of us. Were you planning on going right through it?"

The silent blue sky is full of the big floating clouds, some as tall as castles. They sail along, glowing white and indifferent, and I feel very small next to them in the humming plane. I'm not supposed to go through the clouds, I know that. You only go through clouds once you get your instrument license, which means you can navigate solely by instruments. I steer away from them.

"Aye, aye, Captain," I say, because I've figured out it annoys the crap out of him.

It's windy, so instead of doing touch-and-goes, we're out at the practice area practicing stalls. The first time I did this a couple of days ago, it scared the bejesus out of me as we went up and up until the stall alarm started blaring and then there was a moment like when you're at the very top of the roller coaster, suspended between up and down, and then the nose dropped and it felt like we were going straight down. A few times, we even began spinning around and around because I couldn't hold the wings level, and Stew had to take the controls. That night, I wasn't sure I would ever fly again. But the next day, I went back and practiced some more until I could do it without spinning.

I *am* feeling a lot more comfortable flying. Not surprisingly, since I've spent almost every minute of the last week doing it. The school thought I was sick, Mom and Jill thought I was at school, and in reality . . . I've been flying.

I just couldn't do it. I couldn't face everybody. Just knowing that everybody would be talking about me made me feel like curling up like a roly-poly until the end of the school year. So I called the office, pretending to be Mom, and told them Erin Bailey was *very* sick and wouldn't be at school all week. Then I counted up my savings, money earned from working at the yogurt shop and some money Memaw left me, and went to see Stew.

"I want to learn to fly," I say. "This week."

"What, you mean after school?" He squints at me.

"No, *all* day," I say. "I can pay you. Here."

Stew never asked me why I wasn't in school. He took my money and for the next week we did ground school in the morning, studying charts that looked like upside-down wedding cakes and learning about V-speeds and operating temperatures, and then flew the rest of the day. When Stew had another lesson, I would sit in the hangar and study.

I pull back, sending Tweety soaring up as Stew begins patting his pocket, looking for his gum. He pulls out an empty pack and looks at it in disgust. I reach one hand into my jeans pocket and wordlessly hand him a full pack of gum. After a week spent in close quarters with Stew, I know his gum addiction masks his murderous need for a cigarette. As long as he has gum, he's a much more pleasant person. Relatively speaking, of course.

Stew takes the gum without saying anything, and I go back to my upward climb, turning as I do it so I can practice the stall in a bank. I feel the stall coming on even before the alarm goes off and I concentrate on using the rudder to keep the lift on the wings balanced.

"Head on a swivel," Stew growls, and by now I know that means I'm supposed to be looking out for other aircraft. I crane my neck around, looking for traffic, thankful for the cushion that Stew threw at me after my third flight when I was having trouble seeing out the windows. I see the helicopter in the distance, the one Stew must have heard on the radio. It's going away, so I relax and go back to doing stalls again.

I do them again and again, and everything else seems to disappear until it's only me and Tweety Bird. I don't think about Mom, or school, or genes that won't behave the way they are supposed to. It's like I am not even aware of myself. The rest of the world has faded into a blurry sepia of not-important. This is why I have grown to love flying. This is why I have gotten up every morning this week and gone to the airport, because when I'm in the air, nothing else matters. I execute a perfect power-off stall and think about my father and how he used to do this, and much more, when he was flying professionally. I wonder what it felt like to him when he was just learning to fly, and what he would say to me. Up here, I feel closer to him than I have since he died.

"I saw your dad fly at the National Championships in '94," Stew says into the headphones.

I'm brought back to myself abruptly and turn to look at him in surprise. It's like he read my thoughts.

"You did?" I say cautiously.

"It was really something, watching him fly," he says, and turns away.

I want to ask him more questions, but we're nearing the airport, and I need to get on the radio and tell the ATC, the air traffic controller, that I'm landing. Talking on the radio still stresses me out, despite all the scripts I've studied, so I don't get a chance to say anything else to Stew about my dad.

I find the airport, which is a lot harder than you would think, and then I'm back in the zone as I concentrate on repeating the ATC's instructions and locating which runway I'm supposed to use. I feel a surge of adrenaline as I do all of this without looking to Stew for confirmation that I have it right. I'm in control, this is *my* flight.

Landing is still the tricky part. I line up with the runway

and correct for the crosswind. I cut back the speed as we near the end of the tarmac, halfway expecting the stall alarm to go off, *rahrrr, rahrrr, rahrrr,* to let me know that my speed has dropped too much. But it doesn't, and I breathe a sigh of relief as the main wheels touch down. Up in the air is one thing, but finding that particular point where wheels touch ground still feels like a miracle. I concentrate on easing the front wheel down, and it hits, a little hard but not too bad, and we taxi to a stop beside the hangar.

I look at Stew. He looks out the window, as if the side of the hangar is the most interesting thing he's ever seen.

I sigh.

"I go back to school tomorrow. Do I have enough money left to keep taking lessons in the afternoons?" I say it calmly, as if the thought of going back to school doesn't make me want to gag.

"Yeah," he says, still not looking at me.

I go to get out and he says, "Kid."

I turn back to find him staring at me.

"You did . . . okay," he says.

And that makes me feel like I just won a gold medal.

My first day back at school, I'm sitting outside at a picnic table. I have no one to sit with at lunch anymore. Even the girls I hung out with when Trina wasn't around haven't been welcoming. They've heard about what I did to Trina.

I check my e-mail. It will be at least another week before I get the results of the genetic test, but I'm already checking my e-mail obsessively. I want to know . . . but I don't. I guess while I want to know if I'm negative, I don't want to know if I'm positive.

Michael comes out and leans against the edge of the table. He's wearing a dark hoodie pulled up over his head, even though we're not supposed to wear them up in school.

"Chaz is pretty messed up," he says. "Trina isn't sure she wants to date him anymore."

"I know." I stare at the ground. "It's all so . . . terrible."

"I didn't think you were like that," he says.

This sears. "I'm not," I say. "I'm really not. I . . . I don't know. I just don't know. I don't know what happened." There is no excuse, and I know it.

He looks back at the school. "I guess I thought—" He stops and shrugs. "I guess I was hoping you weren't like everyone else I know."

I nod miserably as he walks away.

Chaz is petrified to be seen near me. Whenever he sees me coming down the hall, he twitches like a rabbit caught in a trap. I think he's afraid if Trina sees him anywhere near me she'll break up with him for good. I'm happy they are still together, but neither of them wants to hear *that* from me.

In physics, Ms. Allison tells me I've fallen so far behind it's going to take an A on my final to even get a C in the class. In English, Ms. Garrison pats me on the shoulder as she passes out graded essays. She's given me a B, with a little frowny face and a "You can do better!" In gym, Molly Jenkins puts up with me talking to her, though she keeps looking back and forth between me and Trina.

"You really kissed Chaz?" Molly asks as we're walking out of the locker room.

"I really did," I say.

She frowns, not getting it.

That's okay, because I don't get it either.

$\sim\!\!\infty\!\!\sim$

When I get home, Mom is lying on the couch. She still has her lab coat on. Nine days after her second chemo treatment and hospital stay, she's able to go to work, which makes her happy. She's worried about chemo brain, which can make her fuzzy and forgetful, but so far she's been okay. Just tired. Very, very tired. We've spent a lot of time watching movies and most of the time she is asleep by seven o'clock. I've taken over cooking, but I'm not very good at it. Everything tastes weird to her anyway. She can't even bear the taste of metal silverware, so we use plastic.

Four more rounds of chemo.

I'm beginning to wonder if she can stand it. If *I* can stand it. What happens if Mom ends up in the hospital again? We heard a woman talking in the chemo room and she'd spent almost the entire month in the hospital, from one complication or another. What if that happens to Mom?

The next chemo treatment starts in less than two weeks. My breath catches funny in my chest. This time we'll be alone. This time Jill isn't coming.

I check e-mail on my phone again as we sit and watch *The Breakfast Club*, but there's still no message about my genetic report. I sigh, and Mom hears me.

"How are you doing, Erin?" She's got her reindeer socks on, her feet propped up on the arm of the couch. She drips some eyedrops in her eyes. No matter how much she drinks water, my mother is a desert of dry skin, dry eyes, and dry mouth. She's been losing her hair, strand by strand, but so far it's not all gone.

"Fine," I say, bright and cheery. *Just* hunky-dory! *Twelve more days until your next treatment, my best friend won't talk to me, the guy I like thinks I'm a tool, and the flying . . . the flying is going great, but I can't talk to you about that.*

"How . . . how did Dad get into flying?" The words come before I have a chance to think.

She rolls over on the couch and looks at me. Then she picks up the remote and mutes the TV.

"Your dad? He always knew he wanted to fly. He grew up near an airport, and I guess he spent a lot of time there when he was a kid. He didn't get along with his parents so he spent all his free time watching the planes. When I met him, he'd already flown in the first Gulf War and was running private charters. He was also getting ready to compete in the US National Aerobatic Championship."

"But . . . you never watched him fly?"

"What? Oh, no. At first, I loved watching him fly. I was there when he won the National Championship."

"But you never went flying with him?"

"He wanted me to. He always said he wanted to show me a glory, which is some kind of circular rainbow you can only see from high up in the air. He said not only were they rare and beautiful, but that if two people looked at the same glory, it would look different to each of them. He liked that. '*Your own personal glory,*' he used to say. I never could fly with him, though. In the end, I couldn't even *watch* him fly."

"So . . . what changed?"

She lays her head back on the pillows and looks at the ceiling. "I thought *I* would change. I thought being near him would change *me*. I thought if I was with him, I would want to do things, go places, be *braver*. But it didn't work. It's hard to change yourself, and you can't rely on other people to do it for you."

"I wish he hadn't died . . . ," I say in a soft voice, looking at his picture on the mantel. "Do you think . . . do you think he would have liked me?"

She sits up and looks at me seriously. "Honey, you are the daughter he always wanted. Sometimes . . . it scares me. I don't want you to be hurt. The world can be a scary, dangerous place."

Mom falls asleep on the couch and I cover her up. I check my e-mail again and I see I have a message from Ashley asking if I'd heard anything yet.

I go out to the garage and sit in the Mustang and e-mail her back.

No report yet. I feel so messy inside, like I'm going to fly apart, like I'm going to fracture into a thousand fragments, and I won't ever be able to find all the pieces of me. Is it wrong to feel the test is going to tell me something about myself I don't know? Knowing the blueprint of my genes, will that explain why I'm falling apart? I feel so different from everybody else. I feel so alone. Why can't I just be normal? Why is this happening?

I put my head back against the seat. I should be studying for my physics final. Finals and the end of school are less than two weeks away. I can't though, not right now. An icy tremble starts in the center of me, and then my whole body is vibrating with unspeakable, arctic emotion.

I don't know if I can take much more of this. Whenever I think of the future, it's covered by a bleak, gray fog. I am getting lost in the limbo and I don't know how to find my way back.

My e-mail dings and I open Ashley's message:

I swam with some dolphins the other day. I was out on the boat and I saw them, so I jumped in. You're not supposed to, because they're wild animals and they can ram you with their beaks if they get scared or just pissed off. Heck, they can take out sharks, they do it all the time.

But these guys were cool. They pretty much ignored me, but every once in a while one would rub up against me, and it was so weird, because I felt part of something so much bigger than me, but so small at the same time. We're all connected like that, down to the genes inside our bodies. We're interconnected, but inside our heads we feel all alone.

I guess I'm trying to say that you're not alone. You may feel like you are, but none of us are. We're a part of something so much bigger.

CHAPTER TWENTY-TWO

Five days before my mom starts chemo again, I feel up Faith.

It goes down like this: I'm late, so I'm hurrying, trying to avoid the dance kids who are doing some sort of routine in the middle of the hall, and as I round the corner by the gym, I see someone there. I put out my hands to keep from running into her and get a handful of boob. This, naturally, is Faith.

"What are you doing, freak?" she cries. "Get away from me!"

My momentum sends me into her and I end up knocking her backward. She lands on her butt. This part, at least, is satisfying.

"Oops," I say.

A couple of her friends help her up and glare at me. Other people are stopping to watch and laugh.

"Aren't you going to say you're sorry?" Faith asks, brushing off the seat of her immaculately white pants.

I think about Va-jay-jay Girl and the picture of me kissing Chaz and don't say anything.

"You're such a *nothing*," Faith hisses at me.

" 'Having nothing, nothing can he lose,' " I say. It's cheesy but it's the best I can do. I make my escape.

"What the eff?" Faith says behind me. "She is so *bizarre.*"

"It's Shakespeare, dummy," volunteers a passing emo in skinny jeans and a scarf who sits behind me in AP English.

At my locker, I'm shaking. I don't know why I care, but I do. Why does she hate me? What is wrong with me?

I get out my phone and check my e-mail. The report should be here and I'm reduced to checking my phone a thousand times a day.

Nothing.

"Hey," Michael says.

We haven't spoken since the day he asked me about what happened with me and Chaz.

"Hey." I tilt my head down so my hair sweeps my cheek. It's automatic, this hiding, and Mom bugs me about it all the time but I can't seem to help myself.

"You okay?" He looks at me.

For a moment I debate telling him about my mom, about the waiting, waiting, waiting on the genetic report, about Faith, and Trina, and my crush. On him. For a minute I want to say everything, and it perches on my tongue like an avalanche just needing a tiny sound to let loose.

"I don't think Faith likes me," I say instead, trying for funny and "Oh well, what do you do?" and ending up with "My life sucks, no one likes me, why don't people like me?"

He hesitates. "She's got a lot going on. When things get bad for her, she goes on the attack. Inside . . . she's not that tough. I guess I understand, feeling different inside than people think you are. Once you get to know her, you get used to her."

"I can probably get used to hanging if I had to, but I don't really want to." Another favorite Memaw-ism.

His lips quirk. "That's why I like you. You make me smile."

"But you *don't* smile. I've never seen you smile. Or laugh either, for that matter."

He shrugs, all lean and slouchy, with his dark, straight hair and dimple in his chin, which I really think I'd like to kiss.

"Maybe—" he says.

Maybe? Maybe we can go out sometime? Maybe we can get together over the weekend? Maybe I might be falling for you?

"Look, I've got to get to class," he says. "Only two more days until summer."

And *maybe* is left hanging.

∞

The world is far below and it's just me and Tweety Bird. And Stew. I want it to be just me and Tweety, but what if something happens? Stew hasn't touched the controls in weeks, allowing me to take off and land and navigate all by myself, but still. Still. He's there. Just in case.

Right now he looks like he's sleeping. I glance over at him, and he's got his eyes closed. It must be nice to get paid to nap. I want *that* job when I grow up.

But I am content. It's a clear day, the wind mild, but even so I feel like we're driving down a rutted-up road as we bounce from one air pocket to another. When you're in a small plane, every bump feels big. I roll Tweety into a big turn, not even flinching as I hang in the harness so I can peer down at my house. Mom's car is there and my chest feels fluttery when I think about her chemotherapy coming up. Four more days. I hate it. I *hate* it.

I know she's worried about me. And that makes me feel bad. I want to be there for her, and she wants to be there for me, but evidently neither one of us can master this trick of *being there* right now. And a little part of me is mad, not at her, but fate, or God, or whatever, that this is happening to her. To me. Why us?

Without warning, the motor dies.

I look over and see Stew has his eyes open, and he's watching me. He puts his hand back on top of his stomach mound, but I see he is clutching the keys in his fat little paw.

"What the—?" I scream. Tweety has already lost speed and begins a steady slide toward the ground. My first instinct is to yank the nose up, but cold concentration centers me. Instead I push the nose down a little to keep up my speed, and pull the throttle to idle. I think about trying to snatch the keys out of Stew's hand, but I'm afraid to take my attention off flying for even a moment. I'm not sure how far he is planning on taking this, so I look around for a place to land. I see a field nearby, and I turn the plane slowly toward it, trying not to lose too much speed and altitude. I'm totally focused, my hands light on the yoke, making as few corrections as possible, because everything I do makes the plane go down quicker.

I line up with the field, and check quickly for trees and power lines. It's clear, except for a fence at one end and a couple of power lines in the distance. It's going to be tight, but I think I can do it.

I wipe my damp hands on my jeans, and get ready to land.

And Stew puts the key back into the ignition.

"Are you INSANE?" I say as the motor roars to life and I slowly pull the nose up and circle away from the field. "I can't believe you're allowed to do that!"

He shrugs. *Whatever.* "You get your medical like I told you?"

I nod. A few weeks ago I went to an aviation medical examiner for a physical exam, and the guy made a big deal about me signing the student pilot certificate. I am now officially allowed to fly solo, whenever Stew decides I'm ready.

He looks at me a long moment, chewing ferociously on his gum, as I circle back around toward the airport. Then he sighs. "Study for the pre-solo exam. I'll give it to you the next time I see you. And then . . ."

I'm holding my breath, not sure whether I want to hear him say the words or not.

"Then I'm going to endorse you to solo. You're ready, so quit farting around."

CHAPTER TWENTY-THREE

The next day, the rumor is I'm a lesbian and that I attacked Faith in the hall. I don't know why she is bothering. But for some reason Faith is getting a kick out of torturing me.

And it *is* torture. I hate people talking about me. I hate the giggles as I walk past, the barely audible comments— "Hey, look it's Va-jay-jay Girl; you better hide, girls!"—and the answering laughter. When I get to my locker, I see someone has papered it over with fliers from the LGBT club. It's stupid, it's juvenile, but it stings.

Only one more day, one more day, and it's over. Blessed, people-free summer is almost here, reading to my heart's content under the old oak in the backyard. Pure bliss until next year. My senior year, which is supposed to be the best year of my life. Somehow, I'm not seeing it.

That night, my mom goes to bed early and I tell her I'm

going to study for my physics final. Instead, I write in my journal. Tears run down my face as I write. I've been checking my e-mail obsessively, but still no report from the BRCA website. I think about stealing one of my mom's sleeping pills and sleeping through a couple of days.

Ding from my e-mail.

It's from Ashley. The last couple of weeks we'd been e-mailing and texting like crazy and I'd e-mailed her earlier telling her about the stupid lesbian rumor and how everybody is laughing at me. *Again*.

Ashley writes:

I'm thinking about jellyfish. I know, weird, right? But here it is. Jellyfish thrive on pollution and since that's what we've been pouring into our oceans, they're creating these huge slimy jellyfish kingdoms where they attack everything: sharks, fish, humans. The funny thing is that jellyfish are usually the not-so-lucky-ones-that-get-eaten, but feed them enough crap and they band together and create this humongous glutinous empire that destroys everything they touch. I'm thinking people are like that too. Every day we get fed a load of crap and we're starting to turn into jellyfish, banding together so we can wipe out everything clean, and pure, and good. I mean, there are good people, but sometimes it seems like most people aren't like that. Most people seem to take unholy pleasure in tearing down anything that shines too bright.

Hold your head up. You're better than them.

The next day, I don't want to go to school. I *really, really* don't want to go to school. I'm so over it, but I have finals to take and it's only *one more day.*

Something has changed when I get there. I'm still getting the whispers and the stares, but it feels different from yesterday. No one is calling me Va-jay-jay Girl, no one is laughing. The room gets quiet as I go into history. I hear my name rustle like a breeze through summer leaves as I sit down. But the tone is wrong. What the heck is going on?

"Hey, Erin, I'm, like, real sorry about your mom," says Lynn Mitchell, who sits beside me. She's been ignoring me since she heard about me kissing Chaz, but now she looks at me with her eyes all big and sad.

"*What* did you say?" I twist around in my seat to stare at her.

She flinches. "I heard about your, you know, mom. That's totally crazy. I'm sorry."

"Just to be clear," I say slowly, "exactly *what* did you hear?"

She's uncomfortable and winds her hair around her finger until the tip turns white. "You know, about the *cancer.*" She whispers the last word, as if it makes it less awful if you say it quiet. Like she's at a funeral.

"And where did you hear that?" I ask.

She twists the hair tighter. "Like, everybody knows. I heard it from two or three different people. So, you know, I'm sorry."

Everybody knows? This is a new form of torture, but from an old source. And I know exactly who it is.

I snag Trina as she comes out of Spanish.

"What the hell did you do?" I say, and I'm not quiet about it.

"Erin." The expression on her little face is guilt and defiance and I know she did it.

"How could you tell everybody that?" I say. We're attracting a crowd.

"Catfight!" someone says. "I put ten dollars on Va-jay-jay Girl." And someone shushes him with *"Didn't you hear about her mom?"*

"How could you do this to me?" I say. "I know you're mad at me, and maybe I deserve it, but *how could you?"*

"Erin, I did it for you!" Trina says. "I know you didn't want anyone to know, but they were saying such awful things about you, and I wanted to . . . I don't know. Help you."

"You think this is *helping* me?" I wave an arm out at the avid audience. "I *know* I'm a freak; does it help for everybody to know how *big* of one I actually am? Looking at me with *pity*? I didn't have much, Trina, but I had ME. And now I don't even have that."

"Erin, I just wanted them to know, so they wouldn't be so mean . . ."

I get up real close to her face and someone says, "Twenty dollars, I'm going twenty dollars."

"This is worse than anything Faith has done to me," I say quietly. "By far worse."

I leave after that and go to the lake, blowing off my physics final. I'm pretty sure I would have failed it anyway.

When I get home that afternoon, my genetic report is waiting for me.

I stare at the screen, my finger hovering over my mouse. All I have to do is click the mouse. The attachment will open and I will know.

Click the mouse.

My finger trembles. I can't do it. I just can't.

I move the mouse to the bottom of the screen and open an e-mail window. I take a deep breath and start writing to Ashley. She's the only one who will understand. She's the only real friend I have anymore.

The report is here and I can't bring myself to open it. I wanted to know, I thought I did, but now I . . . can't. What happens if I'm positive? Everything changes. Already I wake up, and even before I remember, I feel this cold, hard dread in my chest. Will I feel like that the rest of my life? I don't know if I can live like that. But I don't know if I can live like *this* either.

Ashley writes back almost immediately:

I got my results at a genetic counselor's office. It was a whole process, but I'm glad I did it that way. I had so many questions, I'm glad I had a real person to talk to. Anyway, the counselor and I talked a long time on the first visit about whether I even needed or *wanted* to get tested, and what it would mean if I was positive. She did charts, reports, the whole nine yards. I went back to get the results, and by then I guess I knew what it meant. It helped having someone there to talk to about it when I found out.

But even so, I never thought I would be positive. I never thought I could have it. Once I did know . . . I've had some time to come to terms with it. It takes a while. I spent a lot of time on my island afterward, thinking.

You'll get there.

But you don't have to open it. It will be there tomorrow or five years from now if you decide to wait.

I write back.

I wish I was on your island right now. I don't want to be here. I don't want my life.

I sit for a while staring at the screen. I want someone here with me. I want my mom, or Trina, to hold my hand when I click on the report. But my mom doesn't even know I took the test and Trina is . . . Trina might as well be on the moon.

Do I want to know? Do I really want to know I have up to an 80 percent chance of getting breast cancer? And a high risk of ovarian cancer as well? My breasts or my ovaries. Which would be worse? The visible part of me that shows everyone else I'm a woman? Or the secret part that makes *me* know I'm a woman?

How will it feel to know that my very femininity could kill me?

Terrible. It will feel terrible.

But what if I'm negative? What if I don't have it? What if it's a huge relief when I open it and see I'm negative? What if I put this report away for five years, worrying and stressing about it, and come back and open it and I was negative all along?

I have to know. I have to know one way or another.

I'm doing it. I'm going to open it.

My fingers are shaking so much I have to use my other hand to push my finger down on the mouse.

The report takes forever to load. And when it does, I'm not sure what to think. There's no big flashing POSITIVE or NEGATIVE. There's a bunch of medical jargon and words like "deleterious mutation" and ominous statistics I know by heart.

Women with BRCA1 or BRCA2 mutations have up to an 80 percent risk of being diagnosed with breast cancer during their lifetimes. In women with BRCA1 or BRCA2 mutations, breast cancers tend to develop younger and occur more often in both breasts. The risk of developing ovarian, colon, pancreatic, melanoma, and thyroid cancers, as well as other cancers, are increased in women with BRCA1 or BRCA2 mutations.

But do I have it?

I feel like screaming.

I focus, and finally I see it. I'm positive for a deleterious mutation. I'm positive for the BRCA1 breast cancer mutation gene.

I'm positive.

Positive.

CHAPTER TWENTY-FOUR

I sit and stare at the screen, willing it to change, willing myself to see the word "negative" somewhere. It's all medical gobbledygook. Maybe I misunderstood it.

I forward the report to Ashley. Am I positive?

Her answer is one word: Yes.

I press my hands against the edge of my desk, pushing my chair backward onto two legs. The pressure on my palms hurts but I don't care. I close my eyes.

I wanted to know.

I had to know.

And now I know.

Now I know what it feels like to know how I'll die.

Not only that, to know I will most probably be going through what my mom is going through.

I release my palms and my chair falls to the ground with a thud. My stomach lurches and I race for the bathroom. I hang over the toilet, the spit thick in my mouth, but nothing comes up.

After a while I go back to my desk. Ashley has sent an e-mail asking how I'm doing.

I send her back an e-mail, typing quickly.

I can't talk to Mom, because how can I be selfish enough to even think about dumping this on her on top of everything else? But I want to talk to her about it more than about anything. But she'll feel bad for me, that I'm positive like her, especially because she gave it to me, and now I'll have to go through what she's going through. Or cut off my breasts. There's always that option. I've been having morbid dreams about doctors holding me down and chopping them off with a chain saw while I scream. I wake up in a cold sweat, my hands cupping my breasts as if to protect them. The problem is, I need someone to protect *me* from *them*. They're the ones that will kill me. Will my mom, the doctors let me chop them off at seventeen? I'm guessing not. I'm guessing everyone might start thinking little-padded-room thoughts if I even mention it.

How do I deal with this? Everything is so terrible, how do I deal with this on top of everything else?

❦

The next night, my mom wants Dino's pizza. She's too tired to go out, she says, but she's craving pizza. She's not been eating much, and anyway, I'm not too fond of Dino's anymore, but I say, "Absolutely, sounds great!"

I'm not telling her so many things. Failing physics and having to go to summer school is not even the top of my list. I find myself almost telling her about my gene test results again and again. But she doesn't even know I took the stupid test, so I'll have to confess to that.

Mom knows *something* is wrong with me (*Mom, EVERY-THING is wrong with me*) so she took off work for a first-day-of-summer-break celebration. I don't even want to think about what I've done: failing physics means I *have* no summer break. Failing physics means school will go on and on until graduation a year from now. I don't know if I can take it. I really don't.

Even if I get through it, then what happens? College, without Trina, and with no idea what I want to do?

The BRCA thing I've shoved down so deep inside of me, I wonder if it's going to come popping out like one of those springy snakes jammed into a can. But I've decided not to think about it.

I will not think about it. I'm not thinking about it.

So I don't tell Mom anything. We go and get manis and pedis in the morning, which wears Mom out enough that she has to come home and take a nap. Then we watch a Molly Ringwald marathon on cable and decide on take-out pizza.

Trina texts me as I pull into Dino's. She's been texting me roughly every five minutes. I can't talk to her. I can't deal with her right now.

I see them as soon as I go inside. Michael and Faith are in a booth in the back. They're sitting on the same side, close together. Faith sees me come in and she reaches up to give Michael a kiss. He kisses her back. No hesitation. His hands slide up her back and for a minute I think maybe they are going to go at it right there.

They break it off and Faith looks at me. Michael doesn't see me, but he whispers something in her ear and she laughs prettily.

She gets up and heads for the bathroom, which takes her right by me. Michael has seen me now, and the expression on his face is almost priceless if it all weren't so terrible.

The kid behind the counter puts my pizza down in front of me as Faith sashays by. She smirks at me and heads into the bathroom. She doesn't have to say anything. We both know she's won.

Michael starts toward me, and I throw my money at the counter guy and leave without waiting for my change. I'm almost running as I make for my car. I hear Michael call, "Erin! Wait up."

I wave, trying to make it look all cheery and nonchalant. Then I drop my keys and I have to scrabble on the ground to find them and he catches up with me.

"Oh hey," I say brightly, looking up at him. My voice sounds brittle.

"Erin," Michael says and stops.

"What's up?" Like I don't know what the big deal is, like the sight of him kissing Faith didn't feel like someone stabbing me in the heart. I mean, I really didn't think . . . him and me? . . . Not really. Okay, maybe. Maybe I let myself dream a little. And there's where I went wrong. I let myself hope, dream, and this is exactly why I shouldn't, because in the end, life just basically sucks.

"I, uh . . ." Michael doesn't seem to know what else to say. I try to make it easy on him.

"I didn't know you and Faith were an item," I say lightly, like *Isn't that just dandy, you two crazy kids!*

I must not sound right because he looks at his feet. "Erin . . . I like you. I really do. You're different from most people, and I admire you for keeping your head up despite everything. Me, I'm not like that."

Faith is standing in the doorway. She has her phone up, recording us.

"Michael, it's all good," I say. "You don't have to say anything."

"Faith needs me right now. I'm sorry if . . ." He doesn't finish, but instead steps forward and gives me an awkward one-armed hug. "You'll be fine, right? You're a pretty tough chick."

Tough chick? I think, and *Faith needs you? Really?*

I look over toward Faith. She has stopped recording, but she's still watching us. The look on her face is bizarre: there's something like glee, but also . . . worry.

What is *she* worried about?

I look back at Michael. I'm trying to look casual but my face feels like it's about to break in a million pieces. *I need you*, I almost say, but don't.

"No worries, Michael," I say. "Well, it was nice seeing you, but I have to get this pizza home before my mom starves to death!" I hold up the pizza as a prop and walk swiftly away.

"Did you tell her?" I hear Faith ask as I get in my car. "Did you tell her what a loser she is?"

"Oh shut up, Faith," Michael says tiredly, but he grabs her hand and pulls her close as they go inside.

∽〔〕∾

"You got no one who wants to see you do this?" Stew asks, cranking on his gum like *he's* the one about to solo for the first time.

"It's my thing," I say.

He nods, and I get the feeling he understands.

I wait for him to get out. We've done a few touch-and-goes, which were perfect, but he just sits there. He seems to be having second thoughts about whether or not to let me solo.

"What?" I say.

He sighs. "Do like I've taught you. I know you can do this. You're one of the best students I ever had."

"Wow, Stew, watch out, you may start liking kids if you're not careful."

"Fat chance," he growls and gets out. He slams the door and gives me a thumbs-up.

I yell "Prop clear" out the window and start the engine.

It feels good to concentrate on something, to not have to work so hard on not thinking about things. I've stripped it all away until my soul is bare, just a dull, impenetrable cube, small and icy, and I am locked inside.

I tell the tower November Six One Seven Niner Romeo is

ready for takeoff. They give me a runway, and I sit at the end of it and run up the motor until everything shakes. I do my last-minute checks and then take a deep breath and stare down the runway.

I'm scared. Real scared. But I want this, more than anything.

I release the brake and Tweety Bird roars down the runway and makes the leap into the air. One moment I am grounded, and in the next I am free of the earth and everything on it.

My heart pounds and I give a *whoop* of triumph.

"I did it, did it, *did it!*" I chant, but no one but Tweety Bird can hear me. That's okay, though, because this is my journey, no one else's. All the practicing, all the studying have led to this moment, and it's my moment alone.

The plane climbs steadily, and I feel completely in control as I check the instruments and respond to the movements of the air around me. Once I'm clear of the airport, I swing the plane in a wide turn, reveling in the heady sense of freedom. It's glorious. It's the best feeling I've ever had and I want it to go on forever. All the bad stuff in my head has been blown clean away and all that's left is pure joy. *This* is something I can control, *this* is something I can do well, when everything else I touch seems to turn to crap. Below me cars crawl along crowded streets like ants, but around me is open air and freedom.

I fly the traffic pattern, and then reluctantly prepare for the first of my three landings. My stomach clenches at the thought of going back down again, but I pick up the radio to tell the ATC what I'm doing.

And then . . . I put the radio down. I pull Tweety Bird in a steep turn away from the airport.

It takes a few minutes for them to notice. In those minutes, it's like I'm on a seesaw, teetering back and forth in my mind. Something has shifted inside me, and nothing is balanced anymore. I can't find the ground. I don't know if I *want* to find the ground, ever again. Everything is too hard down there, and I can't bear the thought of going back. I *can't* go back.

"Seven Niner Romeo, turn right heading Three Two Zero, the airport will be at twelve o'clock."

They think I've lost the airport. They think I'm lost.

Maybe I am.

The radio continues to squawk until I turn it off.

It's just me and Tweety.

And I fly.

Part Two

CHAPTER TWENTY-FIVE

I'm not thinking much as I fly south. There's too much to concentrate on. I'm flying VFR, which means I'm flying by sight, so I have to look out for other planes. I'm supposed to be on the radio, talking to other planes and to airports when I get close to them, but I don't want to talk to anybody. I know where I am, because of the GPS, but I don't know where I'm going. Not really.

Just away.

I have plenty of gas, so I fly, and I sing at the top of my lungs, and sometimes it seems like Tweety chimes in with a rev of the motor or a whistle of wind. I'm blank. I'm empty. My brain is a mirror of the vacant pure blue of the sky.

I know this is bad, very bad. I should turn back, get on the radio, tell someone I'm fine. I don't know what Stew is going to do. I don't know if they've called my mother by now.

Thinking of Mom threatens to break me, because I don't want her to worry about me.

But she'll be better off without you . . . It has been so hard for her to go through all this and worry about me too. And as much as I want to be there for her, somehow I can't. Not like she needs. I try and try, but I can't do anything to make her better, to ease her pain. And on top of that, I am adding to it. Because I can't seem to help myself. Things have slipped out of my control, like I'm on some sort of slide and keep going faster and faster to who-knows-where but I can't stop.

I don't have a plan. Well, yes, I do. I plan to fly as far away as I can. After that there's nothing. Maybe I will lie down and die. That seems pretty appealing. But short of finding some sleeping pills—

Why are you thinking about sleeping pills? You're more than a thousand feet in the air. All you have to do is let go of the controls and see what happens. It really wouldn't be your fault; it's not like you would drive yourself into the ground or anything. You could take your hands off the yoke and see what happens. Just like that. It would be so easy . . .

I find myself lifting my hands off the yoke, and Tweety is confused. She swerves a little to the right and then drifts slowly downward.

Yes, like that. Sit back and watch the trees get a little closer and what a way to go, right? Doing what you love? You and Tweety Bird. It'll be over quick, it'll be fast, and you won't have to wait for the next five, ten, twenty years for a lump to show up. Done. Finis. All over. Mom would understand, she knows, she KNOWS, KNOWS, KNOWS what hell is like and didn't she say maybe it would be easier if she could just die? Easier. This is an easier way. There, the ground's getting closer and isn't that river pretty, shining in the sun like a glittering ribbon? Concentrate on that. Tweety will take care of everything. I wish Mom could be here . . .

"No!" I scream and snatch the yoke up. "No, no, no, no, no, *no, no, nonono . . .*" I'm screaming at the top of my lungs now, a wordless howl that goes on and on as I drive Tweety back up, up, up. Tears run down my face as all the bad stuff comes out through my mouth in a long shriek of fury and pain. Tweety begins wailing along beside me as I go up so fast the motor begins to strain and we roar together at the uncaring sky.

∽◯つ

Somewhere in the middle of Florida I begin to run out of gas. I still have some, but if I don't land soon, then I won't.

I'm in the middle of the state, so mostly I see rolling fields and an occasional town below me. I don't want to land at an airport, even a small one, because I don't want to talk to *anybody*. This I know. This is all I know.

I see a long flat field below me and it reminds me of the field I almost landed in when Stew stole my keys forever ago. That day I was planning on landing on the field with no power. How much easier to do it with the motor running? I circle around and check out the field. It looks like maybe it's supposed to be growing something, but right now it's dirt mounded up in long furrows. About a mile away is a house with a big barn, but there's nothing, nobody around. I circle again and I'm lining up at the end of the field and getting lower and lower.

Either do it or don't. What does it matter either way?

I do it. I drop down onto the dirt and we bounce some and one big bounce slams my head into the ceiling. Something cracks and Tweety dips to the side and we crash to a halt in a cloud of dust. I rub at my head as I look out of the window. Somehow the ground seemed a lot smoother from the air.

I unbuckle and get out and immediately see I've damaged Tweety's landing-gear strut, the piece of metal that holds the wheels. It's bent and Tweety is drooping to one side. For some reason this makes me cry and I kneel beside Tweety and put my arms around her legs, whispering, *"I'm sorry, I'm sorry, I'm sorry."*

After a while, I stand up. I grab my purse out of Tweety and kiss her nose.

"I'm sorry to leave you like this," I say. "Someone will find you and take care of you, I promise."

And then I walk away.

I find a dirt road and follow it. I don't know where it goes and it doesn't matter.

As I walk, I pull out my phone and look at the dark screen. I turned it off before I ever got in the plane. I don't want to turn it back on but I do.

I have twenty-one messages: ten from my mom, eleven from Trina.

I think for a minute and then send Mom a quick text: im all right pls dont worry. love u

I shut off the phone and keep walking.

Every once in a while a car goes by and I duck into the bushes. But that's only once in a while, so mostly I walk down the middle of the road, swinging my arms and singing. It's only when I see the drops falling darkly onto the white dust that I realize I'm crying.

I'm getting tired when I see a gas station ahead. I don't want to see anybody, but I'm hungry so I go in. A skinny woman with skin browned and furrowed by the sun sits behind the counter, her eyes glued to a small TV. She barely looks up as I put a Diet Coke, a bag of chips, and a sandwich on the counter. I hesitate over Mom's emergency credit card and use cash instead. They can trace credit cards. But that leaves me six dollars and twenty-six cents, so I'm going to be in trouble soon.

I use the bathroom, and as I'm leaving I hear my name on the TV. I stop, using one hand to keep the glass door from swinging shut.

". . . authorities are saying that it appears the student pilot flew off course deliberately and are working to find . . ."

I let go of the door and it shuts with a clang of cowbells. I walk quickly away, and I'm not sure whether the crawling sensation on my back is my imagination or the clerk watching me.

I eat my sandwich and walk. It's hot, it's May in Florida, and before long I'm sunburned and extremely thirsty. My Diet Coke is long gone. I suck on a mint, but as soon as it's finished my mouth is dry again. It occurs to me I could die of sunstroke. I don't care much.

A car comes along and I'm too tired to get out of the road.

It's an old farm truck and the man inside is equally decrepit. He stops and stares at me.

"Where you going, girl?" he asks.

I nod the way I've been walking.

"There's nothing much for miles ahead. Did you run out of gas?"

I shrug.

"Get in, and I'll take you up to Alachua. There's a gas station."

I think about it, "stranger danger" and all that, but in the end I just don't care. I get in and he offers me a drink from a soda bottle that's filled with clear liquid. I'm so thirsty I gulp it down. Thankfully, it's water.

He doesn't seem inclined to talk much, and neither am I. We roll along with the hot wind whipping through the truck and I tap my fingers on the windowsill to the songs still playing in my head.

After a while, he turns onto a two-lane paved road. We begin to see houses and a business or two, and then the gas station.

"You want me to take you back, or you got someone to call?" he asks as I get out.

"I've got someone to call."

I watch as he drives off and I pull out my phone.

CHAPTER TWENTY-SIX

I've never called Ashley and it feels odd. Our relationship was in the Webosphere, and somehow it seemed meant to stay that way.

I listen to it ring and ring and a guy picks up.

"Hello?" he says.

I'm confused and almost hang up.

"I'm looking for Ashley," I say after a moment.

A muffled silence, like he covered the phone with his palm, and then he says, "This is Ashley's brother, Jason. Is this Erin?"

I should wonder how he knows who I am, but I don't. "Yes. Can I talk to Ashley?"

"She's not here. She went fishing."

"Oh," I say and begin to cry.

"Erin. Hey, Erin! Quit it. Stop. Please, stop crying. Ashley told me all about you. You sound like you're in trouble. Can I help?"

"Not unless you want to drive to Alachua and pick me up," I say because I don't know what else to do.

Silence. I'm about to hang up when he comes back. "Okay, I Google Mapped it and it should take me four hours and eighteen minutes to get there. Can you hang on that long?"

I laugh, but it's almost a sob. "That's all I do," I say. "I hang on."

I tell him what gas station I'm at and go and sit under a tree. I'm out of sight of the station but I can still see the parking lot. I drink from a supersize bottle of water and munch on a sandwich I bought with my six dollars and twenty-six cents. Now I have seventy-eight cents rattling in my pocket.

I must have fallen asleep because when I wake, a police car is in the parking lot. I remember then you can track your phone if you lose it, and are they tracking *me*? I turn off my phone even though I told Jason I would keep it on in case he can't find the gas station. I edge further behind the tree. Darned if the clerk doesn't come out with the cop, and they are standing outside the store looking up and down the road. The clerk is talking fast and then she does something that makes my skin crawl. She hands the cop my wallet. I hadn't even noticed I'd lost it.

The cop looks through my wallet thoughtfully and then talks into his shoulder mic. Before long two more cops show up and yes, they are looking for me. This is insane and I don't know what to do. I need to get away but Jason is my best bet. I'd glanced at the time right before I turned off my phone, and I know he should be here any minute. I see it already in my imagination. He gets here. Doesn't see me. Goes in and talks to the clerk and she promptly directs him to the police. And there goes my only ride out of town.

I know I need to do something, but I'm paralyzed.

A ragged blue Jeep turns into the station. It pulls up to the gas pump and a guy gets out. He looks eighteen, nineteen, a little older than me, and he's tall with curly blondish hair pulled back into a ponytail. He's tanned and sloppy-looking, like he's just come off the water, and I know exactly who he is.

I wonder if I can signal him somehow. He doesn't seem to be sweating my absence. He's not looking around or anything. In fact, he looks bored. One of the cops comes over and talks to him and he shrugs and shakes his head. No, he hasn't seen a girl, curly black hair, glasses.

When he goes to get back in the Jeep, I see he's got his hand down low at his side where the police officers can't see him. He's pointing down the road. He gets in without looking back and drives off in the opposite direction.

Great. Now what do I do?

What choice do I have?

I look at my phone and put it on the ground and smash it with my heel. I start worming my way through the bushes in the direction he pointed. After a while, I get far enough away from the gas station and I get up and run. I keep the road in sight but I go for five minutes and don't see him. Did I misunderstand? Was it even him?

But I know it was and somehow I'm not concerned. I keep walking, closer to the road now, and few minutes later the Jeep roars up and swerves to a stop.

"Get in!" the guy yells.

I hesitate because I don't know whether they can still see us from the gas station and then I take a leap of faith and run. I fall into the seat and he is accelerating before I even have the door shut.

"I called in a fire down the road, but I don't think it'll keep them occupied for long." He glances in the rearview mirror. He is big and male and it's hard not to notice that.

"What fire?" I fumble for my seat belt because he's accelerating like Mario Andretti. But he gets to fifty-five and stays there.

"I called 911 and said there was a small brush fire just north of the gas station, figuring those cops would respond," he says. "Hopefully it gave us enough time. Are you okay?" He glances at me.

"How did you know? How did you know those cops were looking for me?"

He hesitates. "Your mom called my house this morning. Looking for Ashley. She looked at your cell phone records so they know you've been texting . . . her."

Something about the way he says this makes me look at him sharply.

"And what did Ashley say?" I ask.

"She said she hadn't heard from you since early this morning before you soloed and she didn't know where you were. They found the plane a couple hours ago, so now they know you're around here somewhere. They're calling you a 'troubled teen.' "

I keep looking at him, not even caring right then about the whole "troubled teen" thing.

"How old are you?" I ask.

He hesitates. "Eighteen."

"And you and Ashley are what? Twins? She never mentioned a twin brother. Or a brother at all for that matter."

He doesn't say anything.

It all makes a horrible kind of sense. The fact he has Ashley's phone, the strange hesitations, the feeling of familiarity . . .

"You're *her*, aren't you?" I whisper. "You're Ashley!"

He won't look at me. Then, "Look, I'm sorry. I didn't know it would go this far. I wanted to tell you, but it never seemed like the right time."

"What, are you some sort of online predator or something? Why were you pretending to be a girl?" I don't know whether to be scared or angry. I put my hand on the door handle, but we're going too fast for me to jump out.

"It wasn't like that!" He looks at me, his eyes earnest. "I didn't mean to do it. When I joined that BRCA forum, I was thinking of my little sister, Ashley. I knew Mom was going to tell her about the gene when she turned eighteen next year, and I was wondering what it was like to be a girl and know you might have the bad gene and have to make all those decisions about what to do. So when I signed up, I used the screen name Ashley, because her name was the first thing that came to mind."

I remembered my own screen name: Thissucks.

"When you posted, it was the first time I'd seen anything

from someone our age. When I e-mailed you, it didn't occur to me that you would think I was a girl. Not until too late. And then you were telling me . . . stuff . . ."

"Oh my God!" I shriek, remembering some of the things I told Ashley. I talked about Michael, about kissing Chaz, my new fun nickname Va-jay-jay Girl, my *period*, for flip's sake. Oh my God, *ohmygodohmygodohmygod.*

I cover my face with my hands.

"You must have thought it was real funny, messing with me like that," I say through my hands. "Ha-ha. Hilarious."

"No!" He reaches over and grabs my leg. Even through my jeans his touch burns. "It wasn't like that. I told you. I hadn't met anyone else my age with the gene, and it felt . . . good to talk about it. I thought if you knew I was a guy you'd . . . I don't know. Stop talking."

"Wait, wait. *You* have the BRCA mutation?" I stare at him incredulously.

He looks at me quickly. "Yeah, I have it."

I guess I knew guys could have the BRCA mutation, I just never thought about it much.

"Things kind of snowballed. I didn't mean to lie to you, but I couldn't find the right way to tell you who I really was. It was stupid, I know, and I've felt bad about it. So many times I wanted to tell you."

I am trying not to mentally go through every e-mail and text I ever sent him. Every time I do I think of something else embarrassing. I thought I was talking to a *girl*, a girl I was beginning to think of as a good friend.

"It's still me, okay?" he says softly. "My name's not Ashley, it's Jason, but that's the only thing I lied to you about. The rest of it's true. It's *me*."

I sit and stare out the window at the trees and bushes rushing past my window. I know I should be mad, and probably worried. You hear stories about this all the time, a guy pretending to be someone else and luring a young girl to her doom. But the difference is that Jason didn't *ask* me to come; in fact he's risking a lot by helping me. And after all the time we spent talking, I feel like I know him even though we just met.

Finally, I nod, because I'm too tired to be angry and because I don't want to lose Ashley, even if she's a guy.

"So what did my mom say? Is she okay?" I ask.

He hesitates. "She's . . . very worried. She wanted to know if you had said anything to me about all of this, if you had planned to leave. Apparently the authorities are questioning your instructor as well about letting you fly by yourself so soon after starting lessons, whether you were really ready to solo."

"I *was* ready to solo! Stew didn't do anything wrong." My heart sinks as I think about all the trouble I've caused.

"Were you coming to see me?" he asks. "Is that why you flew to Florida?"

"I don't know what I was doing," I say after a moment. "I guess if I was thinking of anything . . . it was your island. But I was just flying. I wasn't thinking." It's hard to explain that vibrating emptiness in my head, an echo of which is still there. "I don't know where I'm going. I don't know what I'm doing. I just know I can't go back right now. I *can't*."

"What do you want to do?" he asks carefully.

"I don't know." I lean my head back against the headrest. "How should I know? It's all so messed up. *I've* messed it all up and I don't know how to make it right. I want to be . . . somewhere else for a while."

"You've got to call your mom," he says. "I won't help you unless you call her and tell her you're okay."

I nod. Yes, I need to call Mom, but now I've smashed my cell phone and what on earth do I tell her? What can I say?

"Then what?" I say. "I call her and then what?"

"I'll take you where you want to go."

"The island," I say immediately. "I want to go to your island."

CHAPTER TWENTY-SEVEN

I wake screaming and Jason is saying, "Whoa, Erin, it's okay, you're okay. I'm right here."

I look at him blankly, not at all sure where I am for a moment. I'm still deep in my dream where I come home and Mom is sitting at the table drinking a glass of water, but when she turns to look at me she's a corpse. Rotting flesh peeling away from her skull, the hand holding the glass just bones.

"Erin?" Jason gently shakes my leg, trying to bring me back.

I remember then, where I am, and what I've done. I lean my head against the seat.

"We're almost there," Jason says.

I nod. I'm trying not to think of my phone conversation with my mother. Right outside of Alachua, Jason found a pay phone, and I felt like everyone was looking at me as I dialed my home number collect. Mom cried when she heard my voice.

"I'm okay, I'm okay," I kept saying. "I just need some time. A couple days, okay? Tell them I'm okay. Tell them to call off the search. Can you do that? I'll be home in a couple of days. I'm safe, I promise. I just need . . . a little time."

"You need to turn yourself in," she said, which made my blood turn icy and shivery. "Everyone is looking for you."

"Mom, I can't come back right now. I just can't. But I'm safe, I'm with a . . . a friend. Tell them . . . tell them I'll come back in a few days. Tell them that, okay?"

"I don't know if I can, Erin. This is pretty serious. I don't know if they'll stop looking just because I ask them to. Can't you just come home now?"

"I can't, Momma, I just . . . can't."

It didn't end there, of course, but after a while I told her I needed to go.

"See you later, alligator," she said, and her breath hitched as she said it.

"After a while, crocodile," I said and hung up, shaking.

I think about how hard it was to be apart from her when I was six and scared she would die while I was at school.

Being apart from her right now? It feels like an amputation. Painful, but vital to my survival.

Jason is driving through a small town, colorful cottages clinging to the edge of the road, the water all around. He's humming along to the radio. I can see the side of his face, and I watch him, his eyes flicking to the rearview mirror, his lips moving as he mouths a few words. Jason is big and tanned and freckled across his nose. The slanted sun glows in the golden fuzz on his cheek and his long eyelashes sweep the sweet spot under his eyes. I'm sure a lot of girls think he's cute, but judging from his threadbare T-shirt and his careless, tangled hair, he doesn't care what people think. Trina would say, *He's, like, a magnificently messy nature boy. Yum.*

And then I miss Trina fiercely, and I put her voice out of my mind.

We go over a bridge, and the rest is a blur until we stop in front of some tall green bushes.

I'm numb. My brain is thick and slow, like it got a big shot of novocaine.

"Come on," he says and I obediently get out. We pass a large yellowish rock with some sort of plaque on it, and go down a path through bushes to a tiny muddy beach. The water is out and birds are hopping along stabbing at unseen things in the mud.

"Down this way." When I don't move right off, he takes my hand and I marvel at how big his hand is compared with mine. His fingers dwarf mine. He leads me to the far end of the tiny stretch of sand and gently pushes me down.

"I've got to go get some supplies. I'll be back in a little while," he says. "In a boat. Look for me, because you're going to have to walk out in the water to me. Erin? I'll be back. I promise. *I'll be back.*"

I nod and he hesitates, looking down at me. He tucks my hair behind my ear, a swift, gentle brush, and then moves off down the beach.

I watch him until he is out of sight.

∞

It might have been fifteen minutes, it might have been two hours, but he isn't back. The sun has dropped to where it is shining directly in my eyes. I squeeze them tight, but the golden sunbursts still shatter the darkness, and heat presses against my eyelids. I open them again because he said he would come back.

And there he is, a tall boy in a small boat, his golden mane in a ponytail.

I look around. A few people came out to the beach while I waited, but they have left and now the beach is empty. I stand and start walking out to him. It occurs to me I should probably take off my shoes and roll up my jeans but I don't. The water is warm against my calves and is over my knees by the time I get to the edge of the boat.

Jason helps me in and hands me a life jacket. I look at it and after a moment he puts it on me, moving my arms like I'm a doll. He ties the straps and I notice again the smattering of freckles across his nose and his long, blond eyelashes. He meets my gaze and I see his eyes are an unbelievable mixture of blues and greens and gold. I'm not sure why I hadn't noticed them before.

"You have incredible eyes," I say.

He blinks and then laughs. It's relieved laughter as if maybe he wasn't quite sure of ol' Erin's state of mind, as if maybe he thought Erin might be taking a long walk off a short plank to la-la land.

"Yours are pretty cool too."

"Like grapes," I say.

He frowns, studying my eyes through my glasses. "Hell no, not like grapes. Like bruised violets, all dark blue and purple. Nice."

Bruised violets. I smile and cherish that.

Jason gets up and starts the motor and suddenly we're zipping across the shallow waves. The bow of the boat slides through the smooth, untouched water, leaving a froth of destruction in our wake. The water is clear and brown, and schools of tiny fish veer away from us, flashing like miniature silver missiles. The sun is dropping and the sky glows soft blue and orange. Small islands dot the water, some of them draped with thousands of white birds, and even over the noise of the engine I can hear their screeching. I turn my face into the wind and close my eyes.

∞

"There it is," Jason says after a while.

I open my eyes and look at the island we're approaching. A thin crescent of white sand rings wild, green masses of bushes and a few palm trees. Jason motors around to the back of the island, into a deep cove that goes deeper and deeper into the island, crowded by thick bushes with roots like skeleton fingers dipping down into the water. He slides the boat up onto a small, muddy embankment and looks at me.

"Home sweet home," he says.

He ties the boat to a tree and helps me out. He piles my arms with a sleeping bag and a few grocery bags and leads me up the embankment to a narrow shell path that twists through bushes and abandons me in the middle of a large clearing. It's empty except for the remains of a campfire and several large logs pulled up around the dead fire.

"You should be safe here," Jason says, looking around.

Safe. *Safe.* I don't know what that word means anymore.

We bring up several more bags and Jason quickly erects a small tent and uses a battery-operated pump to blow up an air mattress. I sit on one of the logs and watch him. He lays out the sleeping bag on the air mattress.

"Darn, I forgot the pillow," he says.

I don't say anything. My head is buzzing and I'm concentrating on a lizard sitting on a nearby rock. It's bobbing its head up and down and blowing out a tiny red balloon at the base of its throat. I watch, fascinated.

Jason stands up, looks around at the pile of bags and coolers still scattered around the campsite, and seems to make a decision.

"I know what you need," he says, and holds out a hand to me. "Come on."

CHAPTER TWENTY-EIGHT

I stand and he takes my hand and leads me back down the path toward the boat. But instead of going down to the boat, he takes a right-hand path running beside the little cove and we walk for a while in silence. Small lizards skitter away in front of us and a squirrel chatters from a tree. The air is shaded green and sparkles and shimmies with water diamonds, splashing right through me. The path ends at a small beach and I see we're down the cove from his boat. It is just a patch of random sand among all that wild green, but I smile when I see it.

"Go in," he says. "The water always makes everything better."

I look at him. Then down at my clothes.

"I brought you some of my sister's shirts and shorts, but I couldn't find a bathing suit," he says apologetically. "I'll turn my back and you can go in your bra and underwear. Naked, if you want, the water feels better that way." This is said so matter-of-factly it doesn't even seem creepy. I cannot imagine any situation when I would be comfortable stripping in front of Michael, but I also can't imagine a guy so unlike Michael as Jason. Michael was dark and stormy and dangerous; Jason is clean sunshine and laughter with no dark corners in his soul.

"Are there any sharks?" I ask, staring at the brown water.

He shakes his head. "No sharks here."

He turns his back and I kick off my sopping-wet tennis shoes and unbutton my jeans. I push them down my hips and wriggle out of the wet denim and pull my T-shirt over my head. I look down at my bra and underwear and then leave them on.

I walk into the water, and it's shallow and sandy at first and then it drops off some. I dive in and when I come back up, Jason has disappeared.

I float in the light-drenched water and my head is a black vacuum, echoing and blank. I think of nothing.

Absolutely nothing.

I float on my back for a long time. I see Jason on his boat, fishing. He looks my way and waves, and I wave back. I do not think he can see anything from where he is, but it's hard to care. I feel safer knowing he is nearby.

I close my eyes, and the sun flickers across my body through the shadow of leaves, striping me with heat. My ears are underwater as I float, and sound is muted and watery. The water feels creamy and luxurious on my skin, silky and sweet. After a while I wade to the shallows and sit, my feet buried in sand soft as pudding. The setting sun is still warm, and I lift my face to it, letting it seep into me. I am not thinking about anything but *now*.

"Some people like the mountains, some people love the ocean, but I've figured out I'm an island person," Jason says from behind me. I didn't hear him come up. I have my back to the beach so I cannot see him, but his voice wraps around me like a cottony sheet.

"Why?" I ask after a while, talking to the water.

"Don't get me wrong, I love the water. But being on an island makes me feel like I'm in a castle surrounded by a moat. The bad stuff can't get in."

"I need to be on this island right now," I say softly.

"You need to make *yourself* an island, all placid and calm inside while outside everything rages," Jason says seriously.

"I don't know how to do that." The water is starting to get cold now and quivery chills race along my arms.

He doesn't say anything and I think maybe he has left, gone back to fishing. Then, real quiet, he says, "You're going to be okay. Nothing else might be okay, but *you're* going to be okay."

"I don't know—" I say, "I don't know . . . *I don't know if I can live without her!*" I'm crying, big heaving sobs, and he wades into the water and lifts me out. He wraps his arms around me and holds me while I cry. I can't seem to stop, but he doesn't seem to care, so we stand knee-deep in the water until the sobs drain out of me and I'm hiccuping. He leans back and looks at me.

"Better?"

I nod.

"Okay. Ready to get back?"

He waits with his back turned while I put on my shirt. I look down at my wet, sandy jeans and wrinkle my nose. My

T-shirt comes down to mid-thigh and at this point what does it matter? I pick them up and my shoes and follow after him.

I must have been swimming for longer than I realized, because he has been back to the campsite. A small fire flickers in the fire pit and two camp chairs are set up with a cooler between them to serve as a table.

"Let me grab you a towel and clothes." He ducks into the tent and comes out with a duffel bag. I follow him to the side of the clearing, behind some bushes, where he has set up a small shower, basically a bag of water with a hose hung on a tree branch. He shows me how it works and leaves. I can still see him through the bushes, but he is rummaging in the cooler and doesn't seem to be paying any attention to me. I feel better knowing he's *right there.*

I strip and look in the bag. Towel, soap, shampoo, razor, deodorant, and toothpaste. The shampoo and deodorant look girly and I think he probably pilfered them from his mom or the real Ashley. It all looks heavenly, and I take a long shower, not even caring the water isn't warm. When I'm done, and have pretty much depleted the water bag, I pull on one of the T-shirts and a pair of shorts. They fit, though Ashley is clearly skinnier than me.

I take a deep breath and then go back to the fire. Jason is grilling hot dogs and I realize I am ravenous.

I sit in a camp chair, and before long he has piled my plate with a hot dog, leftover mac and cheese out of a plastic container, and sliced tomatoes. I eat it all, stuffing my face like I haven't eaten in years.

When I look up he is watching me. He smiles, slowly, like

he's pleased. But then his expression darkens. "I have to get home. It's getting late, and I have a final tomorrow," he says. "I graduate next weekend."

"Leave?" Panic buzzes through my veins. "You're leaving?"

He hesitates and then comes over to me. He kneels on the ground in front of me and puts his hands on my knees. He tilts my chin with one finger so I'm looking into his beautiful eyes. "I can take you to my house if you want but I can't stay here. This is what you wanted, right?"

I think about it. It is, isn't it? I wanted to be myself. I wanted to be on the island where none of the bad stuff could touch me.

"Okay," I say. "Okay."

His face is serious as he looks at me. "I will be back. I promise." He seems to know this is what I need to hear. *I will be back, I will not die and leave you alone, I will be here for you as long as you need me.* Things my mom really can't promise me anymore.

I start crying, and he draws me to him in a hug. His body is warm and hard and male and I cling to him. After a while, I stop crying and he pushes me back gently by the shoulders so he can look at my face. He uses one finger to wipe the tears from under my eyes.

"You're going to be okay," he says.

I'm not sure I believe him, but I nod anyway, because I know that's what he wants me to do.

CHAPTER TWENTY-NINE

That night is the scariest of my life.

I'm not a city girl, exactly, but I've lived my whole life in the suburbs of Atlanta. It's not like I've never seen a bird or anything, but the only time I've slept in a tent was with Trina in my backyard when we were ten and Trina thought she might want to be a park ranger. We lasted all of two hours, and then we ran inside and Mom made us hot cocoa.

Up until now, the scariest places I've ever been are the creepy-ass buildings Chaz and Michael love so much.

They seem like child's play now.

I am all by myself. On a deserted island.

And it is dark.

At first after Jason leaves, I sit by the fire and stare into the flames, watching the air darken and the sparks float high into the sky. The mosquitoes come out, and other small biting bugs, but I find some of the bug spray Jason left, and I continue to sit and stare. As the fire dies, I begin to hear sounds.

Big sounds and little sounds.

Small rustling in the bushes, the roar of a faraway boat motor. From the nearby cove comes a cascade of splashes, like a handful of giant silver coins dashed across the surface of the water.

Then I hear something crash through the bushes—*close*—and I begin to think serious bear thoughts, or . . . an alligator!? The thought of a monstrous lizard slithering its way out of the bushes sends me scurrying into the tent. I have a flashlight and a battery lantern and I turn them both on. I don't have a book. Reading at night has always been my way to keep the demons at bay. All I can do is huddle in the sleeping bag and listen so hard it makes my ears hurt. A few mosquitoes have followed me into the tent and they drone around so loudly I want to scream.

The hours pass excruciatingly slowly. I lie awake shaking, every new noise almost sending me over the edge. Shadows move and writhe on the tent walls and I hope they are branches but deep down I know it is the dark trying to get in.

I cannot sleep. I cannot sleep even though it is the one thing I want most in the world because the thoughts in my head are almost unbearable.

∽

I must have dozed off, because Jason is leaning over me when I open my eyes. The light is pearly and gray and even the chirping birds sound sleepy.

"Hey," he says softly. I wonder how long he has been watching me sleep.

"Hey." I am curled up in a tight little ball hugging my knees. For a minute we look at each other and without speaking he leaves the tent. I get up. It's a little chilly, gauzy pink fog stealing through the trees, and I drag the sleeping bag out with me. He is stoking the fire and I sit in one of the camp chairs.

"I brought coffee," he says without turning around. "And a sausage biscuit."

I pick up the thermos and sip. The coffee is hot and black and bitter and tastes wonderful.

"Are there alligators on the island?" I ask. "Something *big* was outside the tent last night." I shudder just thinking about it.

He laughs. "Raccoons," he says, pointing at the trash bag with its contents strewn everywhere. "I should have hung it up in the tree but I forgot."

"Oh." *Raccoons* made all that noise? What, are the raccoons in Florida the size of small cars?

"I can't stay long, I've got to get to school, but I wanted to come check on you," he says. He's got the fire burning nicely now and I stretch my bare feet out to it. He sits on the log facing me.

"How was the night? Do you want to leave? I didn't tell my parents you're here. They wouldn't approve of you being out here all by yourself, but if you want to come back to my house, I'm sure they would be happy to have you—"

I shake my head immediately. Even with the scary noises,

and the living, breathing darkness, I do not want to leave. Not yet.

"I want to stay." I lean forward and put my hand on his arm. He looks up. "Thank you," I say.

He smiles, but it's a small smile, and his eyes are troubled.

"I'll be back this afternoon. I brought you some more food, and a couple of my books. I know you like to read. Are you going to be okay? Say the word and I'll take you home."

"I'm good here." But I'm crying again, tears slipping down my cheeks.

He nods and stands up. He looks down at me and cups my wet cheek with his palm and then he's gone.

∞

I'm not sure what to do with myself. I can't remember when I'd ever been away from the TV, my computer, or my phone for any length of time. It feels odd, and at first I'm antsy. Then I decide to go for a walk and follow one of the trails leading out of the back of the campsite. It leads me to the bigger beach I saw when we came in, overlooking the open water. I wish I had a camera. I sit for a while and watch the sun rise and the boats skim across the water. My tears seem disconnected from me, like a soft summer rain falling gently in the background. A pelican, with a blond Mohawk and startlingly human blue eyes, lands with a *splish-splash* and comes up with a fish in its pouch. I watch in fascination as it gulps down the squirming creature.

I see a fin in the water, and I tense, but then I see the gray back of a dolphin as it porpoises to the surface.

Not a shark.

I think about what Jason said in one of his e-mails, about watching dolphins jump for joy. *Does she think about death? Do animals feel joy because they don't think about death or because they live with it every day?*

After a while I get up and follow the beach around the island. I climb over fallen trees and look at pilings out in the water. *Someone* used to live here, someone used to call this home. I walk until the sun is high in the sky and the sun is burning my arms, and then I turn back. I am still crying. I can't seem to stop and I have given up trying.

I wonder about my mom, what she is doing right now, and if she's okay, and then I start running to make myself stop thinking about it. But even then, pictures of her drawn, worried face leak into my head.

I make my way back to the private little beach. I take off all my clothes except for my bra and underwear and lie in the warm water until it creeps away with the tide and only muddy sand and crabs remain, and still I lie there. I'm shriveled up like a prune when I get out, feeling as tender and weak as a newborn. I put the towel under the shade of a bush and go to sleep.

∽

When I wake, the towel is soaked with my tears. I can't remember my dream, not really, but bits of it flash in my head. Trina dressed up like the Statue of Liberty saying, "Michael is looking for you, everyone is looking for you, where are you, Erin?" and then being in a department store with my mom, mortally embarrassed about going bra shopping for the first time.

I stretch, realizing the sun is going down and that I must have slept for hours. Jason still hasn't arrived, and that scares me. Why hasn't he come back?

I make my way to the campsite, and it is darker among the trees and bushes, and I tremble, even though it's not cold. The fire is dead, and I have to go find some firewood, venturing into the shadowy, whispering bushes. I come back at a dead run with the logs in my arms. I'm already frightened, and the sun isn't even down yet. I am all alone, and no one but Jason knows I am here. What if something happened to him, what if he leaves me here all by myself?

I try to get the fire lit with the long lighter Jason used this morning, but the big logs don't want to light. I sit back on my heels. Eventually I curl up on the blanket in as tight a ball as I can manage, with the flashlight clenched in my fist, and stare at the flameless logs.

CHAPTER THIRTY

It's fully dark by the time I hear the soft *putt-putt* of Jason's boat and hear him walk up the path. I cannot seem to move, and I hear him hesitate at the edge of the clearing as he sees me.

"Erin?" he says softly.

"I need to stop the thoughts," I say, *"but they won't stop. I can't make them stop."*

He comes and pulls me into his arms and rocks with me as the tears slide down my face. I'm aware of his body against mine, warm and big and safe.

"Have you eaten?" he asks when I'm done crying.

I shake my head. I watch while he finds some leaves to put under the logs and lights them. Flames start licking at the logs. He puts some hamburgers on the grill and after a while hands me a plate and I eat.

His eyes are on me.

"Erin," he says.

I look at him, sideways.

"I've got something to show you. Will you come with me?"

It seems an oddly formal invitation, as if this is something important to him.

I hesitate. *No, not really, I don't want to do anything but sit here and maybe if I try hard enough I'll disappear and I won't have to think about anything anymore, ever.*

He takes my hand gently, pulls me to my feet, and leads me into the darkness.

Somehow, with my hand in his, it's bearable.

∞

We walk through the dark green murmur of bushes. The moon cannot find its way completely into this place, and only dribbles and splats of light mark the ripple of our passage. We pass my small beach and walk farther. The bushes are thick here, dark, tangled, menacing, and I clutch Jason's hand.

I see a silver gleam, like the sheen off a frozen winter pond, a moment before we emerge beside a small lagoon. It is a pool of still, radiant light, ringed by the quiet, watching bushes. Jason tosses a shell into the water and shards of light dance across the surface. The luminescent flickers shimmer and shake until finally fading into the silent shine of a looking glass.

"It's—it's unbelievable." My voice feels rusty and unused, as if I have not spoken for days. After I speak, I wish I hadn't, because it feels wrong to speak in the hallowed sanctuary of this place.

"Isn't it, though?" Jason says back, easily. He pulls me down onto a log beside the water. "They'll come soon."

"They will?" *Who will?*

"When I was fifteen," Jason says, "my mom found out she had breast cancer. My grandmother already had it, and it seemed too surreal that my mother had it too. At first, before my grandmother got bad, my mom spent every moment she wasn't in treatment painting. That's what she does. That's *her* secret place she goes when it's all too much. I was trying so hard to be strong for her, but sometimes it got too hard, being strong. I didn't feel strong inside, you know? So, I would come here. I would come and camp for a few days and it was like . . . it was like when I broke my finger playing basketball. It hurt like crap, and I realized the only thing I could do is fix it. So I yanked on it, twice, and the bone slipped back into place. Even though it still hurt, it felt whole, the way it should. That's how it is when I come here. Everything can be screwed up and broken, but when I come here, everything clicks back to where it should be. Does that make sense?"

He sounds a little shy and I turn to look at him. He's watching me, his eyes dark and vulnerable. I get that he needs me to understand what he's saying, and how important this place is to him. It's important to him that I feel it too.

"I get it," I say softly.

He twines his fingers in mine, and I hear a sound, and smell the fragrant odor of grass and mud and the faintly sour smell of digestion. Two cavernous nostrils poke up and gust out a wind of exhalation, and disappear. The casual flip of a tail splashes an expanding ring of moon-sparkles. A head pokes up, large, dark eyes curious and bulbous, a wrinkled face sporting friendly whiskers and a permanently sad expression. Another one sur-faces, and another.

"Manatees," Jason says.

I look at the massive creatures, some as long as twelve feet and pushing two tons. I've heard of them, but never seen one. About all I know is that people are trying to save them from extinction.

"One of their closest relatives is actually the elephant," Jason says quietly. "They're so big they have to eat constantly, sometimes up to one hundred pounds of grass a day."

The manatees' skin even looks like an elephant's, except that it is spotted with barnacles. Ignoring us now, they begin turning over one another, splashing with their flat tails and churning the water.

"Look, they're playing!"

"They're mating. There's one female, and she's in heat. The males will follow her around for three weeks or so, and they mate constantly."

Jason won't look at me as he says this, and when I look at him, even in the moonlight I can see his face is a little red.

My face feels hot. I watch the big sea creatures in silence. Though I cannot see any overtly sexual activity, somehow the knowledge I am watching a mating dance makes me fidgety, but I'm filled with moonlight and am content not to speak.

Time passes, I don't know how long. The angle of the moon's light has changed when the manatees subside, only appearing when they languidly surface for slow, briny breaths. I'm exhausted all of a sudden and shiver in the cool, wet air.

"Are you cold? Here." Jason pulls off his jacket and helps

me put it on. He crouches down to zip it up, his face intent as he concentrates on fitting the zipper together and pulling it up to my chin as if I am a little kid.

"Why does it feel like I've known you forever?" I ask. "You don't feel like a guy. You feel like . . . I don't know."

Safe. You feel safe.

"Thanks," he says wryly. "Just the words every guy longs to hear. Believe me, though, I'm a guy." His hands are on my knees, and he stares at me for a long moment, and suddenly I don't feel so safe. Suddenly I think he might kiss me, and I feel hot and cold and my skin sparks to the touch of his hands.

But he rises to his feet in one smooth movement and leads me back through the dark. The bushes rustle mysteriously and my nose is full of a spicy brew of secret green zest and salty mud.

We don't say anything else, but his hand on mine makes me forget that I should be scared.

CHAPTER THIRTY-ONE

The next day is better. I am numb, but I am no longer crying. Jason brings me a notebook and pen and I spend the day writing, pouring my thoughts and feelings out on paper. Something hard and cold has broken, like there's a whirlpool inside me, one of the great salty, warm maelstroms they found in the Arctic Ocean, dragging up life and muck from an unknowable depth and spinning it out into all that cold, ice-blocked surface water.

I am dreading the night, though. Even at home, my nights were full of dark, swirling thoughts that chased me into sleep. Here, it's like those demon thoughts take shape and crackle the bushes and shake the tent. I'm not sure which are more terrifying: the thoughts in my head or the unseen things that shudder and yowl in the night.

That afternoon, Jason comes to the island and I am fishing in the cove. He left me a pole, but I'm still not exactly sure how to use it.

"Getting the hang of it?" Jason calls as he pulls the boat up on shore.

"I caught a small one." I reel in my line. "But getting it off the line was *not* fun."

"We'll make a fishing ace out of you yet," he says.

"No, *you're* the fishing ace," I say.

Jason told me he is already working as a fishing guide on the weekends, and has even won some big fishing tournaments. This is what he plans to do when he graduates from high school. I envy his calm certainty of what his life will be like, his belief he can shape his future.

"Hey, I have an idea," he says. "Do you want to go fish for something bigger?"

Honestly, I'm not happy about leaving the island. But he looks so excited to be showing me something new that I smile and agree.

"Look at the sun out there on the edge of the ocean." I point at the sky, which is full of oranges, reds, and yellows, like the setting sun is a fiery paintball splattered across the horizon.

"The gulf." Jason is concentrating on a bucket he is tying to the back of the boat, letting it trail behind as we drift. *Chum* he told me when I asked.

I look at him in surprise. "It's the gulf? Like the Gulf of Mexico?"

Now it is his turn to look at me in surprise. "Where did you think we were?"

I shrug. It doesn't really matter where I am. It matters where I'm not.

On the island, nestled like a green jewel in the clear, brown backwater, I'm safe. Out here, the vastness of the water weighs on me, crushes me into something small and insignificant.

Jason doesn't say anything else. A couple of other boats float in the pass, and men with thick poles scan the water. Some of them are drinking beer, but none of them seem to notice the slow destruction of the sun.

We are in a wide, watery pass between two islands. Colorful houses crowd the beach on one island, but the other beach is empty. Both islands are far prettier than my little island (it *feels* like mine now), with sugary beaches lapped by water the color of Jason's eyes. Even though these islands are prettier, I still prefer my secret haven.

Jason works on putting bait on a line and drops it down into the water. He hands me the pole and we sit in silence. I do not feel the need to speak.

"Not until we are lost do we begin to understand ourselves." The line from one of Jason's books drifts through my mind. I'd never read Thoreau before I met Jason and I see why he likes him. Then I start thinking about whether I need to pump up the air mattress a little more tonight, and if we'll eat fish this evening. It's as if I am floating on the uncomplicated, lovely surface of the sea, and as long as I don't go too deep, I am fine. Monsters swim in the dark depths of my mind.

"Uh . . . hey! Hey! I got something," I say as my pole jerks and the line starts zinging out. "It's heavy!"

"Pull back *slowly*," Jason says, "and sit down."

I sit abruptly, pulling back on the pole and reeling when the fish gets closer, holding on for dear life when it decides to go the other way. Jason motors the boat slowly in the direction the fish is going and coaches me to "Pull back, reel, no, don't yank! Slow and steady, pull back, reel" and it seems like forever I'm doing this. As the fish gets closer, Jason tells me I can stand up, and I do. I am concentrating so fiercely I'm surprised when Jason comes up behind me, his stomach against my back, his arms cradling mine.

"You're getting tired," he says, "but this is where it's about to get fun."

He helps me reel, and I see the shadow under the surface of the green water and it is *big*.

"What *is* that?"

"You'll see," he says, and the fish dives, trying to get under the boat. Jason's strong arms move against me, and I try not to notice the way his body feels against mine, but suddenly I'm aware of blood thrilling just under the surface of my skin. He pulls me firmly against him, and I cannot tell if it's because he needs to or because he wants to.

The fish breaks through the water beside the boat and I'm so stunned I almost drop the pole.

"It's a shark!"

"Yep." Jason takes the pole from me, and maneuvers the shark so it's lying right beside the boat. It's about six feet long, brown, with a flat, wide head and a white underbelly.

Its eyes roll back at me and I realize that a *shark* is *looking* at me.

"What . . . what do you do now? Kill it?" I ask, though that feels wrong.

"No, of course not. She's a nurse shark, she doesn't hurt anyone. Here, feel her."

He takes my hand and draws it along the back of the shark, from head to tail. It feels smooth and silky.

"Now the other way," he says.

I rub my hand the other way and am surprised that now its skin feels like sandpaper.

"It's got little scales on its skin, kind of like teeth," he says. "That's why it's prickly when you rub toward its head."

"I can't believe I'm touching a shark," I say and Jason grins.

"Not so bad, is it?"

Somehow this reminds me one of Mr. Jarad's silly sports analogies, and I smile.

With a gloved hand, Jason pulls the shark's head out of the water by the line, and its eye rolls toward me as it thrashes around, splashing water into the boat. It opens its mouth, revealing crooked, yellow teeth, masses of them, and Jason uses a metal pliers-looking tool to grasp the hook, which I can see lodged in the shark's mouth.

"Careful!" I say, because his hand is inches from those wicked-looking teeth.

He is focused on the shark, which is bending its body back and forth, trying to get away. Jason pulls the hook free and the shark drops into the water, splashing us one more time before it disappears beneath the waves.

I let a breath out I did not realize I was holding.

"Let's get back, it's getting late," Jason says as if he didn't just have his hand practically *in* a shark's mouth. The sun is gone, the quiet water holding on to its memory in soft tangerines, pinks, and yellows glowing in the surface ripples.

On the way back he lets me drive the boat, and the feel of the boat dancing beneath me as we skim across the surface of the water, trailing a pod of leaping dolphins, feels like flying.

∽

"Do you think," I say later, after we have eaten and are sitting staring at the fire, "having this BRCA mutation makes us defective? I feel like something's wrong with me, do you?"

Jason stirs the fire with a stick. "Species wouldn't be able to survive and adapt without mutations. Mutations fuel evolution. When they're good, they get passed on so the entire species is stronger for it."

"So, what? If the mutation is bad, we should do the species a favor and die off quickly?" I'm offended, though I know I was the one who asked the question.

He shakes his head. "It's hard to know whether a mutation is good or bad until generations later. The gene mutation causing sickle-cell anemia is both good and bad. People with one of the mutated genes have protection from malaria; people with two mutated genes have sickle-cell anemia. I read one study suggesting the BRCA mutation may encourage neural growth, so people with the BRCA mutation might actually be smarter because of the gene. What if it takes someone with the BRCA gene mutation to figure out how to cure breast cancer? It's a stretch, but you never know. Not until it's over."

I'm quiet. I don't know what to think about that.

"What about guys?" I ask suddenly. "I mean, I know what having the gene means to me. But what about you?"

"It's different for us. No ovarian cancer, obviously, but increased chances for prostate, pancreatic, and skin cancer, and of course, breast cancer."

"I didn't know men could *get* breast cancer." I'm horrified and fascinated all at the same time.

"Well, yes, we can." He looks uncomfortable. "It's rare, but having the BRCA gene mutation ups the chances."

"Do you think people with this gene should have children?" I ask after a while. I've never really thought about children, but I guess if asked, I would say I planned on having one or two. That's what people do. But do I really want to pass this mutation on to a child?

"Do you think your mom should have had you?" he counters.

I open my mouth, then shut it. Who can answer no to that question?

"I don't know what to do," I say. "Women are cutting off their breasts and taking out their ovaries so they won't get cancer. And I understand it, I *do*, because I can't imagine going through what my mom is going through. But on the other hand . . ." I can't go on, because what I want to say is, *I only got my period four years ago! I've never had sex! How can I cut off my breasts and take out my ovaries? What guy would ever want me? And even if I don't, what guy would want me if he knows I have this mutation and that I might die?*

"On the other hand?" Jason is looking at me closely, the firelight all tangled in his curly hair.

"On the other hand," I say slowly, looking at him directly, "is there any guy who would want me if he finds out I'm . . . defective? That I might have to cut off my breasts? I know I could have them reconstructed, but they would be *fake.* They wouldn't be real. Would I feel real?" *Like a real woman?*

"I don't think you'll have any trouble finding a guy to love you for who you are, Erin," Jason says. "A real guy won't be turned off by all this. He'll be strong enough to take it."

"What about you?" I say, and when he looks at me fast and quick, I realize what he thought I meant. "No, not you feeling that way about me—" *God.* My face is burning. "I meant, when you date, do you tell the girl you have the gene mutation?" I'm curious, because I suddenly realize he's never mentioned a girl-friend. Of course, how could he, when I thought he was Ash-ley? But we've been talking about so much, and he's never once mentioned a girlfriend. A secret part of me is happy about that.

"I don't date anymore," he says after a moment, poking the fire strongly with his stick so a swarm of firefly sparks rises in the air. "I'm not planning on falling in love. That way no one has to watch me die."

I stare at him in astonishment. "You think you can do that—just decide not to love anybody?"

"Not *anybody*," he says. "I love my family, and that will never change. But yes, I think I can decide not to love anybody else. I've come this far without falling in love, so why not?"

I'm not sure what to say. I've never been in love either, but I've been dreaming about it since I was a little girl. I can't imagine *not* wanting to fall in love.

"Don't you think," I say slowly, "that you would be happier if you fell in love? You seem to be big into the whole I'm-a-happy-camper thing and all."

He smiles. "That's how you see me, huh? Funny. No, I'm perfectly fine without loving anybody. Why should that change?"

The fire suddenly flares, sending sparks dancing and swirling into the air. We both startle back at the same time, and for some reason that makes us laugh as the dying embers rain down on us.

Jason's question, if it was a question, goes unanswered.

CHAPTER THIRTY-TWO

When Jason arrives the next day, it is almost dark and I have fish fillets on the grill.

"Look!" I point at the fish. "I caught it and decided I would try to fillet it. You made it look so easy. It wasn't."

Jason looks at the mangled hunks of meat on the grill and has the good sense not to laugh.

"Smells good," he says.

We eat the fish, and Jason asks if I want to go for a boat ride.

"It's dark!" Somehow, though, when he's with me, I don't think about the dark. It's only when he's gone that the pitch-black terror returns.

"Yeah, so?" He grins, daring me.

We blast through the moonlit night, ripping through the shiny, dark surface of the water. The wind of our passage beats against my face, scrubbing it clean with salty night air. I'm light and empty, like a vacant house stripped bare of its furniture and doors and windows, just the old wood walls and floor open to the blasting wind. The air, the water, the mystery of the night blows through my head, changing everything it touches.

We slow to a puttering crawl as we enter a dark harbor dotted with elegant sailboats, tall and quiet in the light-splashed night, their masts holding a galaxy of low-hanging stars. The moon is high, raining silver down on the sleeping boats, and it is almost as bright as day. But it is a different light from the sun, quicksilver and shy, full of secrets.

Jason and I don't speak as the boat glides through the silent harbor. Soon we have passed the sailboats and speed up again until we are flying across the dark water.

He runs us up onto a beach, the shells singing under the smooth bottom of the boat. We are on the edge of a pass, and across the water I can see lights, but where we are the bushes are feral and overgrown.

Jason takes my hand and leads me to a fallen tree. It is dark, no houses, or lights, just the wild frenzy of bushes and trees and the tiny tinkle of shells in the salty spank of waves on the shore.

I sit with him, feeling the warm press of his palm on mine. He has laced our fingers together, his larger hand enveloping mine, and it feels right, and not right, all at the same time.

Off the beach, dolphins crest, and the moon-soaked waves quiver.

It is then I see the monstrous shadows stretching across the beach. They are black-etched and contorted, like the reflection of gnarled skeletal fingers.

"What . . . ?" I turn to see what is causing the shadows.

The trees glow sterling in the moonlight, like silver soldiers standing tall in a black sky. Their bare trunks reflect the moon's light, flinging it away into the night.

"Wow," I say.

They are dead, of course, an army of leafless trees lining the shore.

"A hurricane killed them when I was a kid," Jason says. "I like them though, I don't know why."

It seems impossible the goblin shadows could come from the statuesque trees, but maybe life is like that. The shadows are far worse than the reality.

We sit in silence for a while, and I watch the shadows dance as the wind moves in the trees.

"Do you really think," I say, "that you'll never fall in love?"

"Not if I can help it," he says. "I've watched people I love get sick and die. It's . . . soul-killing. I don't ever want to do that to someone else. I don't ever want someone I love to have to go through that."

That makes me sad for some reason I don't want to think about.

"With my luck with guys, I don't think I'll ever find any-one either," I say. "Maybe I should be a nun. Trina was going to be a nun for about five seconds a couple years ago. That way I can do all the surgeries and not even worry about it. What would it matter?"

He turns to me and smiles. "I don't see it happening. You'll find someone."

"I'm not sure I'm good for the people I love," I say after a while in a low voice. "Sometimes I feel like I'm drowning and all I do is drag them down with me. I can't seem to stop hurting them."

Jason stares into the fire. "Drowning people do desperate things. The trick is learning when to hang on, and when to let go."

"It's just all so much. I don't know how to deal with it all." My voice breaks a little. Maybe if it were just one thing, if it was just my mom's cancer, just my positive BRCA status, just Trina's betrayal and Michael's rejection, then I could handle it. But all together, it's just too much.

"When things get bad, I think you have to focus on today. Thoreau says, 'To be awake is to be alive,' right? I'm just happy I'm alive *today*. Who knows what's going to happen tomorrow? I could die in some crazy freak accident, like, I don't know—I heard the other day some chick got strangled when her necklace got caught in her neck massager. If I died like that, I'd feel pretty dumb if I had spent a whole lot of time worrying about some gene that in the end didn't matter at all."

"You wouldn't feel dumb because you strangled yourself with a neck massager?" I say, a giggle bubbling up, surprising me.

"That too," he says, giving me a mock-severe look. "You know what I mean. I try to live every day as if I might be attacked by an angry mutant neck massager tomorrow. Every day matters, you know?"

He is circling his thumb on my palm as he talks, and a fiery-cool deluge sweeps from my hand to every part of me.

"How," I say, serious again. "How can you say you won't ever fall in love if you live each day like it matters? It doesn't make sense to me."

His fingers tighten on mine, and I feel a fresh burst of heat race through me and I close my eyes against it.

"There's a big difference between living each day as it comes and living selfishly. To me, that's like saying, 'If it makes you happy to push someone in front of a train, why not do it?' Hurting someone, especially someone I care about, is not an option. And that's what would happen if I got close to someone. They would have to watch me get sick, and maybe die."

He pulls his fingers from mine and helps me to my feet.

My hand feels cold as we walk back to the boat.

The next day when Jason arrives in the afternoon, I decide I want to go swimming. I strip to my bra and underwear, not even waiting for Jason to turn around. He has seen me like this so many times it seems pointless to pretend modesty.

I wade into the water and Jason casts his pole. He will not

go swimming with me, though I have asked. "I'd rather fish," he says, and "You need it, I don't."

I float in the water while Jason sits on the sand, his eyes trained on the line in the water.

The water is a pure, clean brown, and I can see a school of small fish sliding beneath me, not even stirring the mud in their silent passage. Fringing the cove is a green tangle of mangroves (they build *islands*, Jason said), their exposed roots snarling in an untamed, impenetrable maze. The plants breathe through the roots, he said, and they're a kind of nursery to baby marine life. Dangling from the branches are torpedo-shaped seedlings, ready to drop into the water and float away to a new home.

I can hear the distant call of an osprey and the whisper of leaves in the breeze. *Splash-splash*, clear air, burning sun, the smell of mud, the flop of a fish.

This place is heart-healing, and I never want to leave.

Mom would miss you, Mom would be sad.

I push the thought away, push the pain deep, deep, *deep*.

I get cold, so I wade out and go sit beside Jason. He does not look at me. I lean against his shoulder and watch the play of muscles in his arm and breathe in the salty, musky scent of him. He puts the pole down and stretches out his legs. I curl up next to him and put my head on his legs so I can watch the water.

He tenses but does not say anything.

"Rub my back?" I ask.

His strong fingers press into my shoulders and heat tickles

through me as his hands drift lower, kneading my lower back. I feel the rough catch of calluses on my tender skin, and I gasp a little bit, biting my lip, the heat cascading through me. I stretch like a cat, pushing into his fingers.

Suddenly he curses under his breath and stops.

I sit up in surprise, blinking slowly in confusion and swirling sensation.

"No," he says, and closes his eyes. He's breathing fast.

I look at him in amazement.

He opens his eyes and looks at me. "What are you doing?" He gestures at me, taking in my bra and underwear. "Think about it, Erin. Do you know how you look running around half naked? It was different in the beginning when you were almost comatose, but you're not anymore, you're alive and warm and soft. Do you know how hard this is for me?"

My mouth is open in shock.

"Here." He takes off his shirt and throws it to me.

I pull it on, hugging its warmth around me. I do not know what to say. But I find myself noticing the hard lines of his chest, the white tan line across his lower stomach where his shorts have ridden down a little. I feel the warm fullness of my breasts press against my arms and I am aware of my bare legs. I tug the shirt over my knees.

"I don't understand," I say in a small voice.

He looks away. He's so gorgeous I want to run my fingers through his wild curls and stroke the side of his clenched jaw.

"Do I have to explain this? Really?" he asks in a strangled voice.

I don't say anything. If you paid me a million dollars, I wouldn't have been able to find anything to say.

"You're . . . sexy, Erin." He's not looking at me, and his face is beginning to heat with color.

"You think . . . you think I'm *sexy*?"

"*Yes*," he says on an outward explosion of breath.

I stare at him, but his gaze is focused on the water.

"But I'm . . . I'm *not*," I say.

He snorts and turns his beautiful turquoise eyes on me. "Yes you are." He sighs, running his hands through his hair. "Look. I'm your friend, Erin. I want to be your friend, but it's hard to be your friend when you're running around in your underwear. So do me a favor, okay? Wear some clothes."

He gets up, and I follow as he goes back to camp. It's starting to get late and I don't want him to leave, not like this, but I don't know what to say.

"Here's the thing," he says, after he has hauled in more supplies from his boat. "A front's coming through, so it's going to be stormy and windy tomorrow. I have a charter scheduled in the morning, but I'll be here tomorrow afternoon. If it starts raining before I get back, I brought you some more books, and you can go into the tent and wait for me." He takes me by the shoulders so I have to look in his eyes. "Are you sure you're not ready to go home?"

"No, not . . . not yet."

"Okay." He looks up at the sky, which is the clear, hard blue of a china plate. "Okay." He shakes his head. "It's going to have to be soon, though, Erin. We can't do this for much longer. Do you get that?"

"I know," I say, but it's like the words are buried in the back of my throat.

He busies himself with the rest of his gear, dropping a cooler and cursing in frustration. He seems uncomfortable and jittery, and I just want things back the way they were before.

"I gotta go," he says finally.

"Bye," I say, trying not to sound forlorn but probably failing miserably.

He moves off into the bushes without looking at me again.

∽

I lie awake most of the night. It isn't the night noises that keep me awake, though there are still plenty of them. It's the word Jason threw at me. "Sexy."

He thinks I'm sexy.

I miss Trina so much because she would know exactly what to say; she would help me know what to think about Jason saying I'm sexy.

But he doesn't want to think of you like that.

The first guy who ever told me he thought I was sexy also told me he just wants to be friends.

Is there something wrong with me?

Of course there is. Everything is wrong with me. Why would Jason want to date a girl who is a complete wacka-doodle?

But he said he didn't want to fall in love with anybody.

Sure, but if he really wanted to, he could fall in love with me.

He just doesn't want to.

He doesn't want to because he knows I'm messed up.

Flawed inside and out.

CHAPTER THIRTY-THREE

It is cloudy and blustery when I wake, the tent swaying back and forth like a building in an earthquake. I get out and make sure the stakes are tight in the ground and try to make a fire, but it is too windy. The air has a strange electric tension to it and I feel a weird pressure in my chest. It isn't raining, but the clouds are low and racing across the sky.

I munch on a handful of nuts and follow the path to the front beach so I can look at the open water. It's choppy, sloshing around like giant washing machine, and I see very few boats.

I sit and watch the water turn steel gray and whitecapped, worried about Jason out in those angry-looking waves.

∽৴

It starts to rain that afternoon, quick showers dumping on my head, and then turning off like a spigot. I run around the campsite, throwing anything needing to stay dry into the tent. I eye the big cooler, and decide to put that in the tent as well. By this time, the wind is whipping through my small clearing, and I am afraid the tent might decide to act like a kite and fly. I think about crawling into the tent and curling up warm and snug with a book, but I am too on edge for that. The air feels taut and heavy and I spend the next few hours going from the cove to the front beach, looking for Jason. Something is wrong. He said he would be here.

But as I look out at the scary rolling water and the froth flying high into the air as the waves smash onto the beach, I know he should not be out in this. It's too dangerous, and that means I am on my own.

When it gets dark, I finally go back to the tent. Not that I see the sunset. The air grows murkier until I can no longer see the water, just feel its stinging spray on my cheek.

I drop my wet clothes outside and stand in the rain for a few moments to wash the salt off of me, and a bolt of white-hot lightning sends me diving inside the tent. The rumblings turn into full-fledged booms, and the lightning flashes like strobe lights. I am glad I put the cooler inside, because I am not certain the wind couldn't lift the tent, even with me in it.

I hear something under the crash of thunder, and I strain to listen. I hear it again. It sounds like a *boat*, and *oh my God*, please tell me Jason isn't out in *this*? Because as much as I want, need him here with me, I know it must be really bad out on the water. I could never live with myself if he died trying to get to me.

I unzip the tent and am hit with a wall of blinding water.

Thunder murmurs restlessly as I race along the path toward the cove, lightning splitting the chaotic darkness. I see Jason's boat slide onto the shore and he gets out, shrouded in a yellow raincoat. He ties the boat to a tree branch and grabs my hand.

"Come on!" he yells over the rush of rain.

We start toward the tent and the world explodes in howling, ferocious light, dazzling, blinding, burning, as lightning hits one of the tall, lanky palm trees near us. The pure, encompassing whiteness is punctuated with a boom that sends us both to our knees.

"Storms . . . are worse than they thought . . . ," Jason says.

"Ya think?" I stare at the top of the tree, which has burst into flames despite the driving rain.

"Had to get to you," he says and his teeth are chattering.

"Seriously, you almost killed yourself!"

He is shaking, his hand ice-cold.

I shove him inside the tent and crawl in after him. He falls on top of the sleeping bag.

"Can you take your clothes off or do you need help?" I try to sound matter-of-fact. "Don't look if you can't take it, but I'm getting dry clothes on."

"I'll . . . close my eyes," he says through chattering teeth.

"You better," I say. "Wouldn't want you to think I was trying to seduce you or anything." The words are a little bitter but I don't think he notices.

I strip and pull on dry shorts and a T-shirt, my back turned as I hear him struggle to pull off his wet jeans.

I help him into the sleeping bag and have to zip it because

his fingers are shaking so badly. I lie down next to him, outside the sleeping bag, my head on a backpack.

"Why did you come?" I ask after a while, when his teeth have stopped chattering.

"I said I would," he says.

"But it's storming! You could have been killed!"

"That's what friends are for," he says, a little flip.

"Are we? Friends?"

"I hope so," he says. "I wouldn't want to lose you. As a friend. Are you ready to go home yet?"

I don't answer.

He is quiet for a while and I think maybe he's fallen asleep, and then he says, "My mom is the strongest woman I know. She was going though chemo when my grandmother died. Mom would go to my grandmother's room and sing to her and stay with her for hours. Mom had the chemo port her chest, but she would crawl up in bed with Grandma and lie with her. She was there when Grandma died, singing to her. And after Grandma died, Mom got up and went the next day for another chemo treatment. She did that for *us*, for me and my sister. She knew she couldn't give up. She knew we needed her. She got up out of that bed and went and did what she needed to do to stay alive."

In the light, I can see his throat working, but I don't see any tears.

"And right after my mom went into remission, my aunt, my mom's twin sister, *she* got cancer. After she died, my mom still had to keep on keeping on. I've never seen anybody that strong in my life. All she went through, she still can paint, and smile, and crack jokes, and take care of her family. Because she loves us, and that's what you do when you love someone."

I'm not sure what to say. I'm not sure why he is telling me this right now.

I ask, "Do you think I was wrong? Wrong for leaving like I did?"

He doesn't say anything at first. Then, "What do you think, Erin? I mean, I understand, I *understand*, I do, but yes, I think you were wrong. How many times do you think I wanted to check out, go away, and pretend the bad stuff wasn't going on? But I couldn't. I had to be there for the ones who counted on me. We've *got* to, or family doesn't mean a goddamn thing."

That hurts. Hurts bad. I sit up and wrap my arms around my knees.

"How can you think of me as a friend," I say in a low voice, "if you think I'm so terrible?"

"Erin, I don't think you're terrible." He reaches over, grabs my knee, gives it a little shake. "It's hard. I *know* it's hard. But if you want to make it right, you need to grow up, go back, and *be there* for your mom, like she's always been there for you."

I'm crying and I hold my knees tight.

"I don't know if I can *be* that strong," I gulp through my sobs. "I fell apart completely the last time I tried. I don't know if I can go back and do it all over again."

"You'll do what you have to do," he says.

But what if I can't?

"It's going to be all right." He leans toward me, the sleeping bag falling away from his bare chest, and puts his arm around me. Even though he's done it many times in the past days, somehow this time it's different. We both feel it, and I stop crying, staring into his eyes that are eerily luminescent in the flash of lightning. I wonder what he would do if I rubbed my hands over his chest, because suddenly I want to touch him so badly it hurts.

I lean toward him, and I'm breathing fast and shallow. I want it to happen, I want to kiss him and I wonder if he's feeling the heat like I am, if he's thinking about kissing me. I feel loose and warm, like frozen honey beginning to thaw and sweeten.

He leans forward to meet me, then . . . presses his lips against my forehead. He does that for a while, and I close my eyes, tears slipping down my cheeks.

"Good night," he whispers finally and pulls away.

He lies back down, but I don't think he sleeps most of the night.

I know because I don't either.

CHAPTER THIRTY-FOUR

Though the rain still pours outside, the tent has lightened. Dawn has come creeping, muffled in thick, fluffy clouds.

I look over and see Jason's eyes are open and he's looking at me.

"Are you ready?" he says. "To go home?"

Without answering, I get out of the tent and go to the cove. I take off all my clothes and float in the rain-puckered water. The water feels warm, and the raindrops are cold on my skin. I try to find that place of silence and peace of the last couple of days, but it isn't there anymore. I am a jumble of emotions—anger, confusion, pain, terror—all raging through my head, and I cannot turn it off.

Jason comes to the beach and looks down at my pile of clothes on the sand. He sighs, raindrops caught in the fine hairs of his unshaven face.

"Erin, what are you doing?"

"Swimming. Want to come in?" I know he knows I'm naked. The water caresses me, a silky bronze veil concealing little. My skin feels hypersensitive and I'm aware of the velvety mud between my toes, the tiny flick of a baitfish's tail as it rushes past my calf, the delicious touch of water everywhere.

"Erin . . ."

I don't know why I'm doing it. Not really. Anger thrums through me, pounding through my veins, souring my mouth. I'm mad at him, I'm mad at myself, I'm mad at *everything.*

"The water's *wonderful.*" I move my arms so the water sweeps against my skin, sending shivers from head to foot. I've never felt so aware of myself before. And that's what I want, isn't it? I want to know what it feels like to be a woman before I don't have any of the parts anymore. "Why don't you come in?"

He is looking at me, and his gaze is a heavy, satiny weight touching every part of me, and then he looks deliberately over my shoulder.

"Erin. Stop it. Put your clothes on. We need to go. It's time to go."

"Jason . . ."

"Erin, why are you doing this? What are you afraid of?"

He turns and strides up the path without waiting for me to answer.

I sit in the water with the cold rain falling on my head.

I'm crying as I get dressed. I feel so stupid, and once again, it's all my fault. Did I really think he would come in? Why do I keep throwing myself at guys who don't want me?

What are you afraid of?

I walk slowly, the tears falling. I'm going the opposite direction of camp, on a path I've never been on.

Behind me, I hear Jason call, "Erin!"

It sounds like he's following me.

I walk faster.

"Erin!"

I start running. I crash through bushes and scrape myself on sharp palm fronds, and fall to my knees in the leaves, and then get up and run some more. Ahead of me, I see glimpses of water, and I make toward that and suddenly I burst out of the scratchy embrace of the bushes onto the beach. A heaving expanse of water stretches in front of me, steely waves smashing onto the shore. Birds startle for the sky.

I can no longer hear Jason, and I sit down on a smooth, water-silvered log. The rain is still falling, but I'm shielded by overhanging trees.

I look around. There's not a boat or house to be seen. It feels like no one's alive but me.

What are you afraid of?

I wipe my face with my sleeve, because it's not just rain and spray on my face but tears as well. I want to stay on my little island *forever*, and not deal with anything but whether I'm going to catch fish for dinner. But I told Mom a couple of days and it's been six, and now Jason says it's time to go home and *I'm not ready.*

Oh, Mom, I miss you so much. I don't know if I can survive without you, and God, it hurts, it hurts, and I want to see you and tell you I'm sorry, and I love you so much but it hurts, hurtshurts-hurts. I can't bear the thought of you leaving me so I guess I left you first . . .

A flutter of baitfish throw themselves out of the water as the rain pitter-patters, making dimples on the skin of the water.

What are you afraid of?

A seagull calls and the mangroves rustle in the wind.

What. Are. You. Afraid. Of?

And then I know, and it's like someone punches me in the stomach.

I'm afraid of the dark. I am afraid of getting cancer. I am afraid I will decide to cut off my breasts. I'm afraid I will decide not to cut off my breasts. I'm afraid Trina will never talk to me again. I am afraid Jason will never like me the way I'm beginning to like him.

I am afraid my mother will die.

But above all?

Above all that?

I am afraid of what Mom dying will do to me.

I changed so much after my dad died. I was a fearless kid before, and then everything got so scary. Like a turtle, I pulled into my shell so that nothing could hurt me.

So what would happen if my mom died?

I'd be a pile of Jell-O on the floor, shuddering and quaking, until I eventually dissolved into a puddle of nothing. There would be nothing left of me.

Nothing.

I hold myself as I sob because there's nothing I can do about any of it. People die. People lose themselves.

It happens all the time.

And I can't stop it.

I can't stop it.

I cry for a long time, and when the tears stop, I sit up. I feel empty, hollowed out. All the messy stuff is gone and all that is left is determination.

I know what I need to do.

～∞⌒

When I get back to the cove, Jason is pacing. His eyes are dark with anger and worry.

"Where did you go?"

I was gone longer than I realized.

"I'm sorry," I say. *Will I be saying I'm sorry for the rest of my life for the stupid things I do?*

Jason stares at me, his face hard and set, and for a moment I'm almost frightened of him. He looks grown-up, like a man, someone I've never met. Then he pulls me into a hug. I clutch him back tightly, feeling the hard muscles under the warm skin of his back, smelling the sweat and salt and wildness on him, and I close my eyes. Trying to remember it. This might be the last time. I don't know what's going to happen now.

"It's over," I say when he lets go of me. "Take me home. I'm ready to go home."

"Are you sure?" Jason studies me with his turbulent sea-colored eyes and he is so glorious, so full of life.

"Yes." I start to cry because it is the end or the beginning, I don't know which, but it's sad and scary and I'm still not sure I can do it.

CHAPTER THIRTY-FIVE

It is near dark by the time we get to Jason's house. It sits on a secluded canal, blue with white trim, with a little deck on top overlooking the waving sea of mangroves.

Jason helps me up on the dock and a woman—tall, with a short nest of curly hair and startling blue-green eyes—comes out of the house and hurries toward us.

"Just in time for dinner," she says. "I was worried about you, Jason." She looks at him, relief and love plain on her face, and then turns her gaze on me.

"Mom, I want you to meet Erin," Jason says, almost shyly. "She's been staying out on my island the past few days."

Jason's mother studies me in silence for a moment. Her eyes, so amazingly like her son's, drink me in. She smiles, open and luminous. "It's nice to meet you, Erin. I have a feeling we have a lot to talk about. Let's get you into a shower and dry clothes."

And without any questions, she takes my hand and leads me toward the house.

"Do you think," I say, "do you think I can call my mother?"

Mom cries the entire time I am on the phone with her. She keeps telling me she loves me, she loves me, *God, she loves me and she has been so worried* and then I cry too.

After I shower, Mrs. Levinson—Miriam—sits me and Jason down and we tell her the entire story. When Miriam asks why Jason didn't tell her I was on the island, Jason says simply, "You would have just worried and she needed to be there."

And that was that.

Dinner is a jumble of conversations, happy, *a family*, and I miss Mom so badly I want to jump in a car and drive to her. But Mom says she'll come for me tomorrow and says to *wait right there, please don't go anywhere.*

Jason and his mom look alike, tall and big and somehow untamable, while Jason's dad is thin, with dark hair and eyes and a deliberate manner. He does not talk often but when he does the whole family shuts up and listens.

A skinny, dark-haired girl wanders in when we are finishing. She is carrying a violin case and studying a music score as she walks, and when she looks up, she blinks at me in surprise.

"Ashley," Miriam says, "this is Jason's friend Erin. She's visiting from Georgia."

This is the real Ashley.

Ashley throws a look at her brother and walks over and offers me her hand. "It's nice to meet you," she says quietly.

Ashley gets a plate and sits down and their family is complete. We continue to talk, but I am fascinated with Ashley. Where Jason is bold and bright, Ashley is self-contained and serene, like a jewelry box with all the gems hidden away. You get the feeling maybe she only shares the treasure of herself with the people she trusts.

We eat and talk, and for a little while I'm able to forget everything that is waiting for me.

∽

After dinner, Miriam announces she wants to talk to me alone. I throw a panicked look at Jason, who shrugs, *What can I do?* Miriam tucks my hand firmly under her elbow and draws me with her onto the vast screened porch scattered with colorful outdoor couches and a birdcage holding a large, grouchy-looking green parrot.

"You must be excited to see your mom tomorrow." She sits on a couch and pats the cushion beside her. I sit, and try not to show this whole let's-have-a-talk thing is scaring the *bejesus* out of me.

"Yes," I say. "I've missed her every minute I was gone."

"I know she'll be happy to see you safe and sound." I hear no judgment in her voice.

"I feel so . . . incredibly *guilty*," I say, not surprised that I can talk to Jason's mom as easily as I can talk to him. Both of them have a straightforward quality that inspires honesty. "I ran away when she needed me most. I let her down once, and

I . . . I'm not sure I'm as strong as I need to be. I need to be *there*, and I wasn't the last time. I hope . . . I hope I can do it this time."

"Your mom is going through chemo, and you just found out you have the BRCA mutation. Give yourself a break. It's not surprising you felt overwhelmed," she says. "The important thing is what you do now."

"My mom still doesn't know I got tested. Mom's genetic counselor told her it was best if I waited until I was at least twenty-one to get tested, and even then, there's really nothing I should do until I'm twenty-five. But I had to know. I had to know *now*. I did an online test, and that's how I found out."

"Are you glad you did?" She raises an eyebrow.

I hesitate. Then, "Maybe I should have waited. In some ways it makes me feel so much more helpless knowing that I'm positive but that I have to wait so long to do anything about it. But at the time . . . it didn't feel like I could." How to explain that sense of urgency, that impending doom that I felt? Waiting did not seem like an option. But now . . . Now, I'm not so sure I made the right decision.

She presses her fingers together under her chin. "From what I understand, these online genetic tests, which is the only genetic testing you can get without a doctor's order, test for just a few of the BRCA mutations. In some ways, that gives you a false sense of knowledge, when only a genetic expert can truly help you understand the results and what they mean to *you*."

I sigh. "Well, I did it, and now I know I have two choices. Either I cut off my breasts, and maybe even take out my ovaries, or I wait and see if I get cancer. That seems impossible. I know the doctors do a lot of screening on women with the BRCA mutation, but it seems like with up to an eighty percent chance of getting it—"

"That number is dependent on a lot of factors," she says. "It's not cut-and-dry."

"*Still.* I'm just waiting for the inevitable. I'll spend the rest of my life waiting to go through what my mom is going through. I don't think I can stand it."

She doesn't say anything for a moment. Then she leans forward and takes my hand.

"Even before we found out about the gene, my family has lived with cancer as a sort of unwelcome but necessary houseguest," she says. "We've been battling it for generations. It's a war that sometimes we win, sometimes we lose, but we're always fighting. Living like that, it changes a person. You never feel so alive as you do when death is at the door. Life is hard, but it's the only one we have, and I cannot envision living it in despair." She stares at me without speaking, as comfortable with silence as her son.

"Jason has been . . . great," I say, because my thoughts are like a mass of swirling birds in my mind trying to get out. "I don't know what I would have done without him."

She nods and smiles her lovely smile. "Jason has always loved life, but finding out he had the BRCA mutation . . . it intensified something in him. He made a conscious decision to wring every last drop of joy out of each day he lives."

I think about Jason deciding not to fall in love, but I don't say anything, because it doesn't feel right to tell her if Jason hasn't told her himself.

She sits back, and stares out at the sky and endless mangroves for a while without speaking. At first, I squirm, but then I follow her gaze and somehow get lost in the secret whisper of the mangroves, the smell of the oranges sweetly rotting on the ground under a nearby tree, and the sun-thrown water shapes wavering on the porch rail.

"There is a poem I think about when I am afraid," she says after a while, "when I need to be strong. It's by Hannah Senesh, a young Hungarian girl who volunteered to parachute into occupied territory to help rescue other Jews during the Holocaust and who died by a Nazi firing squad. Her radiant, courageous heart shone through even in her poetry and it makes me feel strong when I read it."

Miriam closes her eyes and pauses a moment before reciting softly:

"God, may there be no end
to sea, to sand,
water's splash,
Lightning's flash,
the prayer of man."

"After she died, they found that she had written 'I loved the warm sunlight.' Past tense, even as she wrote it in her cell, because she knew she was going to die. But still, she was able to enjoy something as simple as the warm sunlight on her face. I remember this when things seem like too much. I remember to notice the warm sunlight on my face."

CHAPTER THIRTY-SIX

I'm standing at Ashley's bedroom window when a strange car pulls into the Levinsons' driveway early the next morning. The last person I expected to see gets out.

Stew.

Not only is he the last person I expected to see, he is the last person I *wanted* to see. I don't want to face him, don't want to try to explain what I can't explain.

Why did Mom send him instead of coming herself?

The doorbell rings, and Ashley speaks from behind me. "Is that your dad?"

I jump. "What? Uh, no. He's my flight instructor."

Ashley is in a white T-shirt and boxers, and she looks so young, though she's actually a month older than me. We talked for a long time as I lay on the trundle bed that pulled from beneath her bed, and she never once complained about the closet light being on. At first it was uncomfortable, because I could not talk to her about the BRCA mutation. Miriam and Jason are fiercely determined that she not know about it until she turns eighteen and I can't help but feel a little jealous of her innocence. Jealous, and sadness for what she has coming. The knowledge feels like a weapon, a life-exploding bomb. I wouldn't wish that on anybody, though a small part of me knows that ignorance is even more deadly. Ashley will turn eighteen in less than a year and then, for better or worse, she will know.

But as we lay there together last night it was hard not to think: *I am on the other side of a divide now. You are on the before side, and I do not want to take that away from you, because the after shatters your soul. What would you say if I told you we may share a death sentence in our very cells? I am a genetic mutant, and you might be one also.*

I'm thinking about cutting off my breasts, I might say, *and what will you do?*

"Aren't you going to go down?" Ashley asks.

"I'd really rather not," I say.

But I do.

Stew is standing awkwardly in the hall with Mr. and Mrs. Levinson, hand pressed to the small of his back, and a coffee stain down his shirt. He looks out of his element away from the airport, like a bird in a grocery store.

"Hi, Stew," I say. *Hi, Stew, you must be superthrilled to see me!*

Stew nods brusquely at me and goes back to his conversation with Mr. Levinson about a detour route to Interstate 75.

Jason comes down the stairs, and he's wearing a pair of shorts but no shirt and I try not to notice because we are just *friends.*

"Who is that?" he says, his voice husky with sleep.

"Stew. My flight instructor," I say in a low voice. "I don't know why he's here."

"Are you ready?" Stew barks at me.

"Uh . . . okay," I say. It's not like I have any luggage. I have my purse, I'm wearing the same clothes I wore the day I walked away from Tweety Bird. I look like the same girl, but I'm not.

"I think we should give the kids a little privacy to say good-bye," Miriam says, and Stew looks like, *No, I'm quite sure they've had enough privacy already*, but he follows Jason's parents as they go out the front door. Ashley drifts silent as a ghost after them, leaving Jason and me alone in the foyer.

I stare at the grayish tile on the floor. I don't know what to say.

"Atlanta's, what, eight or nine hours from here? Maybe I can come visit." Jason is standing close to me, and I can't look at him so I stare at the tiny golden hairs on his wrist, breathing the scent of him, which is warm and musty from sleep. "Erin?"

I force myself to look up into his face. In the bright light of morning, his eyes are shimmering and sparkling with gold flecks. He's not shaven, and he looks older still. Away from the island, I'm not sure I recognize him.

"Will it be the same?" I blurt out. "Will we still be able to be friends now that . . . all this happened?" I wave my hand wildly around and he catches it in his own. Heat floods like molten sugar from my palm to the soles of my feet as he stares at me without speaking. It is not a comfortable silence, but a sizzling one, volatile with unspoken feelings only needing a spark to take shape.

"Nothing's changed," he says after a while, giving my hand a little shake. "We're still buds, okay? We can still talk."

He lets go of my hand and I resist the urge to reach out for his again.

Stew pokes his head inside the door and says, "Daylight's wasting, sunshine," even though it's only been daylight for forty-five minutes. It's that early. He must have driven all night.

"Uh . . . okay," I say, looking back to Jason.

"See you, Erin," Jason says, looking straight at me. His face, usually so clear and open, is shadowed.

"Okay," I say, before I start crying, and I leave.

∞

The ride back with Stew is excruciating. I try to talk at first, to apologize, to explain why I did what I did, but the words don't come out right. It doesn't matter, anyway, because Stew responds only in grunts and won't look at me.

"I'm sorry," I say, "I really, really am."

He looks at me, in his dirty shirt and with tired, angry eyes. "I lost a student once. I lost one and I thought I had again. And to find out it was some asinine stunt? So that you could hang out with your *boyfriend* on some tropical island? Do you know what you did to your mother? To me? You wrecked my *plane*. I thought you had died. And your mother is so worn and exhausted by all this she had to ask me to come get you. How does that make you feel? *This* is why I don't like kids."

He shakes his head in disgust and refuses to speak to me again the rest of the trip.

I don't have a phone or a book, and apparently the radio in Stew's beat-up, old Chevy doesn't work, so I put my head back on the seat and close my eyes, letting the hot, dirty air beat on my face. I already miss Jason, and the island, and am trying not to think about what comes next. So I immerse myself in memories of dark, secret water and manatees playing and sharks that feel like silk.

∽

She must have been waiting at the window because she comes out as soon as we pull into the driveway.

"*Erin,*" Mom says when she sees me get out of the car. She looks frail and exhausted and her hair is almost gone, and I run to her, holding her tight, and we're both crying.

"I'm home, I'm home," I whisper. "I'm so sorry, Momma, I didn't mean to hurt you. *I'm so, so sorry.*"

"I know, Rinnie, I know," she says. "It's the easiest thing in the world to hurt the ones we love, even if we don't mean to."

"I'm here now," I say. "I'm here now."

Part Three

CHAPTER THIRTY-SEVEN

Some people are orally fixated. I'm pretty sure Mr. Jarad is hands-fixated. He has to be doing something with his hands, whether tossing a baseball, playing with his wedding ring, or cleaning his fingernails with a penknife. That's what he's doing today. I saw a real psychiatrist over the summer but when school started two months ago, I told Mom I would rather see Mr. Jarad. Sure, his sports stories are cheesy, but somehow I'm more comfortable with him.

"Mom finished radiation yesterday! She is d-o-n-e. Done, done, done. I'm so happy for her, because let me tell you, the radiation department was *way* more depressing than the chemo department." I swallow hard, because it *was* depressing. I don't know whether it was normal or not, but two or three of the people in the waiting room were quite literally dying. They were only doing radiation to shrink the tumors that were causing them pain in the last few months of their lives. It was weird yesterday to sit in the waiting room looking out the window at the hundreds of pink ducks floating around the pond outside in honor of Breast Cancer Awareness Month and know that the people sitting beside me might not live to see the end of the year. "But anyway. Mom. Yeah, she has follow-up visits and stuff over the next couple of months, but everything looks great and wow, that feels good, you know?" It's hard not to focus on Mr. Jarad's knife; at any moment it looks like it might slip and jam under his nail.

"Hey, that's great," he says, looking up. "I know that must be a relief. How's school? Last week you said Ms. Garrison asked you to be on the e-zine again. What'd you decide?"

I grimace. "It's just not my thing. Besides, I'm trying to get my GPA up. Last year was pretty disastrous. But I got a B in physics over the summer, which was pretty good with everything I had going on with Mom's treatment and all, so I just need to stay on it." No friends and no flying makes Erin a very studious girl. "All in all . . . everything is going *really well.*"

Mr. Jarad has a particularly stubborn piece of dirt, and he concentrates on that for a while after I stop talking. I start fidgeting. Sure, this is getting me out of chemistry, but I'm ready to get on with my life. I'm tired of *talking* about it so much.

"You still having the anxiety attacks and nightmares?" Mr. Jarad asks after a minute.

"Well, sure, the past six months haven't exactly been stellar, you know. I mean, who wouldn't have nightmares, right? Right? But I got through it, *we* got through it. And now that

Mom's going to be fine, I'm just glad it's over, that she's better, because I don't think I could do it again. I mean, I *never-never-never* want to go through that again."

"There's this guy," Mr. Jarad says, and I mentally groan. *Here we go.*

"And he's first round pick and he's really good. Everybody knows he's going to be a Hall of Famer. And his first season, he gets hit real hard. I mean, it gave him a concussion, and you're like, so what? Football players get hit all the time. But this guy, something happened to him. He couldn't get back into the game after that. It was like it knocked the confidence out of him or something. He would get out there, but he was scared the whole time. He would fumble the ball, and he couldn't make a throw to save his life because he was worried about getting hit again. He ended up retiring after the end of his first season, and the last I heard, he was selling insurance. Everybody said he should have come back and tried another season, but he just gave up."

"Isn't that nice," I say, and then, "I mean, what's your point? That I'm never going to, what, be normal again, because of what happened to me and my mom? Or because I lost my dad? I'm fine. I really am. That's what I've been telling you. Sure, I went a little crazy, but I *handled* it, I'm *handling* it, I did what I needed to do, and now it's over." I'm breathing hard now, because I really don't want to hear any more.

"That guy didn't take enough time to work through it all. Just because something is over, doesn't mean it's over in your head. Give yourself some time, Erin."

"I'm *fine*." But the words come out hard and angry.

He nods. He doesn't look convinced.

∽

When I get home from school, Mom is blow-drying her breast, or at least the spot where her left breast *used* to be. I've gotten accustomed to the sight of it, the dark scar running across where her breast was and the heartbreaking flatness of that side of her chest. She's still thinking about whether or not she wants to reconstruct the breast. She could have gotten it done right after the mastectomy, but decided it was too much to do all at once. I can't imagine *not* doing it, but she says she has nobody to impress and she isn't sure she wants to go through the pain and trouble.

"You know you really oughta use some suntan lotion," I joke over the hum of the hair dryer as I walk into the bathroom. Her chest is bright pink, with a few places peeling, exactly as if she'd gotten a good sunburn. Of course, she hadn't, it's from the radiation. She's got tiny, blue dot tattoos across her chest to help the radiation people know where to zap her. "And I always said I'd never get a tattoo!" she said when she came home with them.

"If I could just stay here like this all day, I'd be fine," she says now, waving the hair dryer back and forth over her chest. "Wow, that feels good." She has it set on Cool and it's one of the only things that has brought her relief over the past couple of weeks of radiation.

"So when can you start wearing deodorant again?" I ask,

eyeing the crystal deodorant on the counter, the one Jill sent. That was one of the biggest complaints Mom had about radiation. The treatment itself wasn't too bad. She'd gone in Monday through Friday before work, and it only took twenty or thirty minutes. But she started in the middle of the summer and was horrified to find out she couldn't wear regular deodorant during the month and a half of treatment. August plus Georgia minus deodorant equals a very stinky Mom.

"Soon, I hope," she says, wrinkling her nose. "It got to where I felt like I had to apologize to the radiation techs every time I went in. I smell *funky.*"

"But it's over," I say. "How great is that? It's all over."

She puts down the hair dryer and tousles my hair. "Erin, I wanted to tell you . . . I know this summer was hard on you. But I'm so proud of you. You've been a big help to me through all of this, and I really appreciate it."

"Super-Erin, that's me," I say. "I'm just so sorry I ran away like that. I still feel so stupid. If I had any idea how much trouble I'd get into, and . . . Stew . . . I just didn't know. I wasn't thinking."

Mom picks up a bottle of lotion and begins slathering it on her chest. She had always been sort of modest before she got cancer, but I guess she feels like there's no point to it anymore. "I swear I feel like a *Playboy* centerfold, so many people have seen my breasts!" she told me at one point.

"Have you talked to Stew yet?" she asks.

I sigh. "As far as Stew's concerned, I'm worse than the devil. He hates my guts."

"No he doesn't," Mom says. "He's just angry, and you can't blame him for that. He'll come around. Your dad always said he was a good man."

So come to find out, Stew not only knew *of* my dad, but he was *friends* with him. They met in Iraq, where Dad was flying missions in Desert Storm; Stew was a maintenance-crew chief and they connected when they realized they had both grown up near Atlanta. That's how Stew knew who I was way back when I started lessons. The flying world is evidently very small. Stew, being Stew, hadn't bothered to divulge that little nugget of information.

"What about Trina, have you talked to her?"

"What is this, a who's-who list of those-who-refuse-to-acknowledge-Erin's-very-existence?" I ask. "Plenty of people are still talking to me. Actually, I'm the closest I've ever been to popular this year." I made national news, and it's amazing what that will do for your social status. "It's all good. *I'm* all good. Okay? Don't worry about me."

"It's hard for me not to worry," she says. She winces, and turns the hair dryer back on. "I'm a mother. And somehow I don't think you are really dealing with it all."

"You and Mr. Jarad both," I mutter.

"What?" she shouts.

"I'm going out!" I say. "See? It's Friday night, and I'm going out."

CHAPTER THIRTY-EIGHT

I head to the airport, which is probably not exactly what Mom thought when I said I was going out, but there's still plenty I'm not telling Mom.

She doesn't know I'm positive for the breast cancer gene. There just never seemed to be the right time to tell her. She's been on this big treatment roller coaster, and I didn't want to take her attention off what she needed to do to get better. I suppose I could tell her now, but it seems like a secret either becomes too big to keep to yourself or wound so tight and small that it's too hard to unravel.

I pull into the small airport. It's closed for the evening, and there's only one car in the parking lot, Stew's clunker. As much time as he spends on his planes, you'd think he'd take better care of his car.

I check my phone, and Jason has left a text: Where r u?

Airport, I text, but he doesn't reply. He texted me this

morning, saying he had something to tell me tonight, to make sure I answered when he called. My heart triple-jumps a little, because maybe he's going to tell me he changed his mind, that he thinks we should date after all. But the phone stays silent.

Tweety Bird is in the same place she's been all summer. Parked beside the hangar, forgotten and sad in the golden October light, still listing to the side because of the strut I bent when I landed in the field. They shipped her back on a tractor-trailer a few weeks after I returned from Florida. I keep waiting for them to start fixing her, but as far as I can tell, no one's touched her. I don't know if it's because she's too damaged to fix or because of the ongoing investigation of my accident. If I'd known how seriously everyone was going to take me flying away, I would have jumped in my car instead. Of course, I *wasn't* thinking straight, but I didn't know Stew would get in trouble. I never would have done it if I'd known he could lose his instructor's license. He hasn't lost it yet, but he's under investigation because he let me solo.

Nobody was real happy with what I did, least of all the FAA, the Federal Aviation Administration. I talked to several different investigators, but my explanation for flying away didn't make sense even to me, so how could I explain it to someone else? They pulled my medical certificate, which means I can't fly, and required me to get a psychiatric evaluation while they continue their investigation. I didn't make the appointment for the evaluation until after my mom rang the chemo bell in August. And even then it took me a while to work up the nerve to make the call, knowing that what I said could determine whether I ever got my pilot's license. The talking and battery of tests with the FAA-certified doctors was just as bad as I expected. I'm not sure I did very well at all, I was so nervous.

But it was done, and all I can do is wait to see what the FAA decides. They say it could be months. So we're waiting, me and Tweety Bird, waiting to know whether we'll be able to fly again.

Stew is messing with one of the planes, conspicuously ignoring me. *Yes, Stew, I know you hate me.*

I pull out my phone and get on one of the BRCA websites. I've been doing this a lot lately, coming to the airport to read about other women's battles with BRCA and cancer. I've gotten used to the benign-sounding abbreviations that mean terrible things. "BC" is breast cancer, "BPM" is a bilateral prophylactic mastectomy, when you take off both breasts before you even have cancer. "Ooph" is an oophorectomy, the removal of one's ovaries. And "surveillance" is what they call it when you go every six months to get felt up by a breast doctor, to take a test to monitor for ovarian cancer, and a lot of times, get biopsy after biopsy when suspicious shadows show up on mammograms. When you have the BRCA gene mutation, you might not have cancer, but they treat you like you do.

I guess I think if I read other people's stories enough, maybe I'll figure out what to do.

So far, it isn't working.

I don't want to cut off my breasts.

I don't want to do surveillance.

I want it to all go away.

I want to never have had this gene. And as much as I know I'm not supposed to be worrying about the gene right now, that I have years before I need to do anything, I can't seem to make myself stop.

A cloud drags shadows across the airport and raindrops splatter onto my windshield, popping onto the hood with hollow ringing sounds.

Abruptly one of the panic attacks hits and my heart starts racing. I'm sweaty and cold and shaking.

"Stop it, *stop it, stop it!*" I mutter, putting my forehead down on the top edge of the steering wheel. It's a bad one, and as much as I try to think calming, happy thoughts, the waves of anxiety sweep through me, and I feel like I'm going to drown.

The sound of a car pulling up behind me snaps me out of it, though I'm still panting as I look in the rearview mirror.

A blue Jeep is parked behind me and as I watch, Jason gets out.

He's big, and windblown and oh so beautiful, and I sit for a moment, just watching in the mirror as he walks toward me. Then I swipe my hands across my face, hoping I don't look like I just had a monster panic attack, and jump out of the car.

"What are you doing here?" I ask, going for a hug, and then suddenly feeling shy. It's the first time I've seen him since I left Florida, though we talk almost every day.

He's not shy, though, and sweeps me up into a huge hug, lifting me off of the ground. My feet dangle for a moment and then he sets me down gently. Over Jason's shoulder I see Stew standing in front of the hangar looking at us; he shakes his head in disgust and goes back inside.

"I decided it was time to celebrate," Jason says, leaning up against my car. "Your mom finishing treatment and all. I got someone to take my charters for the weekend, and here I am. All yours for two whole days." He swings his arms wide and I laugh.

"You're here. You're really here," I say.

"Well, since your mom won't let you come see me—"

"Are you kidding? She'll be happy if I never set foot in the state of Florida again."

"—I figured I'd do a mountain-and-Mohammed move."

"I'm so happy you're here," I say, and it's true, I feel the happiness bubbling from some quiet place deep inside of me.

"Me too," he says quietly, and touches my face. It's all I can do not to lean into his hand.

"So," I say, clearing my throat. "What are we going to do now that you're here?"

"I've shown you my Florida," he says. "Show me your Atlanta."

CHAPTER THIRTY-NINE

"You can see *forever*," Jason says as we sit on top of Stone Mountain.

"It's not hard to impress you mountain-challenged Floridians, is it?" I say, rubbing my hands across the warm roughness of the rocks we're sitting on. I'm still out of breath after our hike up the mountain, which of course Jason insisted on doing. Usually I took the Skyride, but I wasn't about to tell Mr. Outdoorsman *that*.

It's a beautiful Sunday, so we are not the only people who had the bright idea to hang out on the top of a mountain. Children squeal and pretend like they are planes with arms held out, people point at the Atlanta skyline, and boys and girls feel like they are all alone under the big, wide-open dome of the sky.

"We've got mountains," he says. "They call them landfills."

He flops over on his stomach and puts his face near one of

the many pools that dot the top of the mountain. "I don't see any shrimp," he says.

"What, you come all the way to the Georgia mountains and you're complaining because you don't see *shrimp*?" I say, and punch his arm playfully.

"You said there's shrimp in dem dere pools," he says, sitting up and leaning back on his hands. "What can I say? I like shrimp."

"You can only see them sometimes. It's crazy, because even when it doesn't rain for a while and there's no water, they leave behind eggs that will hatch when it rains again."

"Ah, they are opportunistic little guys," Jason says. "I like them better and better, these invisible shrimp of which you speak."

"Kind of like cancer just waiting in the wings for the right conditions," I say, and then immediately wish I hadn't. I broke some sort of unspoken agreement we'd had all weekend not to speak about cancer or mutated genes.

He doesn't say anything and after a while the weirdness fades away and we sit in contented silence watching the colorful kites crisscrossing above us and the soaring birds.

Finally, Jason says, "What next, Kemo Sabe?"

∽

Jason has already oohed and aahed over the humongous—I'm talking as big as two football fields—Confederate Memorial of Jefferson Davis, Robert E. Lee, and Thomas J. "Stonewall" Jackson carved into the side of the mountain, so we wander through some of the other touristy attractions until we come to the SkyHike, which is basically a big rope adventure course high above the ground.

"Let's do it," Jason says immediately.

"Uh, no?" I say. "Are you crazy?"

"Why?"

"It's like *in the trees*," I say. "You have to wear a safety harness because it's so easy to fall. No way, José, not my idea of fun."

"Wait a minute. You have an annual pass to this park and you've never been on the SkyHike?" Jason plants himself right in front of me, arms crossed. "Nope. Not acceptable."

"Not acceptable? Really?" I'm laughing though. "It's just that . . . I'm not big into trying new things." It's the reason I don't try out for clubs or do much of anything out of the ordinary, except for that one spectacular thing, which seems so unlike me it's like some other girl did it.

"How do you know you won't like walking barefoot in the grass if you're always walking on the sidewalk?" he asks, pulling me toward the ticket booth.

"Alternatively, walking on the sidewalk would spare me that run-down feeling I'll get from walking in the road," I say, but let myself be pulled. I try not to read anything into the hand-holding thing, because Jason is just like that, but it's hard not to *hope* that it means something.

We get fitted into the harnesses and the attendant lets us go. It's getting late, so there aren't that many people on the course and we climb up to the first level by ourselves.

"Really? You're stopping here?" Jason says. "*Bawk-bawk-bawwwk.*" He doesn't sound *anything* like a chicken.

I stick my tongue out at him and then climb as high as I can go. We are in the treetops here, and I stare down at the narrow board in front of me, spanning two trees. Yes, I have a safety line that will catch me if I fall, but what if it breaks?

"I'll be right behind you," Jason says.

I take a deep breath and edge out onto the board. I freeze for a moment, and then I take another tiny step, and then I'm moving quicker until I make it all the way across, and I twirl on the platform, laughing. Jason is standing on the other side, and he's watching me and there's an intensity to his gaze that makes me hot and cold at the same time, and then he's laughing too, yelling, "I knew you could do it!"

He runs nimbly over the board to the platform where I am standing and sweeps me up into his arms, swinging me in a dizzying circle. I close my eyes. I could stay like this forever.

He releases me and looks into my face, his eyes dancing with happiness.

"So, scaredy-cat?"

"Yeah, yeah, you were right," I say, smiling. I look over at the next part of the course, which is just a single rope stretching from one platform to another with a few vertical ropes to hold on to.

"Watch, it's easy," he says, and steps carefully out onto the rope. Then he moves faster, his feet flying as he practically swings from one guide rope to another, never losing his balance. He is glorious to watch, his feet sure, his muscles moving smoothly under his white T-shirt. He reaches the other side and looks at me.

"Think you can do it?" he calls.

"No problem," I say, and mean it.

We spend hours clambering around on the ropes, and I even try a rock-climbing wall, shrieking with excitement when I reach the top. One the way back home, we're both tired but happy.

"I'm thinking anchovy and pineapple pizza," Jason says, stretching himself out in my passenger seat. He's leaving soon so he can drive all night to make a charter tomorrow morning, but I'm trying not to think about that.

"Uck," I say. "I thought you were making all that money doing the charters. You can't spring for steak?"

"Not when I'm really feeling pizza," he says and grins lazily.

So I take him to Dino's, and it's crawling with kids from school because we have off the next day for a teacher workday. A couple of them wave at me, and I hear someone say, "It's the Flyaway Girl," which is an improvement over Va-jay-jay Girl so I guess I can't complain. Molly Jenkins and Lynn Mitchell gesture for me to come sit with them, but I shake my head with a smile and slide into a booth. I'm trying not to notice Michael, who is drawing at a table by himself in the back.

We eat, and Jason and I laugh and talk, and I completely forget the black hole in the room that is Michael.

"Are you sure you can't stay another night? You've made such a good impression on Mom I think she'd be fine if you decided to move in," I say. Mom was initially surprised by Jason's sudden appearance, and a little skeptical, but by the time dinner was over she was insisting that he stay in our guest room and now seems to genuinely like him. Not that Jason is hard to like.

"Nah," he says, "I can't. I said I would be back tomorrow." He reaches a long arm over my head and snags the bill from the waitress.

"I was just kidding about you paying," I protest. "I can pay half. We're friends, right?" I say it a little suggestively, but he ignores me, as usual. *Yes, we are friends*, his silence is telling me, *let's not make a big deal about this, okay?*

Faith comes in as we're getting up to leave, but she ignores me, as she has been doing ever since we got back to school, and marches toward Michael.

"I wouldn't want to be him," Jason says easily, and I turn to watch as Faith reaches Michael.

"When did you become such a zombie?" she says, loud enough for everybody to hear. "You're supposed to be meeting me at Caitlyn's, but I knew when you didn't show that you'd either be home playing with your little houses or here *drawing* them. What is *wrong* with you?"

"Wow," Jason says and opens the door for me so I have to leave without hearing what Michael says. I notice that Stew's *Learn to Fly!* flier is gone from the door, and I wonder if he decided to take it down so he doesn't get another no-good kid like me signing up as a student.

"That was Michael," I announce as we walk to my car. "And Faith."

"*The* Michael?" Jason whistles, and then laughs. "I'm guessing he wishes he chose you right about now."

It kind of hurts, because it's like Jason is saying he wouldn't *care* if Michael and I were dating. And maybe he doesn't care. Not like that. Maybe he truly thinks of me as his friend, and would be happy for me if I were dating someone.

"It's like Grand Central Station around here," I mutter in exasperation as Chaz's Mustang pulls up. Chaz hops out and throws me an anxious look before scurrying around to let Trina out.

Trina gives me a little halfhearted smile and I do the same, which is what we've been reduced to. At one point, right after I got back, I think we could have become friends again. She and my mom had talked a lot while I was gone, and she came over the day after I arrived home. But I was still messed up in the head, and it was uncomfortable, and she didn't come back. And I didn't reach out, and now we just smile when we see each other, which hurts, but I don't know how to fix it.

They disappear inside, and I look at Jason. "And that," I say, "was Trina."

The front door opens and Chaz comes loping out.

"Erin!" he calls, looking over his shoulder worriedly like Trina is about to come out with guns blazing.

I turn and watch Chaz coming toward us. He's taller, but still jerky and uncoordinated as he comes across the parking lot. But something's different from last year, a newfound confidence in the way he holds his head, a bolder swing to his gait.

Chaz stops about ten feet away from us, like he thinks if he comes any closer I might attack him. It's the first time we've talked since I kissed him.

"Hey, Erin." *Snap, snap, snap* go his fingers. He Proactived out over the summer and his acne is gone.

"Hey."

Chaz looks back over his shoulder again. It seems like he's ignoring Jason, but I don't think he's even registered him. He's focused on me. "She's in the bathroom, and I . . . uh . . . wanted to talk to you about something."

"If you want me to be the maid of honor at the wedding, you probably need to talk to Trina first," I say, beeping my remote at the car to unlock it.

"What? Wait. No." His face turns red. "It *is* about Trina though. She's bummed the two of you aren't friends anymore. I mean, she cries about it." His face squinches up. The thought of Trina in distress is that bad for him.

"I'm sorry," I say. "I really don't want her to feel bad."

His face clears. "Yeah? That's great. You'll talk to her?"

"What? No. I mean . . ." I trail off. What on earth can I say to Trina?

She cries about it . . .

Because of me?

"I don't know," I say. I don't want to talk to Trina. I don't know what I'd say.

"Awesome!" Chaz begins backing away. Our conversation is over, and he wants to make sure I don't grab him from behind.

"Chaz," I say, figuring I'll start with him and see how it goes.

"Yeah?" He turns, halfway, so he's in a position to make a quick escape if necessary.

"I'm sorry," I say. "I really am."

He nods and darts off.

Jason is shaking his head as I turn back toward him. "Is there always this much drama in Erin's world?" he asks.

"You caught me on a good day," I say.

CHAPTER FORTY

In December, I'm late to Creative Writing, but I stop by the restroom to fix my hair, which has escaped its scrunchie and is bouncing enthusiastically into my face. I'm in a good mood, because it's the last day of school before winter break and I'm making all A's except one freaking B in calculus, which I'm pretty sure I can pull up. Things have settled down to almost normal over the past couple of months. Well, as normal as things can be when my best friend and I are still not talking, I'm still not allowed to fly, and I'm a walking cancer case waiting to happen. But normal in that Mom's feeling like her old self and school is school and there's no trips to the chemo or radiation wards in our future. When I was in the middle of all that, it was like I was in a little dark box with no way out, but now that I'm past it, well, it was only six months of our lives. Mom has told me that we're in a wait-and-see mode, but

I know, I just *know* that the cancer is gone and that everything is finally going to be okay.

Perspective. I guess that's what Jason's been telling me; it's how you look at things.

I hear something, and I stop in the middle of putting my hair back into a ponytail.

I hear it again, and it's a toilet flushing on the other side of the big restroom, hidden from where I'm standing in front of the mirror.

Okay, someone flushed the toilet. No big deal.

But as I finish taming my hair into the scrunchie, I hear the toilet flush five more times. Then six. Then seven.

Something must be wrong with it.

I grab my backpack and hear the noises. Animal sounds, like something's in pain.

I'm late but somehow I can't leave it alone. Curiosity and the stupid cat and all that.

Moving quietly, I walk around the bank of sinks and poke my head past the tile wall. One of the stall doors is closed, and I see feet underneath. As I stand there, the toilet flushes two more times. Now I can hear someone crying. And talking.

"You want to text? Try texting me *now*," I hear someone say, the words thick with tears.

I recognize the voice. I need to leave, I need to get out of here, but somehow I can't move.

The toilet flushes again, and then two more times in quick succession. Then the door jerks open and Faith comes out. She doesn't see me at first. She stands at the sink and takes deep breaths, staring at herself in the mirror. She's stopped crying, but her face is a mess, swollen and red, and she has raccoon eyes from her smeared mascara.

The door to the stall swings back and forth, and I see a smartphone in a pink case in the toilet.

Her phone. That's what Faith was trying to flush.

I wonder if she and Michael are fighting. But as far as the school grapevine goes, they broke up spectacularly at Dino's the night I saw them there with Jason. I've seen Michael in the halls, and he's always alone. He's been a loner for a while now, but this year he seems more *aggressively* alone. Like he's on a mission to be alone. He hasn't said a word to me, but a couple of times I've felt his gaze on me, dark and tingly.

Faith takes a deep, trembling breath, pulls a makeup bag out of her purse, and starts applying cover-up in quick, deft strokes.

I take a step backward, with every intention of making a break for the door, but Faith looks up and sees me. Her face twists, and for once she doesn't look cute. She looks like a little girl who just found out her puppy died. We stare at each other for a moment without speaking.

"Do you need me to . . ." I trail off. What, am I going to ask if she needs a hug?

"Just go away," she says, "you stupid dork. Go away."

Okay, fine.

I leave, but I feel unsettled the rest of the day.

After school, I'm parked at the airport again, surfing the BRCA websites. Stew comes out and gives me an indecipherable look, and then I watch him go back inside, my heart breaking a little. I still haven't heard from the FAA; I'm still grounded; Tweety Bird still sits broken and alone beside the hangar. Mom says that the FAA is dragging their feet with Stew as well, and that he still doesn't know if he will be able to keep his instructor certificate.

My phone rings and Jason says, "I'm watching the Godzilla of the heron family high-stepping his way through the shallows. I wish you could be here to see it."

"Are you on the island?"

"Yeah. I dropped off a charter and decided to come for a little while. Then I started thinking about you. What are you doing?"

"Wallowing," I say. "It's cloudy and nasty here."

"It's beautiful and sunny here," he says, his voice full of laughter. "Aren't you glad you're coming to visit?"

"Yes," I say, and my voice vibrates with my need to be away from here, to be *anywhere* else but here.

"Bad day?"

"Uh . . . It's hard to explain. I caught Faith crying in the bathroom today, and seeing her like that . . . it made me realize that I have *no* idea what is going on with Trina. I'm such a coward, but I just haven't been able to talk to her. And I *need* to."

"What's stopping you?" I hear something in the background, the sound of splashing water, and my heart smiles a little when I realize I know what it is: a fish jumping high and crashing down into the water in a spectacular belly flop.

I hesitate. "I guess . . . I'm afraid we'll end up hurting each other more. I don't want that." *It's the easiest thing in the world to hurt the ones we love.* "I wish I had a time machine to go back to before, when everything was still okay."

"But then you wouldn't have met me," Jason says. "I don't mean that in an aren't-I-great way or anything. I just mean that bad things happen, and sometimes they make way for good things. Change isn't always bad, you know?"

"As a rule it is," I say, staring at Tweety Bird, solitary and broken.

"There's my glass-half-empty girl," Jason says.

We hang up a few minutes later and I stare at the browning leaves dancing across the parking lot. They're already dead and don't even know it.

∞

I pull up in Trina's driveway and sit in my car for a while. I know she's home. Retro, her old green Saab, sits in the driveway.

I need to get out.

I need to go talk to her.

But somehow I can't.

Eventually, she comes out to me. She's barefoot, even though it's about sixty degrees, and she's wearing a T-shirt and sweats with Big Bird on the butt. She dresses almost normal now, and I realize I miss her outfits. For the longest time I was embarrassed about the extravagant costumes she would wear to school, to the mall, everywhere. She looks like everyone else now. Maybe that's what she really wanted all along. To feel normal, to feel like everybody else.

She comes up to the passenger window and I roll it down.

"You scoping the joint?" she asks.

"Don't have to. I figure if I wait here long enough Chipper will bring me all your valuables." Their dog Chipper is notoriously friendly.

We don't speak for a long moment, and then she opens the door and gets in, wrapping her arms around herself. I turn up the heat.

"What's up?" She looks at me and I force myself to look back at her. Her hair is its actual color for once and is smoothed back into a blond ponytail. She's got a tattoo on her upper bicep, *Chaz*, all loopy and flowery. Goofy girl. What is she going to do if they break up? But she's talked about getting a tattoo for the longest time, and I always swore I'd go with her and hold her hand. *Dorkster Twins activate.*

I wonder if Chaz held her hand while she got it done.

"I wanted to say . . . I wanted to say, I'm sorry. I'm sorry for everything. I'm sorry for kissing Chaz. I'm sorry for yelling at you last year. I'm sorry for us not being friends."

She looks away, out the front windshield. "I'm sorry too," she says. "I should never have told everybody about your mom. And I'm sorry we're not friends."

We don't say anything for a while.

Then, "How is she?" she asks, looking at me.

"She's done with treatment. Things are good. She's thinking about getting her breast reconstructed, but she's not really all that into it. She says she's fine going uni-tit."

We both smile, and then it fades away.

She puts her hand on the door handle. "I'm glad. So . . . see you around?"

"Sure. I'll see you around."

She gets out and goes inside without looking back.

I sit for a moment longer and then back out of her driveway.

The bridge isn't there yet, but the tiniest spiderweb of tentative hope spans the abyss.

Maybe it will be strong enough.

CHAPTER FORTY-ONE

Aunt Jill arrives the next day with four-year-old Malcolm to spend a few days with us before Christmas. Malcolm, whom I haven't seen since he was two, is an unstoppable ball of energy, bouncing from room to room. I babysit him Saturday night, to let Mom and Jill go out by themselves, and the only way I can get him to sleep is to lie with him in the big guest bed.

After I tell him story after story, he finally lies quietly. He blinks owlishly at me and purses his lips, blowing imaginary bubbles in my direction. He pats my hand and I realize I'm absentmindedly rubbing my breasts. They are black and blue. I can't seem to stop pinching and probing at them, searching for a lump. The thought that something alien and malignant could be growing inside of me feels like fingernails scratching down the blackboard surface of my brain. I can't stop thinking about it.

"Boo-boo?" Malcolm asks, patting my breast.

"I don't know," I say. "That's the problem."

Do I really want to live the rest of my life waiting for a lump to show up?

No.

No, I don't.

~~~

The day after Christmas, Mom drives with me to Florida. Our Christmas was quiet, but nice. I gave her a new sweater. She gave me a new tablet.

On Interstate 75, I check my phone to see if I have a text from Jason or Trina. Trina and I have slowly begun talking again the past week but it feels tentative, uncertain. We're making progress, though. The foundation is still there.

"Erin, please don't text while you're driving."

"I'm not texting." I put my phone down. "I'm checking to see if I *have* a text."

She sighs and shifts in her seat, putting her hand to her back. She pulled a muscle or something, and it's been bugging her. I feel bad, her having to spend so much time in a car when her back hurts. Of course, she could have let me drive by myself, but that wasn't happening. I'm not complaining, though, because it was a feat in itself to convince her to let me go visit Jason at all.

"Erin, I've wanted to talk with you about something."

Buzz, buzz, buzz. Awkward-conversation alert.

"Hmmm?" I check the gas, but we still have plenty. If this gets too bad, I might have to dive for an exit on the pretext of a pee stop. I glance at her out of the corner of my eye but she looks determined. It's still hard for me to get used to her with white hair, but that's how it grew back in.

"I've been wanting to talk to you about Jason. You know, I thought long and hard about whether to let you go to Florida to stay with his family. It's just . . . Look. You'll have plenty of time to . . . expand your relationship with Jason as you get older."

Oh God, she picks *now* to have the sex talk?

"You're still my little girl," she says softly. "I know Jason was a great source of strength to you during my illness, and I know he still is. But . . . don't confuse love and gratitude."

Love? Who said anything about love?

"You don't have anything to worry about. Jason and I are just friends." And he has every intention of us just *staying* friends forever. More and more, this whole let's-be-best-buds thing is beginning to bug me.

"Just . . . be careful, okay? Sex is such an important part of an adult's life, but I just don't think you're ready for it. There are so many confusing, adult emotions involved in that type of relationship. I don't want you jumping into the pool without knowing how cold the water is."

Seriously, this is about as awkward as my first-period talk.

"Jason and I are not going to have sex."

We drive in silence for a little bit. My face is burning.

"I met your dad in college," she says and stops. I can tell she's embarrassed too, which doesn't help at all.

I wait. I never realized how little I knew about my dad before. It sounds strange, but until recently I thought I knew everything there was to know about him. High tosses into the air ("Watch the ceiling fan, Justin!"), bedtime poems, and his laughter as I tried to walk in his cowboy boots. But my six-year-old self's memories aren't enough anymore, and I will never get the chance to know him any better.

"It took a while," she continues, "but then I realized I was madly in love with him. It scared me, honestly. We dated for quite a while before we . . . you know."

"Sure." I squirm, halfway wishing for a tractor-trailer to overturn or something, just so she'll stop.

"You don't want to regret anything."

"Okay."

After a while, I say, "You and Dad were madly in love?"

"Well, yes, of course." She shifts again in her seat, wincing.

That seems odd to me. She and Dad were once just like Trina and Chaz? The way I want to be with a boy one day?

"How did you know you were in love?"

She looks out the window. "I don't know how to explain it. I'm not sure anybody can. It's like trying to explain pain. You can tell someone you hurt, but you can't really make them understand the pain. Love is like that. I suppose if I was going to try to explain it, I'd say love is something you can live without, but when you have it the world seems brighter, a happier place. It's easier to smile and to laugh."

"And Dad? He felt the same way about you?"

"Your dad was so much braver than me. He said he knew the first time he saw me he was going to marry me. It took a long time for me to admit how I felt. Ever since this happened," Mom touches her prosthetic breast, "I've been thinking about how I've lived my life. I . . . have regrets. I regret I wasn't strong enough to stay with your dad. I never stopped loving him. I just couldn't handle the worrying all the time when he was up in the air. But if I'd known he only had two more years to live, I never would have divorced him. I would have spent every minute of it with him, right up to the end. You just never know. You never know what's going to happen."

"I wish I was brave like Dad," I say.

"So do I," Mom says. "Every day I wish I was as brave as he was."

We drive for a while, and finally I say, "Mom, there's something I need to tell you."

She looks at me sharply. I'm guessing her Mommy Alarm is now going *buzz, buzz, buzz.*

"I got tested for the breast cancer gene," I say. "I have it. I didn't want to tell you while you were sick, but now . . . I wanted to tell you."

There is an awful silence, and I sneak a glance to see Mom blinking rapidly, her throat working.

"Oh, *Erin*," she says, when she can talk. "Oh, I'm so sorry." Her voice steadies. "I don't understand . . . How did you get tested? I didn't think you could get tested until you were eighteen. Why did you keep it a secret?"

"I did it online. You can get tested for a bunch of genetic stuff like that. And . . . I didn't want to worry you."

She shakes her head, and then sighs. "I guess I shouldn't be surprised. You kids are so much more savvy than we were at your age. I never would have thought . . . Okay. Well." Her eyes are glazed with unshed tears. "We need to get you in to talk to a genetic counselor. That way you know all your options, what you'll need to be thinking about. I wish you had waited . . . and talked to a counselor. That must have been so terrible finding out on your own. I can't even *imagine*."

"Everyone said that the counselor would just tell me to wait. Mom . . . I couldn't wait. I *couldn't*. I had to know." *But carrying that knowledge around by myself almost killed me*, I don't say. And, *Now I'm not sure I really wanted to know*.

Mom takes a deep breath. "I suppose as they do more and more of this kind of testing we're all going to have to think about how it affects you kids. I suppose . . . what's done is done." She looks real sad, though.

I take a deep breath. "I've been wondering . . . You chose not to take off your other breast, even though you knew you had the BRCA gene and that you may get cancer again. Why?"

She looks out the window and for a minute I think she is not going to answer. Then, "It's a very personal decision. Nobody can tell you what's right for *you*. For me, at the time, just taking the one seemed like the right thing to do. They also told me I need to take out my ovaries, but it seemed like too much. I don't know. I've been thinking more about it. Maybe I will do the surgeries."

"Maybe we can do them together," I say.

She looks at me sharply. "By the time you have to worry about it, hopefully there will be a *cure* for breast cancer. That or better surveillance techniques. I wonder if anybody ever thought about what all this genetic testing means to real people. Yes, hooray, we're able to see the mutations in our genes, but what do we do with the information? We cut off body parts. I pray every day we will find a cure for these diseases we can predict but not stop." She reaches over and pats my leg. "There's no reason for you to worry about it right now. Who knows what the future will bring?"

"But I do worry! I walk around feeling like I've got an expiration date stamped on my forehead. How do you live like that?"

She is quiet for a while. "Whenever I start thinking about it, I think about you, and your father. I think about the people I love, and even if my time is short, at least I had the incredible luck to have you in my life. Which would you rather, to have a long miserable life, or a short, beautiful one?"

CHAPTER FORTY-TWO

Jason and I walk along the shore of our island, and the tide is low, the mud laid bare in all its intimate glory. We go slowly, the clattering crabs racing in front of us, and Jason points out the distinctive five-finger mark of a raccoon, which looks like a small hand. Birds wheel and dive, come to feed on the cornucopia of crabs, worms, mollusks, and other small creatures that are the Happy Meal of the shorebirds.

"The tides are different here in southwest Florida." Jason bends down and slides his hand through the water. When he stands, the water falls like diamonds from his fingers. "Most places the water ebbs and flows twice a day very predictably, little foamy soldiers advancing and retreating." He uses his fingers to make little legs marching along and I smile. "But here, the tides are pretty much a mess. They come and go as they please, some days having two very unequal highs and lows, other days only one high and low. And some days the tide waits and waits until all of a sudden it piles up on shore all at once." He sweeps his arm around, making a *whooshing* sound like the tide just wiped out everything around us.

I laugh. "What I would pay to spend one day in your head. It must be pretty crazy in there."

"Crazy good, or crazy you-need-to-be-medicated?"

"Time will tell," I tease.

We walk in contented silence.

I wasn't sure I wanted to come to the island, which is why we left it to the last day. I'm not sure why I was hesitant, except that the island had become such a magical, healing place in my mind that I was afraid reality would ruin it. I shouldn't have worried though, it was just the way I remembered it.

It's been a great visit, not only with Jason, but with his family as well. Jason lives in an apartment on the first floor of his parents' house, and I stayed upstairs in Ashley's room. She and I talked late into the night, not about the BRCA gene, which she still doesn't know about, but about everything else. After all she has been through with her family, she has a quiet serenity that fills a room. I suspect that the news of the gene mutation is not going to shock her. There's been too much cancer in her family to not know something is wrong. It might even be a relief to her to know one way or another.

"I've been thinking . . . ," I say.

"Uh-oh." Jason turns to look at me. His curly hair is untamed and messy, his blue-green eyes brilliant with the glitter of water.

"Seriously. I've been doing a lot of thinking about my BRCA mutation. I think I'm going to get the surgery to remove my breasts. I don't think I can stand waiting the rest of my life to get cancer."

It's the first time I've said the words out loud, and it's like a sneeze that finally came.

Jason doesn't say anything at first. He sits on a log and I sit beside him, digging my toes in the cool, slippery sand. I listen to the cranky creak of palm fronds moving in the light breeze and the sweet whisper of the light-shattered water.

"Everything I read said I'm going to need to start really paying attention five or ten years before my mom's first onset of cancer, which was when she was thirty-five. Cancer comes earlier every generation, so I'm thinking I'll remove my breasts by the time I'm twenty-five or so, and my ovaries in my thirties. My risk will be a lot lower then. What do you think?"

"Erin . . ."

"I know it seems crazy to be talking about cutting off my breasts when I'm only seventeen, but don't you see? It's the only way to not have to worry for the rest of my life. It's the safest way."

"Life isn't safe, Erin," Jason says.

"I know that. Don't you think I know that? What would *you* do if you had a choice?"

"I don't, though. I'm glad I don't have a choice. I don't want to have to make a decision like you and Ashley will. But if there was some part of my body I could cut off to reduce my risk? No way."

"But it's the only way I can minimize the risk, to make myself as safe as possible. Don't you understand?"

"I understand you want to live your life safely, Erin. I don't.

I want to *live*, period. I don't think you can do both at the same time, not really."

I shake my head, not knowing what to say. Jason always says exactly what he thinks, so why am I surprised he would tell me his opinion? But I want him to understand. I want him to tell me it is all right.

I want him to tell me it is all right because I'm falling for him. I have been for ages, but it is only today, as it is almost time for me to leave, that I see how much he means to me. Thinking about the months ahead when he will be in Florida and I will be in Georgia makes me feel cold and alone.

"Erin." He tilts my face toward him with the tip of his finger. "It's your choice. You have to do what's right for *you*. But if you're asking my opinion, I think you should wait until you're older to decide anything. Don't worry about the future until you have to."

"I wish I could do that," I say in a small voice. "I wish I knew how to do that. But I don't. I'm not like that."

Suddenly, I'm aware of how close he is to me. It's not the first time this week I felt this searing flash of attraction between us, but always before he would turn away, or say something, and nothing would happen. I'm not even sure he felt it. But this time, this time I *know*. I feel it deep inside, in that newly minted woman part of me that can tell when a boy is looking at her *like that*. I'm warm and jittery and without meaning to, I lean closer to him.

And we're kissing, and man, oh man, it's not like kissing Ted Hanson in ninth grade or even Michael. I tangle my hands in his hair, and his hands slide up my back under my shirt and they feel *hot*, burning, and the taste of him is like wild honey.

I'm not sure how long we kiss, but when he finally pulls away, my shirt is unbuttoned and my lips feel bruised and swollen, and I'm already missing the feel of his lips on mine.

"Dammit," he says, looking at me.

"Wow. Not exactly what a girl wants to hear after she's been kissed." I'm smiling though, because I can tell he felt it too, that unbelievable heat between us. "Can we do it some more?" I playfully reach for his hand to draw him closer to me.

"Erin. No," he says, standing up. "We . . . can't. We're friends. It has to stay that way."

"Friends can't kiss?"

"No!" he says explosively. "Not like that they can't."

"Okay." I get up and stand in front of him. "This calls for an experiment. We need to try it again and see if we still feel like friends." I cup his face in my palms and draw it down to mine.

If anything, it's better the second time. How can I even think about removing my breasts when it feels this good to have someone touch them? I had no idea. None whatsoever. I wonder what else I don't know. Then I don't think anymore and just *feel*.

"Erin, stop." He takes me by the shoulders and physically moves me back a step.

"What?"

"*We can't do this!*"

"No, I guess we can't, not as friends. But I think I might like to kiss you some more. So where does that leave us?"

He takes a step away from me. "Don't you understand? I can't fall in love with you. I think I have, a little already. I feel happy whenever you're around, and when I talk to you, I want to keep talking to you forever. But I can't fall in love with you. There's no future for us. I told you. I *warned* you. I will not fall in love. I can't risk us falling in love and down the road you having to watch me get cancer. If we can't just be friends, and after this," he waves a hand at my unbuttoned shirt and I reflexively cross my arms over my chest, "I don't think we can, then I don't think we should talk for a while. We need some distance."

"Are you kidding me? How can you say that?" My heart is pounding and I feel shaky, sick. I can't believe this is happening.

"I'm trying to protect you!"

"I don't need you to protect me!"

We stare at each other angrily, and he sighs, running his hand through his hair. "But don't you see? That's exactly what I've been doing since I brought you to the island. The way you feel about me is all tied up with that. You've got to find your own happiness, Erin. You can't rely on someone else to provide it for you. It's my fault, because I *liked* helping you, I liked being there for you. But I'm not always going to be there, and you need to know you can do it on your own, without me."

"What are you, my father? I don't need a protector, Jason. I need someone who feels the same way about me as I feel about them."

"And I can't be that for you."

"No, you are *refusing* to be that for me."

"I think we should take a break," he says quietly. "Until we can just be friends, I don't think we can be anything at all."

"Then I guess we can never be friends," I say, and my voice is shaking.

"Maybe not." His voice sounds anguished, but his face is determined.

"This is the guy who is always talking about living in the moment and not worrying about the future until it happens. You're such a hypocrite!"

I call the words after him, because he is already walking away from me, along the shore the way we came.

Words crowd my mind as we make the short trip back to his house, but by the time we arrive I've slicked over the fear and anger with a thick layer of glacial determination. If he doesn't want me, well, I don't want him either. I won't let him see how much he has hurt me. I talk with Ashley and Miriam as I wait for my mom to arrive, and my smiles and words skate across the slippery ice of my armor.

When Mom arrives, Jason comes from his apartment and without speaking, helps me load my stuff into the back of her car. When it is time to go, Miriam gives me a hard hug, whispers, "*I don't know what's going on but it'll be okay,*" Ashley gives me a small smile, and his dad shakes my hand firmly.

Then Jason and I are standing in front of each other.

"So long," he says, and it is casual, friendly, unbearable.

"Yeah," I say. "See you later."

My heart is breaking as I get into the car, but there is no way to change anything.

∽

Mom seems distracted on the ride back, but I am in misery and don't pay much attention. I tell her Jason and I are fighting, and she says, "Oh, honey, I'm sorry" and I spend the rest of the trip staring out the window in silent agony.

When we are almost home, she clears her throat. "I have something to tell you, Erin."

I turn to look at her and see she is pale, her jaw clenched in pain. Her pulled muscle didn't get any better the week I was gone.

"What?" I say. "What's wrong?"

"I went to the doctor while you were gone. They did a PET scan and—Erin, the cancer is . . . everywhere. It's in my bones, in my liver . . . It's bad, honey."

"*What?*" I stare at her in shock. "I thought you were better! I thought they cured you! *How could this happen?*"

"It was an even more aggressive form of cancer than they realized. It had probably already spread back when I had treatment before, we just didn't know it."

My mind whirls with horror. Oh no, not again, my poor mother . . .

I try for casual, this-is-old-hat-but-what-can-you-do? "Okay, what next? Surgery?"

She shakes her head. "It's too widespread for surgery. I'll go back on chemo, radiation, to keep it from spreading any more, and hopefully that will shrink the tumors some so I'm not in pain." She puts a hand to her back and in horror I remember talking to a lady in the radiation waiting room, the skin-and-bones one who said cheerfully, "Got to radiate the little bastards before they break my bones. Before long I'll be glowing in the dark!" Talking about the tumors, growing like rocks inside her bones. *Oh God . . .*

"How long will you be in treatment this time?" The thought of more rounds of chemo and radiation is nauseating.

"You don't understand, Erin." Mom reaches over and grabs my hand. "This is not curable. I'll be in treatment for the rest of my life."

Part Four

CHAPTER FORTY-THREE

"How's she doing?" Miriam asks when she picks up the phone on a beautiful spring day in late April. No "Hello, how ya doin'?" because I'm on her caller ID and she *knows* how I'm doing.

"Not good," I say and my voice wavers. "They told her today the latest round of chemo isn't working, and it was so much worse than the last time, so they're going to try something else, but . . . I don't know . . ."

Miriam is comfortable with silence and is not one to offer insincere platitudes, like, *It's okay, honey, I'm sure it's all good, and let's talk about the bright side, you know, getting ready in the morning is so much easier without hair!*

I've been talking to Miriam since January, right after Mom started her first new round of chemo and I spent the entire night holding her as she lay on the bathroom floor. (*Look, Mom, it's nice down here, cold and smooth and I agree! Let's hang out here all night!*) The next morning, I picked up the phone and dialed Jason's mom. I needed someone to talk to, someone who would really understand, and Miriam was the only person I could think of who understood exactly what I was going through.

I'm still talking, babbling, my thoughts gushing from my mouth. "But I go to school, because it upsets Mom when I don't, and everybody *knows*, the teachers know because Mr. Jarad told them that's why I've been missing so much school, but the kids know too. I walk through the halls and everyone is nice to me, and it's just *wrong*. I'm walking along and everybody is talking about stupid stuff, math tests, senior projects, and parties, and what so-and-so is *wearing*, and I'm like a shadow nobody can really see. Don't they understand none of that stuff *matters*?"

"But it does, Erin." Miriam's voice is firm. "It *does*. That's life, every little bit of it. It's silly, it's terrible, it's messy, it's pure, it's *life*. Dying is just one small part of it. The vast majority is made up of those frivolous, glorious moments. That's what those kids are doing, they're *living*. And I'm afraid you're not. You still need to appreciate the funny shape of a cloud, or a joke that makes you want to pee your pants, the way the warm breeze makes your skirt flip up around your knees. You still need to feel the sunlight on your face."

"What, are you telling me to stop and smell the freaking roses?" I ask, incredulous.

She chuckles, sympathetic but with a touch of humor, which is exactly how she's been helping me get through this. "Every once in a while, yes. Give it a try."

I'm silent, because I'm sure she's wrong, but a little part of me knows exactly what she's talking about. I cannot dismiss the words of this woman who has held her mother and sister in her arms as they died.

"I don't know . . . I don't know if I can do it, Miriam. I'm trying, but it's not enough, and I need to stay upbeat for her, but sometimes it's *hard* . . ."

"You're doing it, Erin. You already are. Some things are simply too much for a person to bear. And yet people do. Every day. They do it because they have to. They do it for love. It takes courage to live in joy instead of despair."

"How . . . how is he doing?" I ask after a while, because I always do at the end of these conversations, and the ones I have with Ashley as well. It seems like I am talking to everybody in Jason's family except for Jason.

She sighs. "Erin, I wish you would let me tell him. I feel dishonest not telling Jason I talk to you, and what's more, he would want to know about your mother. It's not fair to him, and it's not fair to me."

"I'm sorry," I say miserably. I know it's wrong to ask her to keep this secret, but I can't help myself. "Please don't tell him. If he knew about my mom it would make him feel guilty and I don't want him calling me out of pity. And I don't want to put this on him either. I wanted so much from him . . . it wasn't fair. I see it now. And I'm scared I'll do it again, because it's easier to lean on him. I just want to know . . . is he okay?"

"He's hanging in there, honey," she says and her voice is soft. "Just like you."

∞

I go downstairs and Mom is lying on the couch, gently crying. The tears stream silently down her face and I'm not sure she is even aware of them as she stares at the TV. I look to see if there is something sad on, but it's some sort of game show. She is lost in her thoughts, staring unseeingly at the screen as the tears drip onto her pillow.

"Mom," I say softly. I kneel beside the couch and take her thin body in my arms and she sobs soundlessly. I don't ask what's wrong, because she does this often, and what is she going to say? *Oh, don't mind these silly little tears, Erin. This cancer thing? A real bummer!*

"I'm scared," she says, clutching me. I am all she has. Jill has come for weeks at a time, and the fridge is stuffed with casseroles from friends and neighbors, but in the end it is her and me, swirling slowly in a sinking life raft.

"I know," I say. "But it's going to be fine. We're going to beat this thing. Look how hard you're fighting. You are a *warrior.*"

She is silent, because she doesn't like it when I talk like this. But I believe if I stay positive the good vibes will zap at least some of those creepy-crawly cancer cells that just *ache* to pack up their wagons and set off for new, unexplored territory.

I hear there's wide-open spaces out there in the femur. Pack it up, Martha, we're going to find us a new home!

"*No,*" she says, and I am surprised by the ferocity in her voice. "I am scared for *you.*"

"I'm fine, Momma. I know I fell apart last year, but I'm different now. I will be here for you. I can do this. I *want* to do this. And when we get you well, we can go to Dino's and get our manis and pedis and laugh about all this."

"I need to know you will be okay when I'm gone," she says.

"*Don't talk like that*," I say. "You are *not* going to die. The tumor board is meeting about your case, and with that many doctors putting their heads together you *know* they'll figure something out. You're starting that stronger regimen of chemo, and even if that doesn't work, there're tons of clinical trials and those are working *wonders*. Don't give up hope, Mom, please. You can do this. You can do this for yourself, and you can do this for me. I need you. I need you here with me. I need you to tell me what to do about Jason. We haven't talked since I left after Christmas break, and there is this big hole in me nothing seems to fill. I need you to see me graduate. I need you, Momma, every day, so please, *please don't leave me*."

She hugs me as hard as her frail arms can and I hug her back, feeling her smooth bald head against my cheek.

"*I'm trying, I'm trying*," she whispers.

CHAPTER FORTY-FOUR

The next day is Saturday, and I go to the airport. It's a blue-sky April day, the air warming gently, the trees sporting their fresh, green leaves.

It's been a couple of weeks since I've come to the airport, and the first thing I notice is that Tweety Bird is gone. My heart sinks. Stew must have sold her. She must have been more damaged than I realized. Maybe he had to scrap her out.

Then I catch a glimpse of yellow in the hangar and realize with relief that Stew moved her inside. Does that mean he's working on her?

I sit for a while, enjoying the tiny glow of happiness. But heavy, dark thoughts keep intruding and it's like a cloud has moved across the sun even though the air is still bright and clear. I pull out my phone and go to one of the breast cancer websites because I can't stop thinking about it, no matter how hard I try. My finger hovers over the "Stage IV" forum, but I can't bear it right now. Instead, I choose one of the preventive mastectomy forums, and I spend ten minutes reading about chest expanders, nipple tattoos, and silicone vs. saline breast implants. These women are determined to rebuild something from scratch, and I admire them for it.

I just don't know if I can do it.

I answer a post, and comment on someone else's post. I've been doing this a lot lately; it helps to have someone to talk to who understands what it's like to face these choices. Miriam will be telling Ashley about the possibility she may have the BRCA mutation in a week. While I'm dreading Ashley finding out, because she's become a friend, at least we'll be able to talk about it. It's been the elephant in the room in all of our conversations, and she doesn't even know it.

I read a text from Trina asking if they are picking me up for our Excap excursion this evening. I hesitate on that one, because I really don't want to go. I'm not in the mood for fun and games.

While I'm thinking about it, someone knocks sharply on my window.

I jump and stifle a scream.

Stew is standing beside the car, tapping a wrench into the palm of his hand. I hesitate and then roll down the window.

"You ready to help fix the mess you made?" he asks. This is the first time we've talked since he brought me home.

"Uh . . . yes?"

"Come on, then," he says.

I scramble out of the car and follow him into the hangar.

Tweety Bird is supported by cables attached to the ceiling and she's missing the strut I bent when I landed in the field.

For the next two hours, Stew says nothing to me except to ask for tools, which I give to him. The silence isn't as fierce as it was on the ride home, though, and I'm glad for it. I don't want Stew to hate me.

"You going to appeal the FAA decision?" He wipes the grease off his hands and reaches for a stick of gum.

"What? Wait a minute. They decided?" How did I miss *that*? I've been paying our bills, as well as grocery shopping, but it's hard to keep up with everything. I realize it's been more than a week since I checked the mailbox.

"I heard the FAA made their decision on you. You didn't know? They revoked your certificate. Permanently."

My head is spinning. The FAA thought I was so messed up that I shouldn't be allowed to fly again? Ever?

"And . . . and . . . what about you?" My voice is so low it might as well be a whisper.

"Me? I got cleared a couple weeks ago. Damn bureaucrats," he grumbles. "Takes 'em forever to make any fool decision."

I close my eyes, feeling a wave of relief. For Stew, at least.

"Thank God," I breathe.

Stew eyes me, and his expression is unreadable.

"Good for me, but what about you?" he says.

"So . . ." I gulp. "They say I can't get my pilot certificate? For . . . the rest of my life?"

Stew shrugs. "That's what they're saying. But you can appeal it. You'll have to go to a hearing and convince a judge that the FAA was wrong, that you should be allowed to continue your flight instruction."

"I'll have to talk? Like at a trial?" I can't imagine it. I really can't.

"What, you think they read minds? Of course you'll have to talk. You'll have to stand up and talk damn good to convince them to give you another chance. The judge will want to know why you did it in the first place, and why he should give you another chance."

My stomach drops. I can't imagine standing up in front of strangers and baring my soul like that.

"I don't know if . . ." I trail off.

"You're telling me you can take an airplane three hundred miles by yourself and land in a field, but you can't get up in front of a few people and convince them to let you keep training for your pilot's license?"

"It's different." As crazy as it sounds, flying was easier than all the other things in my life. It's the closest I came to feeling like my dad, to touch a little of his bravery.

He shakes his head, making a sound of disgust. "I don't see how."

He hands the rag to me, and even though it's dirtier than my hands, I use it anyway.

"Look, Stew, I wanted to say again how sorry I am about everything. If I'd known I would be jeopardizing your instructor's license I never would have done it. I wasn't thinking. I'm so sorry."

He stares at me for a long moment, and then reaches over

and takes the rag from me. "If you decide to appeal the decision, I'll come to the hearing. I'll tell the judge you're dumb
as a box of rocks for doing what you did, but keeping you out
of the air would be a crying shame."

"Thank you," I say, but he's already turned his back on me
and walked away.

CHAPTER FORTY-FIVE

I go home and check on Mom, but she's sleeping. I refill her water glass and make her a salad, because that's the only thing she wants to eat anymore, when she can eat at all. I stand for a minute and watch her sleep. She has lost so much weight she looks like one of the concentration-camp victims I read about in World History. Her head is as smooth as an egg, and her eyelids are purple as they rest above her pale cheeks.

A horn blows outside, and I check to make sure her phone is in easy reach before I go.

When I get into Chaz's car, it's like déjà vu. Michael is in the backseat and he nods at me as I slide in.

"Hey, girlie," Trina says brightly. "Michael decided at the last minute he wanted to come."

She gives me a wink, but because Trina is incapable of winking, she gives me a squinched-up blink and it's a sure bet

Michael saw. She knows all about Jason, and has loyally declared him a total wangchop. For the past several months she's been trying to set me up with Chaz's friends—"Wouldn't it be a blast if we could double date?"—but so far I've managed to avoid her matchmaking.

Not this time.

"Hey." Michael takes a long swig from a beer he's got between his knees. Straight black hair and dark glowing eyes, he's wearing faded jeans and a soft white T-shirt. He's drawn what looks like an eyeball on the back of one of his hands. It's an intricate drawing with a lot of detail and it's like the eye is watching me as I put my seat belt on.

"Hey," I say, trying for what-was-your-name-again? But the truth is he's still hot, and I feel my pulse speed up as he reaches over and snags the cooler from under my feet.

"Want a beer?"

"No, I'm good."

Trina and Chaz are talking about prom and I stare out the window. It's getting dark and I wonder whether Mom has woken up yet. I'm wishing I hadn't come, but it's too late now.

Druid Hills has, like, a gazillion parks, and we must pass every one of them before turning onto the Briarcliff Campus of Emory University. It's a mixture of old-fashioned redbrick buildings and industrial ones as well, all shaded by trees and abandoned-looking. We park in one of the empty parking lots and shadows fall thickly over the trees. As we get out of the car, Michael chucks three beer cans into the bushes.

"Okay," Chaz says. "We're going to reconnoiter. You ladies stay right here until we get back."

Chaz and Michael trot across the parking lot and Trina and I look at each other.

"Reconnoiter?" Trina says.

"*Ladies?*" I say.

And we burst out laughing.

"Isn't he just precious?" Trina says.

"Adorable," I agree.

She puts her fist up and I bump it gently with mine.

Dorkster Twins activate.

"So, what's up with Michael?" I say, trying not to show how good the fist bump made me feel. That it's *us* again. "Not that he's ever been the world's happiest individual, but he seems pretty dark tonight."

Trina grimaces. "Michael didn't get into any of the colleges he wanted. His grades sucked too bad. He's spent every free moment working on his building models and I guess he forgot to study. It's like he's obsessed. When he got the last rejection, Chaz said he busted all his models, and he's been working on them for *years*."

"That's awful." And it is. I know how badly Michael wanted to go to college and get away from here.

We lean back on the trunk of the Mustang. I notice Trina is wearing a black T-shirt with EXCAPS written across the back and a drawing of the abandoned school on the front. Chaz is wearing one today too. People are calling them Chazatrina.

"What's with your clothes?" I ask. "You stopped wearing your outfits."

Trina shrugs. "I don't know. I guess it was like a disguise, somehow, and once Chaz told me he loved me for *me*, I stopped wanting to hide who I am."

Chaz comes loping back, all ungainly swinging arms and legs. "The coast is clear," he says in a whisper. I halfway expect him to ask for a password.

We follow him across the parking lot toward the building.

"You have to see it from the front first," he says. "It really is magnificent, even abandoned. The son of the cofounder of Coca-Cola built it back in the 1920s, and after he sold it, it was an addiction center, and then a mental hospital. Emory University owns it now, and it's just sitting empty, though they sometimes use it for photo shoots."

Even in the dying light, the front of the building *is* amazing. The fading red bricks and peeling white paint and boarded-up windows don't take away the magnificence of the large rectangular mansion with a two-story circular entrance held up by columns, and graceful half-moon windows. I take a picture, liking the way the glancing rays of the setting sun illuminate hidden parts of the house.

We follow Chaz around the back to a window that looks boarded up, but Chaz and Michael pull down the board, which was only placed in the window, not nailed.

"There used to be a menagerie on the grounds, with a bunch of animals, including a tiger named Jimmie Walker and elephants named Coca, Cola, Refreshing, and Delicious. One of the baboons attacked somebody and they donated all the animals to Zoo Atlanta," Chaz says as he climbs through the window and turns to help Trina first, and then me.

The place is unbelievable. Grand and commanding, even with the industrial touches of its mental-institute days, like the exit signs above the doors and the water fountains. As we wander the imposing rooms and the light fades, I find I'm not scared. The building feels abandoned, but somehow I can hear the tinkling of piano keys in the vaulted three-story music room, and the laughter of women in flapper dresses near the fireplace that is almost big enough for me to stand in. In the study, gold drapes still hang, and I imagine the long-dead man working on Coca-Cola figures. All the ceilings, windows, and doors are larger than normal, like the people who walked these halls were bigger than life.

"Check out the detail," Michael says, standing under a chandelier with a bird's nest in it. "Someone really cared about this house. They spent a lot of time making it this beautiful."

He plays his flashlight over a compass rose that has been worked into the ninety-year-old plaster. It is still gorgeous.

I find to my surprise I'm enjoying myself. I suddenly get why people like exploring these old buildings. It's history, long past, yes, but these forgotten buildings were once bustling with people and energy. They might be dark and scary now, but once upon a time they had a good life, one worth living. This house isn't defined by what it looks like now, neglected and old, but what it once *was*: beautiful and full of life. It is a container of memories, laughter, and tears, and the ravages of time cannot take that away.

We stand in a room with windows big enough to drive a

car through and Chaz and Trina snuggle together in a dark corner.

Michael and I watch the moon rise. It climbs quickly and loses volume and color in the process, like a balloon, big and bright in your hand but becoming small and indistinct in the sky. So much better to have it in your hand. Once you lose it, it's gone forever.

Michael brings a beer out of his coat pocket and chugs it, leaning his hip against the wall.

"I heard about your mom being sick," he says. "That sucks."

"It does," I say. "I heard about your college stuff. That sucks too."

"Yeah." He takes another long swig from his beer, his Adam's apple working as he chugs. For a crazy minute, I want to kiss him in that soft, vulnerable spot at the base of his throat. Whatever attraction I had for Michael hasn't subsided.

And what does it matter? Jason doesn't want me.

"Should have known," Michael says. "Should have known it wouldn't work out for me. It never does."

"But you can't give up," I say.

"Sure I can," he says. "My dad did."

I step closer to him and take his hand. He closes his fingers around mine and we stand like that for a while until Trina calls out, "Hey, I got a great idea. Why don't you guys go to prom with us this weekend?"

I know this is not out of the blue. Trina has been bugging

me about prom for weeks but it just all seems so *stupid*. Trina says I'll regret it when I'm older, but I don't care.

Even so, my heart races a little bit, and I sneak a quick look at Michael. My face is beginning to burn. I don't need any more rejection.

"Why the hell not," he says.

CHAPTER FORTY-SIX

On Friday, I'm sitting in the meditation room at the cancer center, waiting for Mom to be done with her radiation to ease the discomfort from growing tumors. This time it's her hip, but hopefully in a week or so, the tumor will shrink enough so she'll be able to walk again.

"There you are," Trina says loudly, oblivious to the hush and quiet of the room. No one else is there, so I don't bother to shush her.

"Hey," I say. It's not the first time Trina has showed up unannounced at one of these appointments, and I'm grateful for the company.

"You know," she says, flopping down on a seat and closing one eye so she can peer at the stained glass.

"What?"

"If you squint, it kind of looks like the white dove took a big crapola. Here. You gotta squint. See what I mean?"

I squint and darned if she's not right. It makes me laugh, and then I'm clutching my stomach, rolled up on the seat, in hysterics.

"I told my mom I could be a stand-up comic if I wanted to. It was one of those you-could-be-anything-you-want-so-why-are-you-such-a-slack-ass conversations, so I told her I wanted to be a stand-up comic and she said, 'I sure as heck don't find you funny,' and I said . . ." She's on a roll, talking so that neither of us have to notice that my laughter has turned to tears.

After my sobs fade to hiccups, she says, "You're still going to prom tomorrow, right? Michael said you hadn't talked to him all week so he was wondering whether he needed to rent a tux. I tend to doubt he'll find one at this late date anyway, but I figured I'd ask."

"I'm going," I say.

"Your enthusiasm is overwhelming." But she doesn't say it meanly, and she sits with me while I try not to think about the blasts of radiation burning into my mother's bones right now.

Mom is excited about prom, so I guess that's good even if my excitement is nil. I've got the dress and the shoes, and Mom actually made me an appointment to go get my hair and nails done tomorrow morning with Trina. Mom's looking forward to prom, even though the chemo isn't working and it doesn't look like she's eligible for any clinical trials, and they are having to radiate her hip just so she can *walk*.

But she wants me to go, and I will.

"Wow," I say as Michael and I walk inside the Ford Pavilion at Zoo Atlanta and see everyone we know decked out in their finest, many of them swaying to a slow song on the dance floor. Michael's hand is warm and firm on the small of my back and I try not to notice. I like Michael, but I still cry some nights holding Jason's sweatshirt.

Later, I'm sitting by myself at our table while Trina and Chaz dance and Michael has gone to the bathroom, presumably to dump more liquor into his punch. He pounded four beers on the way to the dance and has been steadily drinking since. I'm worried about him, but I don't know what I can do. His mood has gotten darker as the night wears on, and I think about Jason's open, sunshine-bright smile and my heart aches.

"Erin," someone says, and I look up to see Faith. She's in a skintight pink dress and there's no doubt she has me beat hands down in the body department. Rumor is she came with a college boy. Rumor is she made it into Stanford. Rumor didn't mention her flushing her phone fifty times down the toilet. "Can I sit down?"

"Uh, sure. Okay," I say. *What the . . . ?*

She perches on the edge of the chair. "Look, I know we don't know each other very well, but I heard about your mom getting sick again. And I wanted to say I'm sorry. My grandmother just died of pancreatic cancer, and it was horrible." She shudders, a delicate little tremor like a breeze through summer-soft petunias. "She wasted away until there was no meat left on her. It was truly awful. Sometimes I think she's the only one in the world who really loved me without expecting anything back from me." She looks down at her clenched fingers and swallows.

My heart is beating hard, and the loud music and flashing lights are making me sick.

"I'm sorry," I murmur.

"I knew you would . . . understand," she says. "When I heard about your mom . . . how sick she was . . . I wouldn't wish that on my worst enemy. I really wouldn't. I hope it all turns out . . . okay. That's what I wanted to say."

She leaves and I close my eyes. Michael comes back and says something to me, I don't know what, and I jump up and head blindly toward the bathroom.

I sit down on the toilet and cradle my phone in my hands. I want to call Mom, but I know she is sleeping, and it's not fair to wake her up just so I can hear her voice, to reassure myself she is still *alive*.

My chest is heaving, and I'm afraid I'm having a heart attack. I lean over my knees trying to catch my breath. I cannot break down, I CANNOT break down. She needs me to be strong, and I CANNOT give up on her. I try to banish Faith's words from my mind. She wasn't being mean, the opposite in fact, but the thought that her grandmother *died*, that Mom could *die*, makes me want to throw up.

I want to call Jason so badly I actually find him on my Favorites list and put my finger on his name. But it's better this way, it's better for him not to have to go through this. This is my battle, and I need to stay strong and not give up, *never* give up, because if I don't give up on Mom, she can't give up on herself. The only thing that gets me through every day is my belief that she can beat this, that no matter what the doctors say, she will be whole and healthy at the end of it all. If I lose that, if I picture the world without my mom, if I picture her *dying*, I think I will go insane. So I refuse, *refuse*, to think about any other alternative.

I press my hands to my eyes and breathe deep for a while. I hear toilets flushing, girls talking, whispering about being felt up, hotel rooms booked for the after-dance party, and it all seems so bizarre to me that life just keeps going on.

Finally, I put my phone back in my purse and go out to fix my makeup. I barely recognize the girl in the mirror. I have gotten taller, and the stomach pooch has disappeared. My hair is longer, past the middle of my back, and I've got it down, loose, dark curls framing my face. I am wearing a dress the color of bruised violets. It is my face that looks the most different, though. The roundness has melted away and I do not know the woman staring back at me.

"Did Faith say something to you?" Michael asks when I come back to our table. He's not quite slurring. "You can't worry about her, she doesn't mean ninety percent of the stuff she says. When she's not trying so hard to be . . . I don't know, a superstar at everything she does, she's really pretty okay. Her mom rides her hard, texting and calling all the time."

I think about the pink phone in the toilet and I turn to look at Michael. Something clicks into place almost audibly in my head. "You're in love with her, aren't you? Wow. Wow." Perhaps it should hurt, but it really doesn't. I don't feel that way about Michael. Not the way I still feel about Jason.

He's turning his steak knife over and over in his long fingers, concentrating on it. "She's going places. I'm not. It would never work."

"What's with you guys? Give it a chance, why don't you? You don't know what's going to happen. Nobody does."

"I'd rather know in advance," he says. "Saves time and . . . pain."

"Well, I wouldn't," I say with feeling. "I don't want to know the future. Ignorance leaves room for hope." *And hope is sometimes all you have left.*

He turns the knife on its edge and presses the palm of his hand against the serrated blade. His face is expressionless and I can't tell if it hurts him or not.

"So, you're doing what? Hanging out with me to kill time until she notices you again?" I say.

"It's not like that. I like you. I always have. You're a cool person. I like what you have to say. I think you're brave, you know, with everything you have going on."

Which is funny, because *brave* is the one thing I never feel.

After that, the night goes better. Michael and I are more comfortable, and I even dance some, though I know the dork in me is never far away.

"Isn't Chaz just *adorable*?" Trina says as she dances up to me. What Chaz is doing on the dance floor is a lot of things (criminal? anatomically impossible?) but adorable is not the word I would have used. But I smile, because she is happy, and I *hurt*, missing Jason, but I'm still happy for her.

She puts her arm around me and shimmies her hip into

mine. "How you doing, girl?" she whispers into my ear. "I know this is hard. But try to have fun. She wants you to have fun."

I nod and smile, and give her a little push back toward Chaz. On my way to the punch, I run into Faith.

"You know," I say. "I'm trying to figure out Michael."

She looks at me sharply. "Good luck with that. I mean, no offense, I know the two of you are hot and heavy, but he's a *mess*. I couldn't care less what Michael is thinking anymore."

But the pain in her eyes belies her words. She does love him. Whatever happened between the two of them is dark and sad on her face.

"He's down," I say. "Real down. I think he needs a friend. One that really understands him."

She sighs. "He talked about dying all the time after his dad killed himself. Everything changed, and I couldn't bear the thought of him . . . doing something to himself. But I'm never really happy when we're apart, either. It sucks. Love sucks. But . . . when I get him to laugh, it feels awesome. God, I don't know." She folds one little fist into the pink, shiny fabric of her dress.

"Seriously? You made him *laugh*?" I stare at her in amazement. "I can't even make him *smile*. You two are meant to be together. Truly. Why don't you go talk to him? I'm heading to the bathroom, and I might be a while."

"Why are you . . . ?" She hesitates, and looks away.

"Being nice when you were such a jerk to me?" I think about it. "Because it took courage to come say what you did to me about your grandmother. It would have been easier for you to not say anything, and I have a lot of respect for people who don't do the easy thing."

She looks a little taken aback, but then nods. "Thank you."

She goes over to Michael, and I go back to the bathroom. This time I let myself cry. How easy it is for them, how impossible for me.

CHAPTER FORTY-SEVEN

Monday after prom, I go to the airport. Tweety Bird is fixed, good as new, and Stew took her up yesterday for the first time. He asked me to go—not to fly, just as a passenger—but I said no.

I don't know if I'll ever fly again and I don't want to be reminded of what I'm losing.

Stew throws me a rag, and I start wiping down one of the planes, a two-seater Cessna 152 with its engine compartment open.

"You decided?" Stew asks.

"No."

He shakes his head and goes back to doing whatever he was doing under the cowling of the Cessna.

I still haven't decided if I'm going to go to the FAA hearing tomorrow. It was one thing to write a letter telling the FAA I wanted to appeal their decision, but when I got the letter back setting my hearing date . . . it all got real, then. If I don't go, I'm guaranteed to never fly again. If I do . . . I don't know. I don't know if I can do it.

"Why not?" Stew asks, his words muffled because his head is in the engine compartment.

"I've got a seriously important hair appointment. Highlights, bob, the whole works," I say.

Stew pulls his head out and glares at me.

I shrug. "I'm scared," I say simply.

"Yeah? So?"

"I wish I were braver. I wish I could go out and do all these things and not be scared of it all. But I can't. I'm not like my dad. He wasn't scared of anything."

Stew doesn't say anything for a while, and then he stands up and wipes his hands. He should look ridiculous with his big belly and tufts of scattered hair, but somehow he doesn't. He points a thick, oil-stained finger at me. "Justin Bailey not scared? Girl, you don't know what you're talking about. He was a great aviator, one of the best I've ever seen. And before every mission, he would throw up. Puke his guts out. He was that scared. But you know what? Afterward, he got up there and did what needed to be done. I think you're confusing bravery with stupidity. Stupidity is not knowing enough to be scared. Bravery is being scared but doing it anyway."

I stare at Stew openmouthed. I don't know what to say.

"If your dad was here right now he would tell you to get your butt to that hearing tomorrow because you need to fly. Just like him. You both need to be *going* somewhere to feel truly alive. I knew him well, and you're just like him, even if you don't realize it. I flew in the 'missing man' flyover at his funeral, you know. Three planes in formation where there should be four. We do it when a good pilot, a good man, dies. That was your dad. A good man and a good pilot, and I have a feeling he was a good dad as well. He would want you to do this."

∽

I stay up most of the night writing. As soon as I get one draft done, I delete it and start over. Around four in the morning, I sigh, and close my laptop. I'm too tired to even brush my teeth, and without thinking I shut off the light. As the room goes pitch-dark, I feel the familiar panic start. My mouth goes dry and my heart starts thumping.

Really? This is the girl who flew three hundred miles on her first solo, caught and cooked her own fish, and stayed in a tent in the middle of nowhere all by herself? This is the girl who has held her mom's hand through countless chemo treatments, and her head as she's puked afterward? And you're still afraid of the DARK?

I take a deep breath and make my way to my bed, guided only by the orange glow of my clock.

And then, for the first time since I was six, I go to sleep with the lights out.

∽

The next morning when I go down for breakfast, Mom is lying on the couch with a glass of water and a thermometer. The new pain medicine they have her on is good stuff. The sight of her without eyelashes and eyebrows is still surprising, even though it's been months. She looks so frail and small and *old* I want to take her in my arms and never let go.

"Are you going to do it?" she asks, dabbing at her nose, which is always running. No nose hairs equals drippy nose.

"I think so."

"Erin . . . I know I've not been all that supportive of your flying. I wasn't on board with your dad's flying either. This one thing that meant so much to him, and I never really shared it with him. I want you to know that if flying makes you happy, then it makes me happy too."

"Okay, Mom," I say, leaning forward and kissing the top of her head.

"It's important to me for . . . for you to know you are capable of touching the world. Don't live your life stingily. I did it for far too long. I can't do anything about that now, but you can live better. Will you do that for me? Will you live your life to the best of your ability?" She is floaty with the medicine, but her eyes are blazing with determination.

"I just don't know . . . I don't know if I'm brave enough to say the words I need to say. That's what I need to do, but I'm still not sure I can do it."

"You can," she says simply as I grab my bag and head for the door. "I know you can."

"At least that's one of us," I say.

⸎

It's as bad as I thought. A courtroom like in the movies, a judge sitting behind a big bench, me at one table by myself, and the FAA guy and a lawyer at another. Several other people are there, but the only one I care about is Stew. He nods at me as I go up the aisle, and I force a sickly smile. The judge begins the proceedings with a lot of mumbo jumbo, and says that he plans to give me some leeway due to my young age and lack of counsel.

It goes downhill from there. People get up to talk about me, and they are condescending and brutal in their condemnation. I am *unstable*, they say, a threat to myself and others in the air. They drone on and on, listing my crimes, and then there's a surprise. Mr. Jarad, dressed in a suit, comes to take the stand. I hadn't even seen him come in. I close my eyes, because it's one thing to hear strangers talk about me, but Mr. Jarad *knows* me and it will be almost unbearable to hear him say the same ugly things as these other people.

Mr. Jarad states his name and profession, and it turns out he's really "Dr. Jarad," with a bunch of very respectable-sounding credentials. He talks about me, saying that he's been seeing me professionally for a year and then he starts using big medical words that seem to boil down to me being a normal teenager who had been going through an incredible amount of stress in the days leading up to my flying away. The judge looks thoughtful after Mr. Jarad says in his medical opinion I am not a risk to myself or others, and that no, he does not think I would act in the same reckless manner again. As Mr. Jarad walks back to his seat, he winks at me, and I see that he's wearing sneakers with his high-dollar suit.

Then Stew gets up.

"I knew her dad," he says. "He flew in Desert Storm. She's just like him, they're aviators. It's in their blood. She's a numbskull for doing what she did, but, Jesus, who among us weren't numbskulls at seventeen? When she's in the air she's more focused on flying than the majority of adults I take up. Grounding her, it's like cutting the wings off a bird. See what I'm saying?"

Then it's my turn.

"If you don't mind," I say, standing, my hands shaking so hard I have trouble fishing my notes out of my bag, "I have something I'd like to read."

The judge shrugs. "Go ahead."

I take a deep breath and look down at my paper.

And then I speak:

Flying solo was one of the scariest things I've ever done. I practiced and practiced, but I wasn't sure I could do it on my own. As long as I had my instructor in the seat beside me, I knew he would save me if I messed up. Maybe I wouldn't solo at all. It would be easier not to, it would be easier just to fly along for the rest of my life as a perpetual passenger.

But in the end, I did it. I soloed. I can honestly say it was a disaster. You know that. That's why I'm here.

I think you want to know why I did it. I wish I could give you a good explanation, but I can't. My mom was getting ready to start chemo again, I lost my best friend, I failed physics, and the guy I thought liked me chose another girl. It felt like life piled up on me all at once. You're not interested in all of that. I get that. And I suppose, that's kind of the point. Because when it came to flying, none of that mattered. When you're in a plane, and a thunderstorm comes up and your instruments fail, and your motor stops, you can't just go someplace else. You can't give up. You have to keep flying.

No matter what.

Learning to fly, to live, is *hard*. You make mistakes, and you have to live with them, to forgive yourself. Someone once told me that to live, you have to be willing to make mistakes. Well, I made a big one. I know that. All I can tell you is that I learned from it. I know I can't just check out when things get bad. I have to keep on going, for myself, and for the people I love.

Hopefully that will make me a better pilot if you give me the chance. I'm not there yet. I still have a lot left to learn and I'm beginning to think that I'll be making mistakes and learning from them the rest of my life. I want to keep flying. Things may go wrong, things may seem overwhelming, but I know now I can't give up.

I look up. The room is silent.

"Please," I say. "Don't ground me. Let me keep flying."

CHAPTER FORTY-EIGHT

The day after the judge decides to let me fly again, Mom decides she has to have Dino's pizza to celebrate, and that I need to go get it immediately. I agree, say, "That sounds *stellar!*"

We both know she doesn't want pizza. We both know anything other than water, and a lot of times that too, comes back up immediately. She is trying for some sense of normalcy for me, and I play along because it makes her feel as if she is in control of *something*. She keeps talking about planning a big party for my eighteenth birthday next week, and I know it frustrates her that she just *can't*. It's too much right now.

I swerve the car back and forth in the lane, pretending it's Tweety Bird, thinking about how it will feel to fly again. I still have a long way to go before I get my pilot's license, but at least I won the privilege to keep taking lessons. I want to fly so badly, so why do I feel guilty about it too?

When I go in to get the pizza, I see Chaz and Trina sitting in a booth.

I slide in across from them.

"How is she?" Trina asks immediately, seeing my face.

People ask me all the time. It's got to where I don't know what to say because it's almost a rhetorical question. I mean they want to know—some of them, like Trina, genuinely care—but they want to hear things like *She's hanging in there* or *You know that mom of mine, she keeps a smile on her face no matter what!* What they don't want to hear is *That mom of mine, she pooped the bed again!* or *You should see Mom's belly, it's swollen up like she's nine months pregnant and she's all yellow, even the whites of her eyes!* Or, even, *The doctor yesterday said we needed to be preparing for the end.*

"She's hanging in there," I say.

"Sucks."

"Yeah."

Trina squeezes my leg and I smile at her before giving a let's-move-on wave of my hand.

"Yeah, so," Trina says. "We were talking about Michael. You heard he dropped out of school?"

I nod. A month before graduation and Michael stopped coming to school.

"Faith is trying to talk him into going to California with her when she goes to Stanford in the fall. She wants to get him away from here. He can get his GED there and maybe go to a community college."

"I hope he does," I say, thinking about the burning-bright kid who had the world by the tail only a couple of years ago. Then life happened and wiped him out like a tsunami.

"What about you? Have you heard back from any schools?" Trina asks. "Chaz and I both got into GSU, so I think that's where we're going to go."

Once upon a time that would have hurt. Once upon a time it was supposed to be me and Trina going to college together. But it doesn't hurt now. Trina is doing what she needs to do, and so am I. Our friendship is different than it used to be, but it's still real and true.

I shrug, and don't answer, which they take to mean bad news. In reality, the letters from three schools lie unopened in our junk drawer. They are fat envelopes, probably acceptances, but it really doesn't matter. I'm not going anywhere; Mom needs me too much right now. Once she gets better, and she *will* get better, then I can think about college.

"Did you ever answer that woman who wanted you to blog for the BRCA website?" Trina asks.

I grimace. "No, I can't decide what to say to her."

The moderator for one of the BRCA websites I frequent sent me an e-mail asking if I wanted to write a blog for younger previvors. She said she noticed my posts and thought I had something to say that might resonate with younger women.

It's flattering, but I don't know if I can do it. I don't know if I can write those words and have everyone read them and know who I really am.

I check my phone to make sure Mom hasn't tried to call, panicked a little I have left her so long. A hospice nurse comes in during the day, but at night I'm the only one she has.

I hear Chaz say, "Hey, buddy, you need something?"

I look up and see Jason standing there.

"Erin," he says.

He looks different, though it's only been five months since that last terrible day I saw him. Bigger, more like a man, and even sunburned and gloriously messy as usual, he still makes Chaz look like a little boy. He fills the space, somehow, like the essence of Jason is too tremendous to be contained in the envelope of his body.

I'm staring at him openmouthed and Trina gazes back and forth between us quizzically.

"*Jason*," I whisper and her expression clears, becomes more wary.

"Jason." I clear my throat. "What are you doing here? How . . . ?"

"I went by your house. Your mom said you were here."

He stands there looking at me with his eyes the color of the sea, and I want to weep, to throw myself in his arms, but I don't.

"You really messed with her head last time," Trina says, going on the attack. "Are you here to do that again?"

Jason doesn't speak for a moment. It's so ridiculous, Trina bristling, Jason looking tired and full of words. "I never wanted to hurt her," he says finally. "That was the last thing I wanted to do."

Trina purses her lips.

"Okay, enough." I slide out of my seat and grab my bag. "Jason, we can talk outside."

Faith comes in as we go out and she turns to stare at Jason, then touches her finger to her arm with a hissing sound. Jason is hot. Like I don't know. Like walking close to him doesn't make me hot and cold and tingly and want to pull him into the backseat of my car.

Jason leans up against a motorcycle and I see the Deadhead stickers on it and know it's his.

"You're taking up suicide as a hobby?" I nod at the bike.

"It gets me around."

We stand for a moment, just staring at each other.

"Do you know," he says softly, "you look so beautiful, all I can think about doing is kissing you and never stopping?"

"Jason," I say, closing my eyes.

"Your hair's grown out some. I like it."

"Why are you here?" I run my hand through my hair, and cross my arms tight over my breasts.

"I couldn't take it another day," he says in a low voice. "Life is too freaking short to waste by yourself when you love someone. I had to at least tell you that. I came here to say that. I didn't want to go through life wishing I had said it to you. To wonder if it would have made a difference."

"No. Wait. Wait." I clear my throat. "You love me?"

"Come on, Erin, you know I do. You're strong and courageous, and you have this radiance, this glow, when you smile, and when you do you're positively beautiful."

He steps toward me and cups my cheek with his big, warm hand, and I close my eyes, leaning into his strength.

"But what happened? I don't understand," I say, and then almost wish I hadn't. I don't want to talk him *out* of loving me. But I have to know. "You said you wouldn't fall in love with anyone. So . . . why me?"

He laughs, soft in his throat. "I was stupid, okay? I was arrogant and stupid, and I had never fallen in love so I just didn't understand what it would be like. I didn't understand that it would hurt more to *not* love than it would to love, and how important it is to love someone and have them love you back. I'm sorry it took me so long to say it. I was just so afraid . . . But Ashley set me straight. You know we told her about the mutation last week, the day after her birthday? Yeah, of course you know, Ashley said you two had been talking. Anyway, once she knew, we started talking about it all. And, God, I'm in awe of her. She's decided she's not going to get tested. She says she refuses to be defined by words on a piece of paper, that knowing wouldn't change how she plans to live. She'll be careful, she'll do surveillance, but she's not going to let it rule her life. She also told me I was acting like a dumb-ass. She asked me how I'd feel if the roles were reversed, if you left me because you were afraid I'd have to watch you die. I realized that I want to be there holding your hand when you died, hopefully when you're a hundred and twelve, but earlier if necessary. That I wanted to be *that* person for you, the one who's there through the good and bad. And I see now that it works both ways. Maybe you want to be the one to hold my hand at the end too."

"*Yes,*" I say. "Yes, I want to hold your hand through all of it, the good *and* the bad. But I'm worried because I leaned on you too much. I took advantage of you, and it wasn't fair, but I couldn't seem to stop myself. And I was afraid if I had you back, I'd do the same thing again."

"Erin, that's exactly what I'm saying. That's how it works. I see that now. You lean on me some, and someday I'll lean on you." He steps closer to me, and lifts a strand of my hair in his fingers. "That's the deal we make when we love someone."

I close my eyes, feeling *him*, feeling the warmth of his love.

I start crying, and he takes me in his arms and it feels so *right*, so *good*, that I cling to him, inhaling his sweaty, gorgeous maleness, wanting to climb inside of him. We hold each other for a long, long time, until I realize Mom is waiting for me, that I haven't even gotten the pizza, that I'm supposed to be meeting somebody at my house.

"I've got someone coming to look at Dad's Mustang," I say. "The guy wants it for parts." Which seems sad and good all at the same time. Anytime I saw an older Mustang on the road, would I wonder if maybe a part of Dad's Mustang was in it, making it a stronger, better car? "And I need to get back to Mom."

"She didn't look well," Jason says. "She looked like . . ." He doesn't finish.

"Yes."

"Erin, why didn't you call me? Man." He shakes his head. "I'm so sorry."

"It's going to be fine," I say. "She's going to pull though this. I know it. *I know it.*"

Jason looks at me with his worldly, timeless eyes but says nothing. I've seen that look before, and I don't want to understand it.

CHAPTER FORTY-NINE

On my eighteenth birthday, I take Mom flying.

As a student pilot, I'm not allowed to take a passenger by myself, so Stew comes with us.

Jill pushes Mom in her wheelchair to Tweety Bird and Stew helps Mom into the back of the plane, handling her as if she's labeled "Fragile Handle with Care." Jill's been staying with us for the past week, and she fusses over Mom, making sure she's comfortable.

When Mom first asked if she could come flying with me, I didn't know what to say. She's so weak that brushing her teeth exhausts her. The medication now just takes the edge off her constant, gnawing pain. I don't want her to wear herself out.

But she insists I take her, and when she talks about it her face glows with feverish determination. She says it will be a good birthday gift for the both of us.

Stew buckles my mom in, his hands gentle, and I hand him her blanket. He tucks it around her.

"Your husband was a good man, Mrs. Bailey," he says. "A good friend. I'd like to look after his daughter, if that's okay with you."

She looks at him and smiles. Her face is shiny with sweat and radiant. "Yes. I'd like that," she says.

I refuse to understand what they are talking about.

I do my flight check and my hands are shaking. When I get in, Stew beside me, I sit for a long moment with my hands on the yoke, trying to find that place of calm that I know is somewhere inside of me. I imagine it as a moon-drenched lagoon where manatees come and play.

I tighten my hands on the yoke and I look over my shoulder at my mom, wondering if she's frightened. She is looking out the window and her face is still. As she has gotten sicker, it's like the essence of her is shining through stronger and brighter, like a candle put in straight oxygen. All the impurities have been burned away and it is just *her*, that distilled, purest part of her that remains.

I take a deep breath.

"You okay?" Stew asks me through the headphones. He looks at me sideways. "If you want me to, I can do the flying."

"No," I say. "I need to do this."

I need to show Mom I can do it, though even on my eighteenth birthday I feel younger and less secure than ever before. Will it always be like this, feeling less equipped to deal with life each year that passes? Is this what being an adult feels like, realizing the choices don't get any easier, just more important?

As I neared my eighteenth birthday, I've been thinking more and more about my BRCA mutation. I wish now that I had waited to get tested through a doctor's office. At Mom's insistence, I've gone to see a genetic counselor, and the woman gave me all the information I was craving for all those months after I found out I could have the mutation. My options are still the same, but I feel like I understand them more clearly. I am now old enough to get a mastectomy if I want, though most doctors would advise against doing that at my age. I can schedule the surgery and it would be over; I would never have to worry about breast cancer again.

But does it take more courage to cut off my breasts, or to wait and see what happens, trusting life can be strange and wonderful and surprising? I don't know. I truly don't. I want to have the strength to make the right decision, but I don't know if I'm strong enough.

I'm taxiing now, and the trees soften with speed, and there's the moment I have come to love, when we are free of the earth, the stomach-dipping lightness that means that I am flying.

I climb steadily over houses and tender green trees; hawks float in air currents far below us, rising and falling effortlessly. The sun has found an opening in a far-off cloud bank, gilding it gold and spilling gauzy rays of light toward the ground. The sunlight looks tangible; if you stood beneath those beams, you know you would feel a warm drizzle of sun on your upturned face.

"*I have slipped the surly bonds of Earth, / And danced the skies on laughter-silvered wings,*" Mom says softly through the headset.

I nod, because I feel Dad with us too.

We circle over our house, and Mom puts her hand on my shoulder. It is May, and spring is in full riotous glory. Pink and purple azaleas bloom madly, forsythias glow yellow, and dogwoods drip snowy blossoms. From the air it looks like a child has taken a paintbrush and spattered Easter-egg colors over the canvas of the landscape. The earth is coming alive again.

"It's beautiful," Mom says through the headphones. "I never knew it could be this beautiful. How much I have missed . . ."

I reach back and she puts her hand in mine, and I feel the coldness, the sharp bones.

"You're here now," I say. "Once I get my license I can take you up anytime you want."

She squeezes my hand and lets go. I let myself fall into the sheer pleasure of flying, feeling happy as I can only feel in the air.

Always, always when flying you must keep a lookout for other planes—"Head on a swivel!"—and it's while I'm peering out the side window that I see it.

"Look!" I point at the perfect, circular rainbow against the side of a puffy, white cloud bank. Inside the rainbow is a tiny plane, Tweety Bird, and I think if I had binoculars that I could probably see *us* inside of it.

"It's a glory," Stew says, and I stare at it in awe. Rings of reds, yellows, blues, greens, and violets radiate outward from the shadow plane, and it's almost as if I'm seeing another plane, another us, reflected from heaven.

I remember something then, and say into the mic, "Mom! Remember? Dad always wanted to show you a glory, didn't you say that? He liked that no two people saw the same thing, that everyone saw their own personal glory."

Mom doesn't say anything, and I glance over my shoulder to see she is asleep, her head resting on Jill's shoulder. She looks like a child.

Jill holds my mom in her arms, tears slipping down her face as she stares out the window at the glory in the clouds.

CHAPTER FIFTY

On May 14, my mom collapses trying to make it to the bathroom. On the way to the hospital I call Jill, and Jason,
frantic, crying so hard I can barely see the ambulance in
front of me.

I walk down the cold hallway until I find her room. I stand
outside, taking deep breaths. I scrub my cheeks, trying to
remove the vestiges of my crying jag, put a smile on my face,
and walk into the room.

She is awake, but barely. She tries to smile when she sees
me but the effort is simply too much.

"I wanted," she says slowly, "so badly to see you graduate."

The words echo in the still room.

"You will," I say. "You *will*. They'll patch you up and
you'll be out of here in no time."

She closes her eyes and turns her face toward the wall. I sit
beside her and hold her hand while she sleeps.

Later that afternoon, she opens her eyes. For a moment, they are blank as a baby's, uncomprehending. Then they cloud with pain and despair. She knows where she is.

"I love you, baby," she says, "more than I've ever loved . . . anything in my entire life. If I've done . . . nothing else in this world, I brought *you* into it . . . and that makes me so proud." There is a long silence and she reaches up and brushes my hair out of my face. She says so quietly I almost miss it, *"Promise me, don't ever hide your beautiful face."*

"Momma . . . I love you too. But don't talk like that. You're going to pull through this. I know you will."

She lies still and quiet.

"Hurts," she says at one point and she is so drugged the words are slurred, indistinct. *"Hurts so much."*

I cry, but she is asleep and doesn't see me.

That night Jason and his mom arrive. I refuse to let Mom be by herself and they sit with her when I have to go to the bathroom, but I am selfish with her time. I stay with her by myself most of the night, singing and talking. She floats in and out, always smiling when she opens her eyes and sees me sitting there.

The next day, Jill arrives, and she is solemn and quiet after talking to Mom's doctor, but I refuse to listen to her when she tries to talk to me about Mom.

"No, no, no," I cry. *"Stop it.* You have to keep believing, you can't give up on her. I won't give up on her, do you hear me?"

Jason holds me. Jill, looking weepy, goes in to relieve Miriam by my mom's bedside and I ignore the look that passes between Jason and Miriam. And when Jill comes out an hour later I go back in.

My mom is crying, the pain is so intense, even though they have given her a pain button.

"I'm right here, Momma," I say. "I'm not going anywhere. You're not going anywhere. I'll be right here when you wake up. Think about when you're better, think about all the things we'll be able to do. You need to get better by graduation so you can come. I need you there, Momma, don't you leave me."

She squeezes my hand, and falls asleep.

Jill goes in when I come out, and Miriam says, "Erin, let's go get some coffee."

I shake my head, but she is insistent. Finally I let her lead me to the cafeteria and sip at the coffee she puts in front of me.

"Erin, your mom is in a lot of pain," she says.

"I know, I *know*," I say. "She needs to hang on so the doctors can figure out how to make her better. She just needs to *hang on*."

Miriam reaches over and holds my hand. "Erin, your mother is hanging on as best she can. For *you*. She is holding on for you. She is in a lot of pain, and she is dying. There is nothing left for the doctors to do."

I'm shaking my head, going *no, no, no, nonononono*.

Miriam continues, her words hitting me like blows. "She is hanging on for you, *for you*, Erin. It's hard for mothers to let go, it always is, but you need to tell her it is okay, because she needs to, honey. She needs to let go. She needs to find her peace. She needs to be released from her pain. It's time for you to say good-bye."

I start crying, huge, gulping sobs. "I *can't*, I can't give up on her. I'm all she has, she's all I have. *I can't give up.*"

"You're not giving up, honey. You're letting go."

She holds me until I stop crying, and we go back upstairs. Jason knows. He has been through this before, will probably go though it again. Without speaking he takes me into his arms and I fight to keep the tears at bay because I have to be brave. I don't know if I can do this thing, *but I have to be brave.*

Jill looks up as I come into the room, and she has been crying. She goes, and I climb onto the bed with Mom and hold her in my arms. Her body feels light and sighing, like a dry whisper with nothing left in it.

"Momma," I say, and my voice breaks.

She opens her eyes and smiles when she sees me.

"Momma, I'm saying good-bye now. You—you've done an awesome job raising me and I will be *okay*. I will miss you. *I will miss you so much*, but—but I can do it on my own now. You did your job, you can rest. I'm going to be just fine." I'm crying, but I make my voice strong so she can hear me, so she *believes*.

"Rinnie . . . ," she says and the tears slip from her eyes. "I love you."

"I know, Momma, I love you too. And . . ." I choke back the sobs that threaten to overtake me. "And, it's time for you to leave, Momma. *Let go.* Don't wait around for me any longer. *Please.* You can let go, I'll be fine. It's not good-bye. It's never good-bye, because we'll see each other again. You can watch over me, be my angel, until I see you again."

She reaches up her hand and pushes my hair out of my face. *"See you later, alligator . . ."*

"After a while, crocodile," I say softly.

She falls asleep and I hold her, and wait.

It takes her another day to die, and she is in and out the whole time. But I stay with her, and she knows I am there when she opens her eyes, and I think she knows I am there when she is asleep as well.

I do not need the flatline monitor to know when her soul flies away. A butterfly-wing kiss brushes my forehead, and I lie with her for a while longer, feeling her body grow cold.

I get out of bed. Her eyes are closed, and she is so pale and beautiful, she looks like an angel already.

"I love you, Momma," I say.

And then I go out to face the rest of my life without her.

CHAPTER FIFTY-ONE

Nine days after my mom's funeral, I attend my high school graduation. In the audience are the entire Levinson family, as well as Jill. They leave an empty seat beside Jill where my mom should have been. Jason sits on the other side of it, his face bright with his love for me. I smile at him across the crowd and he mouths *me too*, knowing what I mean.

As names are called and my proud-looking classmates go onstage to receive their diplomas, I look down at Memaw's sapphire ring on my finger. I know my mother and Memaw are inside me because my heart is stitched with their love and dreams, creating a unique quilt of lasting beauty. I miss Mom intensely. I miss her with every fiber of my being. But she is gone and I am here, and there is nothing I can do to change that. Mom and Dad and Memaw helped me weave the tapestry of my childhood, and now I must find my own pattern to follow.

I shuffle forward behind Caityln Baer, and above the stadium I see an airplane high in the sky, its engine just a faint thrum in my ears. I think about Mom's funeral. As I stood beside my mom's casket, I heard the roar of engines and looked up into the endless blue of the sky, my face touched by the warm sunlight. Led by Tweety Bird, three planes roared overhead in a V. One plane was missing in the formation, three planes when there should have been four. It was Stew's tribute to my mother, and I thought about how as we go through life we lose people we love, but we also gain some.

Caitlyn turns and gives me a nervous smile. "Hey," she whispers. "I read your blog. Faith sent out a link to everyone. Wow. Just . . . wow."

I smile back. Two days ago, I wrote my first blog entry for the BRCA website. I wrote about Mom's death, and while it was heart-wrenching, a sense of peace filled me when I wrote the last sentence. I stared at it, thinking about Mom, thinking about what she wanted for me, feeling her fingerprints on the tender surfaces of my heart. Then I pushed the Publish button, sending the blog sailing into the world, like a baby bird flying for the first time. *I'm doing it for you, Momma, but I'm doing it for me too.*

By last night I had twenty comments, and something thawed in me as I read them and saw how people responded to my words. Courage is not always big and bright and loud; sometimes it's as silent and small as true words, a smile when you'd rather weep, or getting up every day and living with quiet dignity while all around you life rages. You cannot truly love, live, or exist without courage. Without it you are simply biding time until you die.

I'm not saying I have all the answers. This summer I am going to stay with Aunt Jill as both of us learn to live with our loss, and Jason and Trina have both said they will come and visit me. I will go to college in the fall, but right now I don't know where. As alone as I've felt for a long time, it has been surprising to me how many people have opened their homes and hearts to me.

One day, I know, I will have to make a decision about my BRCA mutation. But I will not make that decision right now. Every tomorrow brings new challenges and joy. Life can be surprising and beautiful and tragic, and I plan on living it to the best of my ability. The days of my life are pearls on a string, some scratched and marred, some lustrous and pure, but all of them mine alone. It's not the ugliest, or the most beautiful of them, that define me, but all of them together that make me who I am.

"Erin Bailey," our principal says. I take deep breath and walk across the stage to receive my diploma. The audience gasps. I look and see that every senior has a cell phone out, the screen set to a candle, holding it up toward me.

I smile, but I'm crying too.

I love you, Momma, and I'll never forget you. But it's my turn now and here I go. Watch me fly, Momma, watch me fly.

AUTHOR'S NOTE

As I began my research on this story, I was—and am—amazed by the grit and bravery of ordinary people facing the unthinkable. However, I found that some in the BRCA community were uneasy with the subject matter of this book.

First, I was writing about a teenage girl, who I was told should not be even *thinking* about the breast cancer gene until she was at least eighteen, preferably twenty-one or twenty-five. How, I asked these well-meaning people, can you tell someone *not* to think about something? I'm sure this advice works for some, perhaps most, and they are able to go about their normal lives until it is time to tackle the issue of their possible BRCA mutation at an appropriate age. But what about those who can't stop thinking about it?

Second, these professionals were disturbed by the fact that Erin decided to test through a direct-to-consumer company, rather than through a genetic counselor or a health-care provider. I understand their concerns. In fact, I share them. But books are not written about people who always make the right choices. This story is Erin's journey; every woman's journey will be different, and who can fault a teenager's desire to pursue answers, especially when she is encouraged not to even think about the questions?

When I began this book, I researched one of several companies that offered direct-to-consumer (without a doctor's order) genetic testing that included the BRCA gene. As of this writing, this company had suspended health-related genetic testing, dependent on FDA marketing authorization. This is a fast-changing and dynamic field, and I believe that for reasons of privacy, personal empowerment, or just plain curiosity, people will want and demand access to this type of personal genetic testing in the future.

It is important to note that at the time that I was researching this book, the company I used as a model only tested for three of the hundreds of known BRCA mutations. This fact was made very clear in their reports. However, if Erin didn't have one of these select few, she still could have carried another BRCA mutation. This highlights the importance of talking to a qualified medical professional about the results of any genetic test.

Another important note: Erin uses the figure of "up to 80 percent" to describe her lifetime risk of getting breast cancer. This is a fluid number that changes from case to case, but for now, it is a commonly used percentage, and the one that genetic counselors I interviewed were the most comfortable with.

Regardless of whether it is provided through a doctor's

office or through a direct-to-consumer company, genetic testing is here to stay. With courageous celebrities like Angelina Jolie, who openly talked about her BRCA mutation and her decision to undergo prophylactic surgery, more and more people are becoming aware of the role genes play in our health. As genetic testing becomes more common, it is inevitable that there will be serious implications for family members, including children, who will learn about their genetic propensities whether or not they wish to.

For people like Erin, I wonder where this will lead.

ACKNOWLEDGMENTS

I would like to thank Mary Kate Castellani and Caroline Abbey for their invaluable editorial advice (you have no idea how *good* these chicks are), and the entire Bloomsbury team for making the words on my computer screen look so marvelous in print.

Two doctors, Gloria Morris, MD, PhD, from Mount Sinai Hospital, and Jessica Young, MD, from the Roswell Park Cancer Institute, were extremely generous with their time and knowledge in helping me portray Erin's mother's breast cancer treatment as accurately as possible. If I were to ever have need of breast cancer treatment, I would be honored to call either one of these ladies my doctor. Any mistakes are mine alone.

Thank you to Mary Ann Orlang for kindly giving me a tour of the Lee Memorial Health System's Regional Cancer Center.

A big thank-you to Christine McElwain and Shelly Van Bulck for sharing their stories with me.

In addition to reading the plethora of excellent books on the subject, I also spent a lot of time on various BRCA websites and forums reading the heartbreaking stories of women dealing with the BRCA mutation. I am in awe of your strength and bravery. I would also like to thank the genetic counselors and experts with whom I spoke.

I've been flying with my stepdad, Chuck McClinton, since I was twelve years old, and I would like to send a big shout-out to him for being patient with my endless questions, some of them quite strident as my deadline neared. Thanks, Chuckie! It's not your fault if I got it wrong.

My portrayal of Erin's legal issues was guided by my questions to the FAA and the AOPA, as well as Atlanta aviation lawyer James S. Strawinski, who absolutely rocks. Again, any mistakes were either done in the name of literary license, or were simply my own dumb fault. (Let's go with literary license.)

The urban exploring parts were facilitated by my haunting of many urban exploring articles and sites (search "Atlanta urban exploring" and you'll see what I mean). The John B. Gordon School was slated for demolition the last time I checked, and I haven't been able to bring myself to find out if this has come to pass. The Excaps' method of entry into the abandoned buildings may or may not be accurate, and one of the buildings may or may not be alarmed. Be warned!

Thank you, Ashley Elston, for crying.

Mom and Aunt Joyce: thank you for being my extremely tolerant sounding boards and first readers. It would be so much harder without you.

To Eddie, Zack, and Gavin, the three loves of my life. Thanks for putting up with me, guys. I know it's not always easy.

Without Sarah Davies, my splendiferous agent, none of this would be possible. Thank you, Sarah, for helping me grow Erin's story to its full potential.